IT'S COLD
NEXT DOOR

IT'S COLD
NEXT DOOR

Peter de Polnay

W.H. ALLEN · LONDON
A Howard & Wyndham Company
1984

© Peter de Polnay 1978

Reprinted 1984

Printed and bound in Great Britain by
Biddles Ltd, Guildford and King's Lynn
for the publishers W. H. Allen & Co. Ltd,
44 Hill Street, London W1X 8LB

ISBN 0 491 02235 2

ONE

'It's cold next door,' called the little old man, standing in the doorway of number 36. A strange remark to make on a warm September morning, thought Osbert Hinley. The little old man wore a black jacket and striped trousers which were too long for him. His waistcoat was covered with cigar ash.

Osbert gave him a polite nod, then went into number 34 next door. A girl wearing glasses sat at a table facing the door. 'I've an appointment with Mr Bone,' said Osbert.

'The waiting room's to the right,' said the girl, apparently in a bad temper.

In the waiting room a man and a woman sat side by side on a sofa, he lean and about forty, she a few years younger though overtaken by middle age spread. He was holding her hand, and their knees touched. Pretending to ignore them (he did that well) Osbert selected a three weeks' old weekly, and seated himself at the other end of the room. It was an impersonal room with dark leather covered furniture. On the wall hung the framed photograph of a long dead senior partner.

'I won't abandon the children,' said the woman.

'The question is, do you or don't you love me?'

Horrified Osbert tried not to listen. What shameless people, and he held the weekly in front of him as if to shield him from their words. He succeeded in not hearing the woman's answer. A youngish looking partner appeared, the man and the woman rose, and followed him through the door. Osbert sighed his relief.

A grey haired woman poked her head in a little later, saying, 'Mr Hinley, I'll take you to Mr Bone.' So Mr Bone was more important in that he didn't come to fetch his visitor himself. That won't frighten me, said Osbert to himself.

In the large room she took him to a vast Victorian looking glass stood on top of the chimneypiece in which Osbert saw himself shaking hands with Bone. Neat was Osbert's description of himself, and in appearance and movement he lived up to it. His fair hair, his sober clothes, his slim figure and clean shaven face were part and parcel of his picture of neatness. Bone, as he saw in the glass, was a man who loved power, therefore wanted to impose himself. He was stocky, but stood as straight as you expect a much thinner man to stand, hence even his handshake was stiff. He relaxed only when he had sat down behind the heavy mahogany table.

'I'm glad to meet you,' Bone said. 'Ever since I made your aunt's last will I felt like wanting to meet you.'

'Nobody could be more astonished than I am,' said Osbert.

Bone offered him a cigarette from a silver box on the table. Osbert took it, Bone held out a gold lighter, then said, 'Our firm has many old ladies as clients. Nevertheless, your aunt was an exception. I understand no love was lost between you, you and she hardly ever met, yet in every will she made – she made a new one every two years – she left her estate to you.'

'Most extraordinary. I haven't been to Maidwood these last twenty years, that is not since my father died. So you can understand my surprise.' Osbert pushed his chair back as if wanting to give his words more strength. 'And I'm not the person who wants or needs a large estate in North Oxfordshire.'

'It'll grow on you,' said Bone.

'Or not. Mine is the life of a self-sufficient, well

6

organised bachelor. I'm a legal man myself, a barrister who doesn't practise at the Bar, but as legal adviser to some of the big shots in the antique trade I manage to collect a few good bits of furniture and china.' He laughed deprecatingly.

'Quite,' said Bone, frowning.

'What I want to emphasise is that I won't have time to look after Maidwood, and I don't want it to interfere with my well organised existence.'

Bone stood up, went to the window which was open, closed it, then sat down again. 'You won't find any difficulty in keeping Maidwood out of your life. Mawson will see to that.'

'Who's Mawson?' Osbert asked.

'He's the estate manager. Every time your aunt called me down I expected her to tell me that she intended to leave the estate to Mawson. I'm sure Mawson expected that too. For it was he who made and makes the place tick over. However, it was always you. She changed her wills because she suddenly decided to leave a hundred pounds to the Carmelites or two hundred to the Cistercians or something like that. She left Mawson the sum of one thousand pounds which isn't a king's ransom nowadays.' Osbert nodded. 'As I'm more or less your solicitor too I want to warn you about Mawson, I mean his disappointment. He's the younger son of a rich farmer, the love of land is in his blood, they're land hungry those lovers of land, so one must beware of them. He's managed the estate, which consists of a whole village and four farms, these last eight years. It was in a sorry state when he took over, and he's made it prosper. Now he finds himself uprooted and unsure of himself because of your aunt's death and you becoming the owner, you whom he never met, you about whom he knows nothing.'

'I'll be only too happy to let him carry on. He need have no fear on that score.'

'People don't think or argue like that,' said Bone who was enjoying himself. 'He's worried and deeply disappointed. There's nothing to stop you from getting rid of him, putting in somebody else, or, which I'm sure he fears most, meddling and interfering. He has a very high opinion of himself.'

'He may rest assured that the last thing I want is to meddle or interfere. I'm far too passive for that.'

'You say so today, but you might think differently when you become accustomed to being the master of Maidwood.'

'Not I,' smiled Osbert.

Bone's wristwatch said that an old lady was waiting for him downstairs. He should have made the appointment for a little later. Still, he couldn't keep her waiting too long. 'You weren't at the funeral,' he said.

'I was in New York on business, a boring but complicated business.'

Everything seems boring to you, thought Bone. I know your sort, no appetite, no enthusiasm, in brief Mawson needn't worry. 'When,' he asked, 'are you going down to Maidwood?'

'Whenever you want,' said Osbert. 'All I remember is the drawing room which looks like a Gothic chapel.'

'It still looks like one. You should go down as soon as possible. Why not tomorrow?'

'I can't,' said Osbert. 'I've a dinner party, and wouldn't miss it for anything. Great friends of mine.'

A dinner party, thought Bone. That's all he can think of.

'I could go down the day after tomorrow,' said Osbert.

'Are you driving down?'

'Haven't a car, too much trouble.'

'I'll ring Mawson to tell him to meet you at Banbury station. There's a train that arrives at four ten, if I remember rightly, and I usually remember rightly.'

'You're lucky,' said Osbert.

Bone wished he could strangle him. 'When you return,' he said, rising, 'give me a tinkle. I'll be very interested to hear your impressions.' He moved to the door. 'As I'm now your solicitor we must see quite a lot of each other.'

I hope not, said Osbert to himself. He stopped in the doorway as he said, 'When I arrived here I saw a funny old man on the doorstep of the next house. "It's cold next door," he said in a friendly warning voice. Who is he?'

'Old Ramsbottom,' said Bone, tapping his forehead. 'He's dotty and very old, and says a lot of stupid things. The house is his, so nothing can be done about it. He stands for hours in the doorway, calling to the passersby. Take no notice of him.'

'It's cold next door impressed me. I liked that very much, food for thought. It's almost like "cultivate your garden".'

These Catholics, thought Bone, find some meaning in everything. It's cold next door will become a sort of mystery for this pretentious fellow. Then remembering the old lady waiting for him downstairs he held out his hand. 'Don't forget to ring me when you come back. Mawson will be at the station. He's tall, dark hair, and his Ford is dark grey. You'll recognise him easily. He wears a porkpie hat. He'll be looking out for you.'

The girl with the glasses glared at Osbert as he went past her.

I've never met such a conceited fool before, said Osbert to himself, coming out into the midday quiet of Westminster. Old Ramsbottom wasn't in the doorway which he regretted. Should he take a taxi? A bus would do.

His flat in Bloomsbury was on the second floor of a Queen Anne house. The flats weren't self-contained in that each had two entrances from their respective landings: one through a narrow passage that separated the drawing room from the bedroom, the other through the kitchen. Hats, coats and umbrellas had to be left on the landings. Below Osbert lived a large woman who worked for a publisher; on the floor above a man who liked to refer to himself as a high ranking executive. His wife had left him recently which he didn't seem to mind. It was a house with a fine staircase but without children or dogs. However, the staircase smelt now and then of cat's urine.

Osbert remembered that Vivienne was coming to lunch. He went straight into the kitchen to get the meal ready for her, a cold meal because his visit to Bone hadn't given him the time to prepare a meal worthy of his reputation as a cook. He was proud of his dexterity as a creator of good dishes. The kitchen looked like an operating theatre. Vivienne often said that his kitchen reflected his personality, cold, precise and no feeling whatever. He laughed when she said that, and took it almost as a compliment, for he was convinced that awful fires burned within him. Keeping them under control he considered an achievement he deserved to be proud of. The smoked salmon he had bought yesterday afternoon, the chicken he roasted last night, the Stilton came from Jermyn Street, and now he would make a fruit salad with maraschino. When the salad was ready he moved to the sitting room, smiling at the sunrays playing with the green carpet. His collection of French porcelain filled a large bookcase. Books he got mostly rid of after he had read them. He abhorred the idea of the bookworm bachelor with a skull cap sitting in a stuffy room. The furniture was Queen Anne, and it had taken him years to collect it. He poured sherry into a small glass, then jumped up to go down to answer the doorbell.

Vivienne Long was tall and smart, and changed the colour of her hair so often that now and again (said

Osbert) she forgot the colour she wore. She was the widow of a City magnate. She had been Osbert's mistress for five years, nothing wild or complicated about it, and when the last embers had died they decided to remain friends without the joys of the flesh, both discovering in time that it was much pleasanter like that. Once a week she lunched with him, once a week he dined with her.

'Had to leave my car round the corner,' she said.

'Thank God, I haven't a car,' he said.

'Slowly you'll strip yourself of everything,' she laughed, preceding him up the stairs.

'And keep only my china, and then perhaps I'll get rid of the china too. What was the concert like?'

'The usual fare, Bach, Beethoven and . . .'

'Mozart.'

'No, my dear. Elgar for a change.'

They entered the sitting room from which the sun had withdrawn. She sat down on a highbacked walnut chair, to be able to contemplate her elegant figure in the cheval glass at the other end of the room.

'What a fine sight you are,' said Osbert, holding out a glass of sherry.

'Thank you. Now tell me about your inheritance. Frankly, I can't see you as a country squire. You're too urbane for that.'

'I can't see myself either,' said Osbert, sitting down in the only comfortable armchair in the room. An eyesore he called it to apologise for its Edwardian presence among the Queen Anne chairs. 'It's very strange. My father had a sister who was ten years older than he. Nobody liked her, I mean neither of my parents cared for her, and her inheriting from an enormously rich aunt the Maidwood estate didn't endear her to my parents either. As a girl she wanted to become a nun, but her parents stood in the way. We Catholics admire and respect monks and nuns but don't care for our children to become monks and nuns. So Aunt Theresa didn't become a nun. Her revenge was to lead a life of chastity once the inheritance made her independent. I think I met her only twice. The first time I don't remember because I was too small to take notice, the second time was twenty years ago when my father and I were staying with friends in the neighbourhood. That was shortly after my mother's death.'

'I'm so glad that I was an orphan at the age of five,' said Vivienne, uncrossing her well shaped legs. 'So I don't have to pepper my stories with father and mother.'

'I sit corrected,' said Osbert after lighting a cigarette. 'My father and I called on Aunt Theresa who received us in the drawing room which looked like a Gothic chapel. I thought of it the first time I went into the Sainte-Chapelle in Paris. My father – forgive me for mentioning a father again – and she were practically strangers to each other because of the age difference which counts in one's early youth. They talked like two well mannered strangers whom nothing draws to each other. She asked what I was doing, I said I was reading for the Bar, she said, "I see," or something like that, and then we bowed ourselves out. She meant so little to us that we didn't even discuss our call after we left her.'

'And now she left you a large estate.'

'For reasons I'll never understand. But the point, Vivienne, is that not a single particle of mine wants the large estate.'

'And the responsibilities that go with it. I understand you only too well, my poor Osbert.' She let out a tinkling laugh. Like a tiny bell, he thought.

'Don't mock me. There is, however, a silver lining to that vast dark cloud. It's the estate manager whose name I've forgotten though the solicitor gave it to me. He's been running the place for donkey's years, loves it, dotes on it, in short he'll continue running it, thus saving me from all responsibility, I mean work.'

Vivienne had a cramp in her foot, so stood up, shook the leg, then went to the window, and put her glass on the windowsill. 'I'm convinced,' she said, turning round, 'that one always receives what one doesn't want. You're a barrister, and have enough brains to make a brilliant counsel, but you chose to take it easy, and for a bit of old Sèvres you persuade antique dealers not to buy stolen stuff. Yours is the career of least resistance.' How she loved listening to her own voice, he thought. 'And now out of the blue drops a large house and estate on your unwilling shoulders. Any one else would be blissfully happy, not you, my dear, because it means thinking and acting beyond your well controlled instincts.'

'There's nothing to add to that,' he smiled. 'This morning I went to see my late aunt's solicitor. On the doorstep of the house next to the solicitor's stood a little old man who looked at me as I'm sure he looks at everybody who enters his orbit. "It's cold next door," he called, his eyes resting on me for a brief second.'

'Was it cold at the solicitor's?' asked Vivienne, leaving the window.

'I'm sure he wasn't thinking of the solicitor's office.'

'Then what was he thinking of?'

'If I knew I'd be a wiser man.'

Vivienne gave him a smile he knew from old. It said I don't understand what you mean but I won't admit it. 'And what's the solicitor like?' she asked, holding out her empty glass.

'He disliked me at first sight,' said Osbert, 'which is understandable as it was our first meeting.' She allowed herself a little laugh. 'On his table stood a photograph of his grim wife and three small sons. As he spoke to me his eyes said: you'll never have a grim wife and three small sons because you're not man enough to have . . .'

'A grim wife and three small sons,' laughed Vivienne, pleased with herself.

'Exactly.' He poured sherry into her glass. 'His name is Bone.'

'He ought to be an orthopaedic surgeon.'

'Ha ha.' He stood up, opened the dining room door, and as she went past him the telephone bell rang. 'Blast.' It was the solicitor's grey haired secretary to give the estate manager's car's number. He scribbled it on a piece of paper.

The dining room was like a narrow passage with hardly room for the round walnut table, a small china cabinet and a sideboard. However, the window was wide, filling the room with light. Smoked salmon, cold chicken, stilton and fruit salad were on the sideboard. 'You've perfected the art of being on your own,' said Vivienne, a slight reproach in her voice. 'I depend so much on other people.'

'You don't depend on them, you just use them.'

'Are we going to be nasty to each other?'

'We don't have to,' he laughed.

So he still remembers our great days, she thought with satisfaction. 'What is your new house like?'

'I remember it very vaguely. You'll have to come down there once I've found my way around.'

'Will you give up this flat?'

'I might give up the house, but never this flat.'

'Don't be too sure,' said Vivienne.

Speaks like the solicitor, he said to himself, and as it happened at all their meetings since they had ceased to be lovers he wished she had got the hell out of his life, immediately repenting because that wasn't a civilised way of thinking for a civilised man.

'Mawson,' he suddenly said.

'Who's that?'

'The name of the estate manager. Told you I forgot it. This Mawson will play an important part in my life because I'll do exactly as he wants, that is let him run the place without interfering, without putting my foot down.'

'Have you got one?' asked Vivienne.

'Without putting my foot down even if it's necessary, and if he gets the place into a mess I'll sell it with him inside it like a Scottish castle with a ghost.'

'What is he like?'

'All I know is that he wears a porkpie hat.'

Being a greedy eater Vivienne spoke little till she finished the fruit salad, then she remembered she had an appointment with her dentist. He saw her down, and as they parted he couldn't help thinking with satisfaction that she no longer figured in his rare confessions.

TWO

On the Banbury station platform stood a man wearing a porkpie hat. He had the sad face of a fat sheep. Switching on a smile Osbert stopped in front of him, saying in a sure voice, 'Mr Mawson?'

'My name's Smith,' said the man, his fat cheeks colouring.

'I'm so sorry,' said Osbert, blushing scarlet. He had never felt, he thought, so humiliated in his life.

As he came out of the station a tall, hatless, thin man accosted him. 'Mr Hinley?'

'You must be Mawson.'

'That's it. Mr Bone phoned me you were coming down with this train. My car's over there.'

Mawson looked younger than Osbert had expected, not only younger, but in no way resembling Osbert's picture of a land and power hungry man, and there was nothing dislikeable about him. A man, he was sure, he would get on well with.

'Bone said you wear a porkpie hat,' Osbert chatted, sitting beside him in the car. 'On the platform stood a man, wearing a porkpie hat, and stupidly I thought he was you. "Mr Mawson?" I asked. He said his name was Smith. I don't know about you but at such moments I want to sink into the ground.'

'I wear a hat only when I stride round the estate,' said Mawson.

Osbert examined him from the corner of his eye. His cheeks were pale, his nose straight, and he hardly had a

16

chin. Bone must be a rotten judge of human nature, for the man seemed to have no strength whatever. It was difficult to picture him running a large estate like Maidwood.

'I've been to Maidwood only once since I grew up,' said Osbert. 'I don't know the place at all.'

'I gathered that,' said Mawson. 'I used to see Miss Hinley every day, she was a talkative old lady, yet I can't remember her ever mentioning that she had a nephew.'

'There you are. So you can see how surprised I was when I received Bone's letter telling me I was the heir to the estate. I'm here as a complete stranger. I'll need your help and knowledge.'

'I'll do what I can,' said Mawson, his eyes on the road.

Does he always speak in such a flat voice? Osbert wondered.

'Is anybody looking after the house?' he asked as they got out of Banbury. The sky was pale blue, the sun full of warmth, and trees ran past the car like soldiers spread out on a strategic road.

'Nobody really,' said Mawson, looking rigidly ahead. 'There were two sisters, both in their sixties, one parlourmaid, the other cook. When they found out that Miss Hinley left only a hundred pounds to each they stalked out in anger.'

'That means I'll have to make my own bed,' laughed Osbert. Let him see that the townsman couldn't be frightened away.

'Linda, my wife, will see to your not having to make your bed.'

'Very kind of her.'

'Mrs Hackett, the gardener's wife, has been looking after the house since the sisters left. This morning Linda and she got Miss Hinley's bedroom and the study next door ready for you.'

'Perfect. The house, if I remember rightly, is enormous. How will all those rooms be kept clean? Wouldn't it be the best thing to close the house up and just use a few rooms.'

'Discuss that with Linda. She knows the house inside out. The reception rooms haven't been used for years, I don't really know them as my daily calls on Miss Hinley consisted of going up the stairs, knocking on the study door, then going in and reporting on estate matters which she didn't listen to.'

'Were you fond of my aunt?'

'She was my employer,' said Mawson in his flat voice.

Is he trying to put me in my place? Osbert asked himself. If he does he won't get far since I haven't a place in Maidwood.

'The drive,' said Mawson, turning off the road.

Beeches and oaks flanked the drive, though only on one side. The house loomed up at the end of the drive, and Osbert gasped because it was larger and uglier than he remembered it. Like a Victorian orphanage, he thought. It was out of proportion too as the west wing had burnt down at the turn of the century, and not having been rebuilt the house seemed unbalanced. A soldier of the Crimean war who lost an arm, he said under his breath. It would be a waste of breath to say it aloud as Mawson wouldn't understand. Downstairs all rooms had french windows, their frames painted white, the upstairs windowframes were vicarage brown. The house was built of red brick that the years had darkened. An illkempt lawn was on each side of the front door which was surprisingly low as though the house were unwilling to let you in. 'What terrible taste those people had,' said Osbert in a voice that sounded desperate to him. Mawson didn't seem to hear him.

'Linda and Mrs Hackett are in the house,' said Mawson. 'We'll go right in.'

Osbert entered an enormous hall with a light oak stair-case, to the left, and a long light oak minstrels' gallery running round the first floor landing. The walls were dark, and rigid Victorian armchairs with red upholstery stood pushed against them. A fine Regency chandelier hung from the high ceiling.

'Ghastly,' said Osbert, and Mawson pretended again not to hear him.

'Linda,' he called in a loud, rasping voice that filled the hall.

'How dark this place is,' said Osbert, wishing he were back in his light filled flat.

A door opened on the first floor, then he heard foot-steps in the minstrels' gallery. A tall woman appeared on the top of the stairs, wearing a green dress that Vivienne would have abhorred. Not my sort, thought Osbert as she came down the stairs. She had straight shoulders, and small hips, her thick, short hair was naturally fair, her eyes grey, and she moved with purpose, every movement showing that she was com-pletely sure of herself and of whatever she did. Without that bosom of hers I'd take her for a guardsman, Osbert smiled.

'This is Linda,' said Mawson.

'How do you do,' she said, her voice deeper than her husband's.

'I've explained to Mr Hinley,' said Mawson, 'that there's no staff left in the house, but with the help of Mrs Hackett you got Miss Hinley's rooms ready for him.'

'Which is very kind of you,' said Osbert who didn't care for the grey eyes calmly summing him up.

She gave him a nod, then said, 'Come upstairs.'

'I'll leave you to Linda,' said Mawson. 'When you've a moment to spare come to the office. I'm going straight there.'

Osbert took his small suitcase, and followed her up

the stairs. A vast red sofa almost cut the landing in two. 'I don't think anybody has ever sat on it,' said Linda without turning her head. They went through a door, entered a wide L-shaped passage with doors on each side. 'This is the study,' said Linda, opening the first door on the right. It was a surprisingly wide room with a marble fireplace, an armchair to the right, another to the left, a writing table facing the window, and two built in bookcases. On the wall hung a copy of Leonardo's Annunciation. On the windowsill were potted plants.

'This is where your aunt spent most of her time,' said Linda.

'Not an unpleasant room,' said Osbert.

'Here's her bedroom which we got ready for you,' she said, opening a door opposite the fireplace.

The bedroom was crammed with furniture, small chairs, large chairs, round tables, square tables, two poufs and in the bay window a dressing table with a pink curtain and an ornate silver looking glass. Above the brass bed hung an ivory crucifix. 'Most remarkable,' said Osbert. 'Anyhow, the bed is made. I see there's central heating.'

'Only on this floor,' said Linda.

On the dressing table stood a framed photograph which he recognised since he had a copy of it himself, his father when he was fifteen. Here I am aged thirty-eight, he thought, looking at my father aged fifteen, perfect proof of my being out of my element. 'I feel rather old looking at my father aged fifteen,' he said.

'This house makes you feel old,' she said.

'I won't spend too much time here,' he said, and saw relief in her eyes. Or was it something else?

'There are two bathrooms side by side at the end of the passage,' she said.

'I'll explore the passage. Strange this brass bed. I never imagined an old spinster sleeping in a brass bed.

Now could we go downstairs? I remember a colossal drawing room that looked like a Gothic chapel. I'd like to see it again.'

'Come along,' she said.

They went down, she opened a door under the gallery, and he caught his breath as he entered the drawing room. For it was bigger and more ridiculously out of place than he remembered it. Gothic, he said to himself, was hardly the word for it. The walls were blue with gold stars painted on them, the vault-like ceiling was blue too with similar gold stars. The curtains were red brocade, the windows Gothic in shape, only stained glass was missing. The furniture was fake Tudor, and the carpet was red. There wasn't a single painting on the walls, but there were screens near the carved sofas.

'A good place to play hide and seek in,' said Osbert.

'I don't think anybody has ever played hide and seek here,' she said. She was standing beside him, so he had to turn his head to hear her voice. 'What you must bear in mind,' she went on, 'is that this is the house of lone women. It had no master for over a hundred years. I know its story from Miss Hinley who was proud of there having been no male owner for a century. The house and estate had belonged to a Mr Curtis who died two years after his marriage to a Miss Blendhurst.'

'She was a great-great-aunt of ours.'

'Mrs Curtis was twenty-one when her husband died falling off a horse. She lived to be eighty-four, always alone, never leaving the house. She left it to her niece, that is to your aunt who lived here alone for over fifty years. So you see it's more than a hundred years since this house has had a master.'

'Poor house, it won't find much of a master in me.'

'The little that has been done to this house,' she continued, ignoring the interruption, 'has been done by women without men, who didn't entertain, who didn't care what they ate, and certainly didn't care what they drank. The cellar is empty, and four generations of servants stole most of the silver which in any case was seldom ever used.'

'I like listening to you,' said Osbert.

'You flatter me,' she said without looking at him. 'I used to teach English literature in a girls' boarding school in Norfolk before I met Jack.'

'Jack?'

'My husband. His real name is Jonathan, but everybody calls him Jack. What I try to say is that as a man you must forgive this house a lot. It's like a convent without prayers.'

'But my aunt was a devout Catholic.'

'She prayed only upstairs. During the time I knew her she never entered any of the downstairs rooms or the other rooms on the first floor. I'll show you the deserted dining room. I mean as deserted as all the other rooms.'

'Tell me first, whose idea was this monstrosity.'

'Mr Curtis's father's. The house was built in his time. Miss Hinley said that he had been a much travelled man.'

She crossed the room, disappeared behind a screen, then called, 'This way,' and he followed, wondering whether she wanted to frighten him the first male after a hundred years, out of this sanctuary of lone, desiccated women. This house must be the negation of sex, Maidwood the right name for it.

'The dining room,' she said.

It was on a large scale too with plenty of unpolished mahogany in it, and paintings of horses on the walls. One, he thought, might be a Stubbs. A Chippendale wine cooler seemed to be waiting hopelessly for some old claret or vintage port. 'One can see,' he said, 'that the female rulers left this room alone.'

22

'The library,' said Linda, 'was left alone too. Miss Hinley only read books her confessor approved of, in fact brought her. You've no idea how upset she was when he died two years ago. All there was left for her was to read the books he had brought.'

Was she trying to be funny? He looked at her across the oval table, and their eyes met. He knew he would be the first to look away, for her gaze was calm and unflinching. You got no answer from them. 'Let's see the library,' he said.

At once he saw that no new book had entered the library the last hundred years. Bentley's Novels that stood in a long row on the lowest shelf must have been the last acquisition. The books were strictly part of a gentleman's library in the mid-nineteenth century, some quite valuable, but none of them ever read. 'Surtees,' said Osbert, stopping in front of a shelf. He took down *Mr Sponge's Sporting Tour*, and his hands were grey with dust. 'Not the stuff for women,' he laughed.

'I'm fond of Surtees,' said Linda.

'I wasn't thinking of you.'

'Don't let a hundred years of chaste loneliness wear you down,' said Linda, opening a french window. 'Here's the park, twenty-four acres of it, very neglected. Your aunt wasn't interested in gardening.'

'What was she interested in?'

'Prayer. In the Middle Ages she would have chosen to be walled in for life. In our time all she could do was to be driven to early Mass to Banbury and spend her afternoons on her prie-Dieu.'

'Where is it?'

'There's a curtain to the left of her bed. If you pull it you'll find a little recess with the prie-Dieu and a small wax statue of the Virgin. She was in there from three to seven every afternoon, and nobody was allowed to disturb her. At seven she went into the study, at seven-thirty she dined, always fish, then she read religious books and went to bed at nine. She rose at six, and received Jack when she came back from Mass. I came to see her at ten, and stayed with her for about an hour, which I frankly loved because she was a beautifully extraordinary woman.'

'If they had let her follow her inclinations and become a nun her life would have been much more satisfactory. For her, of course.'

'She was satisfied with her life,' said Linda, still in the french window. 'She used to say that she had more time for meditation here than she would in a convent among a lot of chatty nuns. I got very fond of her, and never blamed her even in my thoughts for taking no interest in anybody. It even surprised me that she left gifts to Jack and to the sisters who were cook and parlourmaid.'

'Did she leave you anything?'

'I think she respected me too much to leave me anything. When she was dying she told me that she would pray for me up there.'

'Now I understand why she left the estate to me. No respect for me and lack of interest in worldly matters.'

'Do you want to look at the park?'

'Some other time,' he said, 'Your husband is expecting me in the office.'

'I'll show you the way.'

She marched in front of him, and he thought of the guardsman again. No sense of humour, or too much of a sense of loyalty to his dead aunt, irksome both, and he laughed to himself as he hurried behind her through the drawing room, then the hall. She stopped between the two lawns. 'If you turn to the left you'll see a red-brick box with two windows. That's the office.'

'Thank you for showing me round.'

'As there's no arrangement for food yet – Mrs

Hackett will see you in the morning – Jack will bring you to our cottage for dinner.'

'That's awfully kind of you.'

She gave him a smile which nearly took him aback, for it was a smile you don't expect from a woman you met only an hour ago. It was full of warmth and understanding, the sort of understanding only close intimacy can account for. Then she turned on her heel and stalked off. She knows I'm watching her, he said to himself.

He lit a cigarette before he moved on. She was a strange and curious woman who might be dangerous too. Dangerous in what sense? He shrugged his shoulders because all danger was within you, and he trusted himself enough not to court disaster. Nothing could be more disastrous than becoming too friendly with his estate manager's wife. I exaggerate, in my male vanity I probably misunderstand her completely, he said to himself, and went to the red brick box at the end of the path. Clouds had come up, hiding the sun.

'This is Rex Wheeler, my assistant,' said Mawson as Osbert appeared.

Wheeler was short and fat and perspired profusely. The office, thought Osbert, looked like a sheriff's room in a Western, only star, handcuffs and jail door were lacking. Mawson, he felt sure, enjoyed it, and would put his feet on the table the moment he left.

'Your wife,' said Osbert, 'showed me round that most astonishing house.'

'Rex,' said Mawson, 'do you mind leaving us alone?'

'Most certainly,' said Rex, and left the office as if it were on fire.

'Mr Hinley,' said Mawson, standing up, 'I'm a straightforward person, and therefore far too blunt, I fear. But being straightforward and blunt is, I'm sure, the best policy in the circumstances. I've been running

Maidwood unhampered for eight years. Miss Hinley trusted me implicitly, never interfered with my work, left everything to my judgment, and if you look at the books you'll see that my judgment could be trusted. Miss Hinley is dead, and the estate is yours. Tell me frankly what your intentions are.'

'I've only got one, namely not to be hampered or encumbered in my peaceful, organised life by Maidwood. I'm no countryman, I don't know a cow from an ox, an oak from a beech, and I prefer the paved streets of London to muddy country roads.'

'You might want to sell.'

'What for in this age of inflation? Besides, I've enough to live on.'

'Nobody ever has,' said Mawson with a knowing smile.

'I must be the exception,' smiled Osbert. 'If you continue running the estate you'll be doing me a favour. Carry on as you did in my aunt's time, and you'll take a great load off my shoulders. I don't think there's anything more to be said on the subject.'

The fool doesn't believe me, he thought. He's convinced that I've got some secret plan up my sleeve.

'Mr Hinley,' said Mawson after a short silence, 'rest assured that I'll be worthy of your trust. I'll carry on as before, I'll look after your interest as I looked after your aunt's.'

'That's settled then,' said Osbert, ready to rise. He didn't, he admitted to himself, feel at his ease with Mawson, not in his own territory, that is the office, at any rate.

'The estate books,' said Mawson, lifting two heavy ledgers.

'Tomorrow morning. I want to look at the park, get the feel of the place. Your wife has very kindly asked me to dinner. Where do you live?'

'In the village, that's two miles away. Linda will come at seven to fetch you in the car.'

'I'll be there.'

Osbert walked off, irritatingly dissatisfied with himself, though he couldn't explain the reason. Perhaps it was because in a subtle manner the house, the estate, Mawson, and his wife had intruded more than he had bargained for. Take his aunt who had been a shadow that had as little substance as any shadow. Yet now, thanks to his coming to Maidwood and meeting Linda he knew about her as if he had spied on her from a dark corner, the time she got up, her drive to Mass, her hours on the prie-Dieu, even the food she ate. Most disconcerting for one for whom she had had no existence outside that one visit twenty years ago. And the same would happen with the house, the Mawsons, even with that Rex fellow who bolted at the first word.

He reached the house, went in, looked up on the minstrels' gallery, and it wouldn't have surprised him if a lot of faces had appeared, each waiting to burst into his life. In the drawing room he sat down on a wide sofa, probably the first man to sit on it in a hundred years. Ought to give me a kick, he smiled. One thing was certain, namely that Maidwood would play a part in his existence whether he wanted or not. Frankly, he didn't, but Maidwood wouldn't take any notice of that, and the same went for Linda. That woman had entered his life, coming in through the front door so to speak. He should ask Vivienne down as soon as possible. She had the gift of putting women in their place, instinctively knowing where it was. Where was Mrs Mawson's place? Beside her husband in the estate office, he said half aloud, rising from the sofa. He switched on the lights of the three Dutch candelabra to see what the gold stars looked like in full light. However, the candelabra gave only a dim, lugubrious light, leaving the stars in the shadow. He saw that one of the french windows opened on the unkempt garden beyond which extended the neglected park. A few rain drops fell from the inky clouds.

It was a picture of desolation, the oaks, beeches and conifers seemed to shiver from neglect. Two Frisian cows grazed in the distance. A little life at least, he thought, approaching the ha-ha that separated the garden from the park.

As if by magic a red faced man, wearing gumboots, appeared, doffing his cap. His hair was ginger and grey. 'I'm Hackett,' he said.

'The gardener.'

'And plumber and electrician and mason and caretaker and everything else, sir. These two hands keep the house from crumbling, the roof from falling in, and rain water pouring into the rooms. The wife will be looking after you, so says Mrs Mawson.'

'Do you smoke?' asked Osbert, holding out his packet of cigarettes.

'Only a pipe, sir.'

That was to be expected. 'Whose cows are those?'

'Mr Simpson's. He farms the Home Farm. Miss Hinley let his cattle graze in the park. His sheep come too which keeps the grass down. I wish he'd donkeys to eat the thistle. How do you like the house?'

'It's big.'

'If I was you I'd pull it down and live in Rose Cottage in the village.'

'Rose Cottage?'

'The lease falls in this year, the nicest cottage in the village, but if you don't like it you could build a bungalow here, I mean once you pulled down Maidwood House.'

I forgot that there's the village too, said Osbert to

himself. 'I want to get my bearings before I take any decision.'

'That's it,' said Hackett in an approving voice.

'Where do you and your wife live?'

'In the house, sir. Second floor, I mean what's left of it.'

Osbert despised himself for the comfort Hackett's words gave him. Stupid fool, was he afraid to be alone in that manless house?

'Was butler's quarters, so they tell me,' continued Hackett. 'We knocked two rooms in one because they were small, then two more rooms in one, so we're all right, and now that them sisters have left nobody spies on the wife and me, not that Miss Hinley ever listened to spying.'

'What did she listen to?' Osbert couldn't resist asking.

'To her saints, and that's all I think. I didn't often have a glimpse of her. The wife told me to ask you if I see you what you want for breakfast and what time? She'll bring it to the study then.'

'Nine o'clock if it suits her. Tea and boiled egg, four minutes.'

'No cornflakes or bacon?'

'Just a boiled egg.'

'I can hear a car, sir.'

'That must be Mrs Mawson. Glad to have met you, Hackett. We'll have many more chats, I'm sure.'

'I'm round the house and gardens the whole day. See that vegetable patch behind that big cedar? That's ours, Miss Hinley's special orders, but you can have any veg you want, sir, you're welcome to them.'

'Very kind of you. Good night.'

'Good night, sir. Tea and boiled egg at nine sharp.'

Osbert met Linda in the middle of the drawing room. As he had forgotten to switch off the lights she appeared to him as if she were the first guest arriving at a party he was giving. She had changed into a dark, tight fitting woollen dress, and it was difficult to keep his eyes off the shape of breasts and hips. They must be the sort of breasts women-hungry men dream of.

'I don't think I've ever seen the lights switched on in this room,' she said. 'You're certainly changing the place. To its advantage, I think. The car is at the door.'

That same intimate voice of the person who guesses your thoughts because you are such old friends. Probably she spoke like that to everybody, no cause to take notice of it. She switched off the drawing room lights as they went out. The drizzle had ceased though the clouds remained.

'In the abomination of desolation, that is the park, I met Hackett,' he said, getting into the car beside her. It was the same dark grey Ford.

'He talks too much, so does his wife. You'll have to keep them at arm's length.'

'I think you'll be a very useful guide.'

'I'll do all I can.'

What was he to do? Kiss her on the cheek, or just put his arm round her shoulders, the two lovers needing no words to express their feelings?

'Thank you,' he said. 'The idea of a house without men for over a hundred years continues to fascinate me. Therefore, my aunt too. I met her only twice in my life. Did she ever mention me?'

'Never. Once I asked about the boy in the framed photograph. "That's not a boy," she said. "That's my late brother."'

'And you didn't know that the late brother had a son.'

'I didn't,' she said, 'but now I do.'

'Obviously,' he laughed, disliking his laugh.

'One couldn't put questions to your aunt. Questions

and answers just weren't part of her life. She put no questions to me, and it wouldn't have occurred to me to put any question to her. No how did you sleep, or how do you feel today. None of that.'

'What did you talk about?'

'It's difficult to answer. She talked about the books she read, mostly lives of saints, the writings of Cardinal Newman and everything Blaise Pascal had written. I would come in, and she would start where she left off the day before. "I was thinking, Linda, about St Augustine," and off she was. I think the only question she ever put to me was "Have you any children?" and that years after she met me.'

'Have you?'

'No children. We've reached the village.'

The houses were built of Cotswold stone, many of them had thatched roofs, and there was a fountain with benches round it in the little square.

'The poor man's Broadway,' observed Osbert.

'Not so poor. We've a few City commuters. Here we are.'

The Mawsons' cottage had a thatched roof too. Very olde worlde, said Osbert to himself as he followed her in. The hall was small and narrow, an oak chest the only furniture. The sitting room was straight out of a chintzmaker's coloured advertisement. 'All this is Jack's,' she said as if to show that she had guessed his thought. 'We brought it from Norfolk.'

Mawson appeared, smoking a pipe, his welcoming smile a special effort. 'Have you met Hackett?' he asked. 'I'm sure he was the first person you saw when you went back to the house.' Osbert said he had met him. 'He's a good worker, knows his different jobs, but don't listen to him. Anyhow, he talks too much.'

'Would you like whisky or gin?' asked Linda.

'Whisky, please,' said Osbert, and Mawson, who took nothing, continued talking, hardly letting Osbert put in a word edgeways. From Hackett he moved on to Simpson, of the Home Farm, from Simpson to Jackson on Pond Farm, then to Yailor on Rock Farm, and Linda, who sat in an armchair, smoked one cigarette after the other, remaining aloofly silent. A scratch on the door was followed by a whimper, Mawson opened the door, a basset hound trotted into the room and sat down at Linda's feet, his eyes filling with pathos as she scratched his long ears. She seemed completely engrossed in the scratching, and Osbert couldn't help thinking that she had become unaware of his and Mawson's presence.

'I'll see if the meal is ready,' she suddenly said, rising from the armchair. The basset hound left the room with her.

'Dealing with farmers,' went on Mawson, taking no notice of their departure, 'is the trickiest part of my job. It's a matter of saying no all the time.'

'Saying no to what?'

'To all they ask and insist on. But one must be a farmer oneself to be able to say no.'

'And you are a farmer, so Bone, the solicitor, told me.'

'I was born on a farm, and worked on that farm with my farmer father and farmer brother. I took this job when my father died. Being in partnership with a brother isn't my idea of a happy relationship.'

'Why?'

'Dinner is ready,' said Linda from the door. So Osbert got no reply to his question. Besides, he forgot it at once as Mawson didn't interest him enough to want to know more about him. He felt he had summed him up enough for his purpose, which was to keep his distance from him, the farmers and the running of the estate. No involvement, he said to himself several times while Mawson continued holding forth.

The dining room was exactly as a cottage dining

room should be. That's his taste, not mine, Linda's eyes said. It was all oak, and on the sideboard stood a Spode soup tureen which, Osbert was sure, had never been used. The food matched the room, no imagination yet you couldn't complain about it. Beer was served with the meat, then Mawson produced a bottle of tawny port. Linda remained silent during dinner too. The basset hound slept beside her chair. A giggling girl from the village brought in the dishes, left them beside the soup tureen, stared at Osbert, and when she went out closed the door noisily. Mawson had reached the accountant who came monthly from Banbury to examine the books. 'He's twice divorced,' said Linda, her only contribution to dinner talk.

'I'm sure you don't want to stay out too long tonight,' said Mawson as they rose from the table.

'Your guess is right,' said Osbert, hating Linda for her silence.

'I'll drive you back,' she said.

'I'll take you tomorrow morning round the estate in the landrover,' said Mawson, seeing him to the door.

'Are you always so silent?' Osbert asked as they drove off, leaving behind the whimpering basset hound.

'I saw no reason to interrupt Jack. He wants to put you into the picture, and I've nothing to do with the picture.'

'I think I feel like you.'

'Jack is fanatically devoted to the estate. The less Miss Hinley bothered about it the more he attached himself to his work.'

She's trying to sell me her husband, he thought. 'That's a great relief for me,' he said. 'In that respect I'm like my aunt. I don't want to bother either.'

'You can let Jack do all the bothering. He's very much the bothering sort.'

'Oh good.'

The car stopped in front of the house which to Osbert looked sinister in the pale moonlight. If he rang the bell a ghostly footman with a grinning skull would appear holding a taper. Luckily he didn't know where the bell was.

'I'll come in and show you where the switches are,' said Linda.

'Do.'

She went in, he followed, she switched on the enormous Regency chandelier which gave as dim a light as the candelabra in the drawing room. Too many dark corners here, said Osbert to himself. 'I wish I could offer you something to drink, but I'm sure there's no drink in this house.'

'Your aunt never had a drink. Tap water was served with her meals.'

She stood facing him with her back to the staircase as if wanting to bar his way. Again her eyes looked straight into his, though this time he felt no compulsion to look away.

'Perhaps you'll have a cigarette with me,' he said, holding out his packet. She took it, he lit it for her, and felt her breath as she let out the smoke of the first puff. He ought to step back: he remained where he was. 'Tell me,' he said, 'did my aunt know that she was dying? You made me curious about her.'

'She was expecting death ever since I knew her.'

'Was she afraid of it?'

'She looked forward to it. For her this was a world of shadows. The real world was up there.' She says up there and not Heaven, he thought. 'Life for her would begin in death. She'd a heart attack two years before she died. "Most disappointing," she said when she recovered. The last time I saw her was in the morning during our daily chat. She had made me read *Les Pensées* of Pascal. . . .'

'Whom I never read.'

'You ought to. I left as usual. I always came on foot to see her, and on reaching our cottage I heard the telephone ringing. It was Jack to tell me that the parlourmaid had raced over to the office with the news that Miss Hinley had fallen on the floor on her way to the study. She always received me in the bedroom. She was dead by the time I drove here. I telephoned doctor and priest in Banbury.'

'What did she look like in death?'

'Exactly as she looked in life. I understood then that for her death wasn't an effort.' Her voice quavered. 'I don't know how to express it.'

'I understand, so I think at least.'

'I miss her terribly.'

'I'm an awfully curious person, perhaps because of my barrister training. Why did you come on foot to see my aunt?'

'To be able to look forward to our talk, and to meditate on what she said on my way back. Good Lord, I must chase home. Good night, and don't fear her ghost. It's a very gentle one.'

She went without looking back, feeling his eyes on her. She got into the car, waited a little as if expecting the door to open. She smiled to herself, lit a cigarette, and drove to the cottage. The basset hound barked as she entered the sitting room. Mawson sat in an armchair, smoking his pipe. She threw herself on the sofa on the other side of the fireplace.

'Well?' he said.

'It's going too well, in fact too fast.'

'It can't be fast enough for me.'

'You're becoming frightened of your own shadow, Jack.'

'His shadow, and it's a very substantial one. Listen, Linda. I studied him during dinner. It's all an act. These dapper fellows with smooth manners are more dangerous than men who throw their weight about.

This one is all smiles, but I bet the smiles go when he's alone.'

'I don't think they do,' she said, playing with the basset hound's ears.

'I'm nobody's fool,' said Mawson, which was his favourite expression. 'No man who comes into an estate like Maidwood will behave as he behaved before he came into it. He pretends he's unimpressed, just an act. And why does he act? He acts because he doesn't want to show his cards yet.'

'Cards?'

'Cards. He needs me now because he needs me, understand? Once he got the hang of things he'll get rid of me, and then what am I going to do? What are we going to do? I don't want to lose Maidwood.'

'He won't want to get rid of you, rest assured of that.'

'He'll want to, and that's why I need your help. You're involved in this as much as I.'

'Because I haven't enough imagination or strength to think up some other sort of life.'

Mawson knocked out his pipe on the fender, then with his hands in his pockets he faced her, his small brown eyes narrowing. Hers were fixed on the basset hound's ears.

'He likes you,' he said. 'It's easy to see. In the beginning he'll definitely be lonely here. You can easily become the guiding light.'

'And if I fall for him in my attempt? Have you thought of that, Jack?'

'You're not the sort to fall for anybody,' he said, filling his pipe.

'Once being enough? I might become that guiding light, he most certainly needs someone to explain things, but if he is the man you take him for will my guiding light suffice?'

'That's up to you.'

36

She stood up, and folding her arms she asked, looking hard at him, 'How far do you want me to go?' He smiled at his pipe, 'Answer.'

'You're clever and intelligent enough not to go too far,' he said.

'One can't ever get an honest answer out of you.' There was no anger or passion in her voice. She was simply stating an obvious fact.

'The real danger lies two years ahead,' he said, after lighting the pipe. 'In two years time Simpson's lease ends. I want that lease.'

'And remain the estate manager?'

'I can cope with the farm and the estate. You know I can.'

'I admit you can. Nobody will ever accuse you of not being keen on work. A lot can happen during the next two years.'

'I must be firmly in the saddle when the two years are up. Since Miss Hinley's death I don't feel there's a saddle at all.' His voice shook with anger. 'I'd every right to expect her to do something for me before she died. Where would Maidwood be without me?'

'I always had the feeling that in your conceit you thought she would leave Maidwood to you.'

'She said so once.'

'Jack, you're lying. All she said to you was that she couldn't imagine Maidwood without you.'

'With Osbert Hinley I might lose Maidwood altogether. How do we know that he hasn't got some pal he wants to give my job to? He can give me a year's notice if he wants to. Miss Hinley was devoted to you, yet you didn't use your influence.'

'Make her change her will?'

He went to the window, pulled the curtain aside, gazed at the moon which shone on the edge of a cloud, then retraced his steps to the fireplace, enough time to leave her question unanswered. 'It's no good crying over spilt milk, but we don't want it to be spilt again, and that's your job, Linda.'

'My impression is that all Hinley wants is peace and quiet, and for his peace and quiet he needs you.'

'We can't take risks, and we don't know the man. When Bone phoned me I asked him what he was like. Bone doesn't think much of him. He said he wasn't the sort he would trust, and advised me to watch my step.'

'And you want me to watch his step.'

'We don't want to miss the bus a second time.'

'We missed the bus the first time because you thought in your immense conceit that Miss Hinley might leave Maidwood to you. She left you a thousand pounds, so you didn't miss the bus completely.'

'What's a thousand pounds when my whole future is at stake?'

'It isn't, you'll see that it isn't.'

'I trust you, Linda, the man definitely likes you.'

'I'm going to bed. Come, Nick.'

'I won't be long.'

She went upstairs with the basset hound, and opening the bedroom door she asked herself for perhaps the hundredth time why they continued sharing the same bed, but to move to the guest room or tell him to move to it would break their tacit, almost instinctive, understanding that their relationship wasn't dead as long as they didn't speak about it. She undressed in front of the wardrobe glass, and when she was naked she examined her reflection as though it were a stranger's. The stranger in the glass had firm breasts, hardly any belly, and the thighs and legs were well shaped. She gave the stranger a quick smile, then hurried to the bathroom, for she wanted to be in bed with the light out when Mawson came upstairs.

He came half an hour later, making as little noise as he could, pretending he didn't want to wake her though he knew that she was awake. While he undressed in silence she said to herself without anger or rancour that this was the man for whom in her passion she had given up everything. But so had he. He got into bed, and if their knees or backs met in the course of the night neither of them noticed it. Nick snored in an armchair.

THREE

When Osbert heard Linda's car leaving he sighed like one who is deeply disappointed. Did he expect her to come back, holding his hand, and take him to the bedroom? Still sighing, he mounted the stairs, found the switch of the L-shaped passage, then went into his aunt's study. Here Linda had sat at the old woman's feet, listening to her dissertations about St Augustine and Pascal, a picture he couldn't imagine, so he dismissed it from his mind. It came back, however, as he looked at the books on the shelves. Lives of more saints than I ever heard of, he said to himself. He opened the bedroom door. He would sleep there because the bed was made, tomorrow he would move to a room less crammed with furniture. Tomorrow? Tomorrow night he would be back in his Bloomsbury flat, the prospect of which ought to give him the strength to spend the night in his aunt's bed. He lifted a curtain next to one of the many tables. Beyond it was the recess with the wax statue of the Virgin and the prie-Dieu. Here the old woman had prayed for hours. He sunk on the prie-Dieu, considering that the fitting thing to do, and he would, since he owed it to her, pray for the eternal rest of her soul. But hadn't her soul been at rest on earth too?

Instead of praying he found himself wondering what her prayers had been like. What sort of prayers did people who asked for no earthly pleasures or goods send up? Grant me this, grant me that, was the usual run of prayers. She had wanted nothing on earth since (according to Linda) death was no effort for her. No effort is needed where there is no fear. I fear fear, he said half aloud, and it wouldn't have surprised him if his practically unknown aunt had appeared to tell him that the fear of fear was the fear of death, and you feared death only if you didn't trust enough the resurrected Christ. He rose from the prie-Dieu, and went in search of the bathrooms. He found them, chose the first and on his return to the bedroom he drew the curtain of the recess before getting into bed.

Silence was disturbingly complete, not even the screech of an owl to remind him of the living world. I'm beginning to understand, he thought, that convicts in their cells welcome the visit of mice. A few years ago, when their affair was burning high, he had observed to Vivienne that fear was his only fear. The fear of being frightened by a burglar, the fear of panicking if a doctor were to tell him that he suffered from an incurable disease, in short the fear of being afraid of dying. Vivienne, who loved such conversations, said that death was better than dying because the dead weren't afraid any more. 'Before the exam and after the exam,' she said. He loved her too much at the time to tell her that she didn't understand what he meant.

The fear of fear, he repeated to himself, and old Ramsbottom appeared, saying in a cautionary voice, 'It's cold next door,' and cigar ash streamed down his waistcoat. Osbert slept soundly till seven in the morning.

The water was hot in the bathroom which he found surprising. His aunt surely washed in cold water. He heard footsteps in the passage, it must be Mrs Hackett, and he went back to the bedroom, leaving the bathroom door open, to show her that he hadn't evaporated in the night. When he was dressed he pulled the curtains, and looked out. The windows gave on the park, and in the sunshine it seemed less desolate. The golden days of Aranjuez are on their way back, he smiled to himself. There was now a whole herd of cattle grazing among the oaks and beeches. The sky was cloudless and the sun shone gently with September restraint. Mrs Hackett was moving about in the study. Let's meet her, he said to himself.

Mrs Hackett was about fifty, and wore a mini-skirt. She had thinning red hair and her nose was long. 'Good morning, Mr Hinley,' she said with a strong Oxfordshire accent. 'I laid your breakfast on this table. Is it okay?' He said it most certainly was. 'I don't know which table Miss Hinley used because it was Mary, the parlourmaid, who looked after her, not too much work, I can assure you. Hackett tells me he met you last night. He said you want a four minutes boiled egg. It's in the eggcosy to keep it warm.'

'Thank you so much.'

'Hackett is my second husband. I was widowed when he courted me. My first hubby was a garagekeeper.' Her voice implied that marrying Hackett had been a mesalliance. 'He died stupidly, God rest his soul.'

'Stupidly?'

'He repaired the engine of a car, then got into it to try it out, and a lorry drove bang into it, killing him outright. It was Ken who came to tell me.'

'Ken?'

'Of course, you don't know nobody here. Ken's the grocer's errand boy. That boy's everywhere. You can't take a step without Ken turning up on his bike. They say in the village that he cycles round even on a Sunday so to be everywhere. Sit down, Mr Hinley, or egg and tea will get cold.'

He sat down, and she hovered over him like a bird of prey while she chatted on, Osbert wondering how she and Hackett managed as both were fast talkers.

'Hackett was unmarried,' she was saying. 'He says

he'd some secret sorrow when he was in the Army. He was a regular soldier. All men say they've secret sorrows, just to make themselves important. He proposed to me with his secret sorrow. Why not? I said to myself, and so I came here, and that was seven years ago. Mr and Mrs Mawson were here already. He went to fetch you at the station, didn't he?'

'That's it.'

'He's been running the estate a long time, as you surely know, but it's Mr Wheeler who comes to the house most often. He's from Bucks. They say he's getting married to some girl from Bicester.'

'I see,' said Osbert who wished he could get the chatterbox talking about Linda, but refrained from mentioning her because it seemed to him unfair and below the belt. Or was it because he didn't want to hear anything nasty about her?

'Have you come to settle in?' Mrs Hackett asked.

'I've got a flat in London and my work keeps me there most of the time.'

'Isn't Mr Mawson lucky,' she exclaimed.

'Lucky?'

'Miss Hinley she never went out, and now you won't be here much either. Can I say something?' He nodded, then buttered a piece of burnt toast. 'Mr Mawson goes about like he was the real lord of the place.'

'That doesn't worry me.'

'I'm not saying that to say something bad about him. Hackett and me think he's a very good landlord.' She ogled Osbert as she said that. 'But what I always say is if you don't buy something then it isn't yours.' Osbert couldn't help grinning. 'We'd a garage hand when my Tom was alive, a good boy, but once I caught him – I was looking out through the upstairs window – saying to a gent who stopped his car and asked for the boss that it was him. I flew down and

43

gave him hell, not that Mr Mawson would ever think of saying he was the boss, but what I mean is Hackett and me thought when we heard that you was coming that ... well, it would be a little different now.'

'Mr Mawson will continue running the place. I'm afraid I'll be a bit of an absentee landlord.'

'You let Hackett and me know always when you come so to have things ready for you.'

'I most certainly will. When I come down next time I'd like a different bedroom.'

'Finish your tea, and I'll show you the bedrooms. Six are furnished. The best is the porch room that looks on the drive. You can see who comes from a long way.'

'May I come in?' called Linda.

'Come in,' called back Osbert, the door opened and she appeared, wearing brown corduroy trousers and a yellow sweater that showed the shape of her breasts. If I went up to her and kissed her I would find it the most natural thing in the world, he thought. His fingers itched to touch the breasts, which would be the most natural thing in the world too. Before either of them could speak Mrs Hackett said, 'Mr Hinley's asked me to move him into another bedroom.'

'Don't you like your aunt's?' Linda asked, turning her grey eyes on him. A lighthouse, he said to himself before saying that he liked the room, but would prefer one on a smaller scale.

'I myself don't like sleeping in a deathbed,' said Mrs Hackett. 'I'm going to show Mr Hinley the porch room.'

'Can it wait?' asked Linda. 'Jack wants to take you round the estate.'

'Of course it can,' said Osbert. 'When I come down the next time. It might be this coming weekend, I'm not sure, but I'll let you know, Mrs Hackett.'

They left Mrs Hackett in the study. Going down the stairs Linda asked, 'Did you sleep well?'

'Better than I expected.'

'I told you it's a gentle ghost. I decided to accompany you and Jack, if you don't mind.'

'You know I don't.' Why should she know, she who twenty-four hours ago had been a complete stranger to him? 'Is there a telephone anywhere?'

'In the hall under the staircase.'

'I must ring London.'

Nick, the basset hound, sat with soulful eyes in the middle of the hall. He came forward, wagging his tail as they appeared. 'There it is,' said Linda, pointing at a table in the dark shadow under the staircase. He lifted the receiver, she went to the front door accompanied by Nick, and stood with her back to him while he spoke to Vivienne. To give himself a sense of reality, he thought as he heard his voice asking her whether she was free that evening. She told him to come in when he got back from Maidwood.

'Is there a train,' he asked Linda, 'that gets me to Paddington around seven?'

'The five-ten from Banbury. Are you going back tonight?'

They were walking up the drive, their shoulders nearly touching, Nick trotting in front of them. Her gait was fast, and being more a stroller than a walker it was well nigh an effort for Osbert to keep up with her.

'I might come down for the weekend. It depends. I was almost sure there wasn't a telephone in the house.'

'I see what you mean. Your aunt never used it. Mary, the parlourmaid, or May the cook needed it, not she. Everything was prearranged with her. The taxi driver, who lives in the village, came every morning to take her to Mass. The butcher and the baker called with their vans twice a week. She had no friends, and if the doctor were wanted – I mean when I thought that he ought to see her – either the sisters or I rang him. When she wanted to see her solicitor it was I who arranged it.

As Jack and I came daily she dealt with the outside world through us, not that she had many dealings with it.'

'You were very fond of her.'

'More than I can tell.' Again her voice quavered a little.

They reached the top of the drive, he wished she would stop to let him regain his breath, and lo! she did, calling to Nick not to cross the road.

'I'm not accustomed to striding out so fast,' he said. 'I'm no countryman, but I've said that before.'

Nick trotted back, a lorry rattled past, and she stood facing Osbert, her grey eyes fixed on him. He no longer wished to turn his away.

'Don't tell them too much that you're not a countryman,' she said.

'Who are they?'

'Jack to begin with, and the farmers you'll meet this morning. You don't want to develop in them a sense of protecting and guiding the townsman, not in your interest.'

'I hope that you'll be protecting the townsman.' He shouldn't have said that, for it was going too fast, but going where?

'You can rely on me,' she said in a solemn voice, and he loved the light in the grey eyes. 'To begin with,' she laughed, 'get yourself gumboots. It's very muddy here in winter.'

'I'll buy gumboots first thing in London. What else?'

'Don't tell the farmers that you won't spend much time here. Better for them to think that you take an interest in the estate.'

'How do you know,' he laughed, 'that I take no special interest in my inheritance?'

'You made it plain to me. No reason to make it plain to them too.'

She moved on, though slowly, for which he was grateful. She guesses every wish of mine, he said to himself. The wind blew from the east, driving clouds like a flock of sheep, and it being her natural gait she strode out after a while, another effort to keep up with her. Nick lagged behind. So she doesn't guess every wish of mine, he thought. Perhaps it was better like that.

Mawson stood outside the office, waiting for them. They look like a well matched pair, he said to himself, switching on a huge smile. 'I trust you slept well,' he said.

'Very well,' said Osbert. How could she be Mawson's wife? He had never seen two people less made for each other. He shrugged his shoulders because that was no answer to his question.

'The landrover's over there,' said Mawson, pointing with his pipe.

Osbert sat beside him, Linda in the back. Mawson spoke about Simpson and the Home Farm, the best of the four farms. Simpson's lease would fall in in two years time, if Simpson mentioned it he, Osbert, should say that he left such matters to the estate manager. Jack's going too fast, thought Linda.

'Naturally I leave all that to you,' said Osbert.

The morning with the farmers neither bored nor amused him. They went out of their way to be friendly and hearty, he was friendly though not hearty, for he lacked the gift of heartiness which he didn't regret. He saw cattle, sheep, poultry, arable land and pastures, orchards too, and not once did he say to himself that all that belonged to him. He decided that Mawson was too good to be true, and he went on to think that behind the façade there might be more than met the eye, that being perhaps the answer to Linda marrying him. Of her he was constantly aware during the visits to the farmers.

'Want to be dropped at the house?' asked Mawson.

'I'd like you two to lunch with me in Banbury.'

'I can't,' said Mawson, 'but I'm sure Linda will be delighted.'

Again you're going too fast, her eyes warned him as she said that she would like to lunch with Osbert very much.

'Could you drive me first to the house to collect my things?' asked Osbert.

'You're off?' said Mawson. Osbert nodded. 'When are you coming back?'

'Perhaps this weekend, don't know yet.'

'We haven't discussed anything,' said Mawson.

'Plenty of time,' said Osbert. 'Maidwood existed without me for hundreds of years, so it can wait a little longer.'

'You shouldn't have said that,' observed Linda as she drove him to the house in the Ford.

'I said it only to your husband.'

'You didn't say it to my husband: you said it to the man you employ.'

'I say,' he smiled.

'I'm serious. Didn't you ask me to protect you? They all feared your aunt though they hardly saw her, and the few who did feared her even more. I think I was the only person who wasn't afraid of her. I used to say to myself, I don't fear that gentle smile. Yet the others did, none more than Jack, but the fear kept him working hard.' She shook her head. 'I'm getting away from the subject. You must make them respect you. If you know nothing about farming...'

'I can assure you that I know absolutely nothing about farming.'

'In that case dignified silence is the answer.'

'You're a dear,' he said.

She pretended she hadn't heard it. Anyhow, the house loomed up, Nick barked on the backseat, and when she and Osbert got out of the car, Nick's bark became shriller.

'Let me do your packing,' said Linda. 'A woman is quicker than a man.'

He sat on a chair while she put pyjamas, yesterday's shirt and dressing gown into the suitcase which he had left on the bed. As she leaned over the suitcase he couldn't help admiring her behind. Just a push, and they would land on the bed. 'Have you left anything in the bathroom?' she asked, turning round.

'My shaving things in the first bathroom.'

'I get them,' she said, leaving the room.

He got up, and went to the window. A narrow escape, he said to himself. Did she guess his thoughts this time too? Standing at the window, gazing past Hackett who was digging in his vegetable patch, he became frightened. If he continued harbouring such thoughts and desires it would end with their falling into bed in which case matters would become too complicated for his peace of mind. Besides, the outcome might easily be a personal disaster with Mawson going, dragging his wife away with him leaving him without Linda and nobody to run the estate for him. Careful, he said to himself, very careful. Linda appeared, he turned back, looked at her, and fear left him.

It returned, however, as the train took him to London. When the train had arrived in Banbury station, he leaned forward, planted a kiss on her cheek, murmuring, 'Thank you for being such a help.' Without glancing back he climbed into the nearest carriage, thus couldn't see her reaction. She had a smooth skin. Was that an excuse for his behaviour? And what did she think? The frightening thought was that his pecking her cheek was as natural to her as to him. It had been like that during the lunch in the country inn to which she had taken him. He felt all the time they were wasting their time with a table between them. Nothing should be between them, no chairs, no tough roast duck, only their bodies heaving together. Or not even heaving, just lying in each other's arms while chatting as they chatted in the restaurant. He was willing to bet his last penny that she too had the same sentiments while she struggled with the duck.

He had known a number of women, and he hadn't felt that sense of belonging with any of them. Vivienne and he were two different entities, and if he guessed what went on in her mind there was nothing uncanny about that since with old friends that isn't difficult. But to feel as he felt with Linda was definitely uncanny. Why hadn't they known each other all their lives? He had never put that question with any other woman.

'Pardon me,' said a bearded man who sat opposite him. 'When do we get to Bicester?'

'This train goes through Oxford, so there won't be Bicester.'

'Dear me,' said the bearded man, and went on reading his newspaper.

The trouble was that she happened to be Mawson's wife. Were she on her own she would now be sitting in the bearded man's place. Being Mawson's wife he must control himself if he didn't want to race to disaster. He might not be a pious, staunch Catholic as his aunt had been, yet he wasn't the man to break up marriages. Besides, he couldn't marry a divorced woman for he wouldn't sleep in peace if he cut himself loose from the Church. Anyway he wasn't the marrying kind. He must stop, and it is easier to stop at the beginning of the road than in the middle of it.

'Pardon me,' said the bearded man, 'is this Oxford?'

'It's Reading.'

'Dear me.'

Vivienne must come down for the weekend. If she couldn't manage this weekend let her come down the following weekend. Her presence in Maidwood would dissolve the silly dream. What he was feeling was a silly dream, and nothing else.

'Look, sir, we're in Paddington,' the bearded man exclaimed as the train entered the station. 'At last I can get out.'

The taxi queue was too long, so Osbert went down into the tube, changed at Oxford Circus, alighted at Holborn, and when he entered his flat through the kitchen he firmly declared to himself that Linda had become a pale shadow. His trouble was, he thought, that he like imagining things that ended badly. Linda was intelligent enough to understand that the little peck was just a sign of gratitude. He looked at his engagement book that lay on the vast writing table: tomorrow he had two appointments. Life was going on, silly fancies would vanish as he moved with it. Probably to find other silly fancies, he laughed to himself. As long as they're not the estate manager's wife. It was time to go to Vivienne.

She let him into her flat herself. When she had guests for dinner she hired a Mrs Hickson, who was a lady in her own right in as much as her late husband had been an unsuccessful painter of some distinction. She cooked to make both ends meet, and expected to be respected as an artist's widow. Hence it was out of the question for her to open the door.

'Simon is here,' said Vivienne.

Simon Payne was a man of wealth and erudition. He didn't like mentioning his wealth which his forebears had acquired in the nail trade. He preferred to talk about Palladian villas and the paintings of Le Nain.

'My dear Osbert,' he said as Osbert appeared in the Louis XVI drawing room, 'I hear you came into a white elephant.'

'If you saw Maidwood you'd say that the white elephant came into me.'

'Stamped on you,' said Vivienne.

'And poor Osbert is squashed flat,' said Simon. 'What is the place like?'

Osbert described the house, not forgetting to mention that his first impression was that he looked at a soldier who had lost an arm in the Crimea.

'Dali ought to paint that,' said Vivienne.

'And sell it as a railway poster,' laughed Simon.

'What is it like inside?' asked Vivienne.

Osbert spoke of the drawing room with the gold stars.

'You ought to put an organ into it,' said Simon.

'Whose organ?' laughed Vivienne, which made prudish Simon frown. 'Osbert, darling, tell Simon about the man on the doorstep, so fascinating.'

'I went to see a solicitor in Westminster,' said Osbert. 'On the doorstep of the house next door stood a little old man whom I've never seen in my life before. As I went past he called to me in a warning voice, "It's cold next door."'

'Very significant,' said Simon. 'Very deep.'

'Significant? Explain, darling.'

Mrs Hickson poked her head in to say in a dignified voice that the cold trout in aspic was on the kitchen table, the roast duck in the oven, and the apple charlotte on the shelf above the table. 'And now I wish you good night,' she added. 'Perhaps you'll send me a cheque tomorrow or the day after.'

'She doesn't accept cash,' said Vivienne as the door closed on Mrs Hickson. 'She wants a cheque however small the sum is. Thinks it's more dignified like that.'

'When I spoke about the little old man and it's cold next door, you said it was significant,' said Osbert. 'What did you mean, Simon?'

'Forgot,' said Simon in a plaintive voice. 'When I'm interrupted I invariably forget. On my deathbed I'll forget my famous last words because the doctor or some other fool will interrupt.'

'What a loss to humanity,' laughed Vivienne. 'Come, we're going to dine.'

They helped her to take the food into the dining room which was almost smaller than Osbert's in Bloomsbury. Significant, thought Osbert while Simon told Vivienne a long story about the weekend he had spent in Le Touquet. It's cold next door might signify that Linda was next door. It couldn't be cold wherever Linda was. So she couldn't be next door, which was precisely what he feared. Should he ask Simon down too? No, Simon going down with them wouldn't achieve his aim. It must be Vivienne alone. He wouldn't speak about it till Simon left.

'You're very silent,' said Vivienne.

'The white elephant is weighing him down,' said Simon.

'What you people must understand,' said Osbert, 'is that it's worse than a white elephant in that it's more alien to me than would be a pink or a white elephant if I were asked to look after it. This morning the estate manager took me round to see the farmers. It didn't sink in. Why should I waste or spend my time chatting with those hefty men in leggings? As a matter of fact none of them wore leggings. I explained to my mind that they were my tenants. My mind refused to believe it.'

'You'll get accustomed to it,' said Simon whom the predicaments of other left always cold. 'I was reading last night a very interesting book about Byzantine art. I begin to reach the conclusion that only decadence can produce great art.'

Osbert wasn't listening. Linda had appeared, leaning over the suitcase, his eyes drinking in, as it were, her behind while every particle of him wanted to throw himself on top of her, with the same anguish of acute desire as in the bedroom at Maidwood. Vivienne must come down, for her cynical matter of fact presence

53

would keep Linda at a safe distance. What he meant, he admitted, was keeping him at a safe distance from Linda. Vivienne was saying that the Renaissance was the contrary of decadence, thus Simon's theory didn't hold good.

From decadence Simon moved on to the post-impressionists. This duck, thought Osbert, isn't as tough as the duck in the inn, and now he saw Linda sitting opposite him at the inn, speaking about his aunt. Wasn't it strange for a young woman full of the force of her age to cherish the memory of a desiccated old woman whose contribution to life had been nil? He had said so, and she answered, 'If you could have heard her speak as she spoke to me, with the quiet strength of her faith. I think she's posthumously converting me.' That wouldn't help matters either, would it? He lifted his napkin to hide his smile. Damn it, hadn't he come to Vivienne to forget Linda, or rather consider her and his feelings for her as so much nonsense and fantasy in Vivienne's flat which had long existed in his life, whereas the day before yesterday he didn't even know about a person called Linda Mawson?

After dinner they went back to the drawing room, where much brandy was drunk. Then Simon remembered that he was going to a late party, so would they forgive him if he left at once? His goodbye smile took in Vivienne and Osbert, and when he had left Vivienne observed, 'The poor innocent thinks that he's leaving us to bash our way through the night.' Her having been Osbert's mistress in the past and a close friend in the present was a matter of pride with her, and she couldn't help harping on it.

'I want you to do me a favour,' said Osbert, ignoring her words, 'a real and urgent favour. Come down to Maidwood this weekend. I want you to see that monstrosity and the people, the estate manager, his wife, and the man and the woman who look after the monstrosity.'

'Of course, I'll come down. You know that my curiosity is boundless.'

'Thank you from the bottom of my heart. I entered there a sort of fourth dimension, if you get my meaning, and I don't see why you shouldn't enter it too. The house, those new faces, even the memory of my aunt, surrounded me there like a band of highwaymen surrounding a solitary wayfarer. I don't mean there's any evil intention, but surround me they do. Your presence will make me feel less surrounded.'

'Vivienne to the rescue. I'll drive you down. I'm free from Friday morning on.'

They decided to leave Friday morning around eleven, and lunch on the way. When she saw him to the door she said with happy smiling eyes, 'Isn't it wonderful to be able to part without desire or rancour? The perfect relationship.'

'Indeed the perfect relationship,' he said, asking himself whether there could ever be a perfect relationship between him and the estate manager's wife. His next thought was that he had now an excuse to ring Linda.

However, he succeeded in keeping himself back from ringing her before Thursday afternoon. Mawson would be in the office, and she was surely in the cottage, reading one of his aunt's books, the only tangible presents she got from her. For the thousand pounds had been left strictly to Mawson.

Her voice on the telephone was slightly different from the voice he expected. In fact, not as deep as when she spoke direct to you.

'This is Osbert Hinley speaking.'

'Oh hullo,' she said.

'I'm coming down on Friday with a friend, Vivienne Long, so could you please ask Mrs Hackett to get two bedrooms ready for us.'

'I'll tell her,' said Linda after a brief silence. 'What time do you expect to arrive? I could fetch you at the station.'

'She's driving me down. We'll arrive some time in the afternoon.'

'I see.'

'Could you do me a favour? Get in drinks and things like that. I know I've no right to ask you ...'

'I told you I'd look after you,' she laughed.

'You're too kind.' He wanted to say, you're a dear. 'I'll manage the rest. I'll bring down some food for the first night.'

'I can get in food if you want.'

'Vivienne and I'll manage.' He was proud of that. 'Could you and your husband come in for drinks in the evening? I want you to meet Vivienne.'

'I look forward to it,' she said.

She remained seated in the armchair, a life of Sainte-Thérèse-de-Lisieux in her lap, but she didn't pick it up. After a while she called to Nick, who lay stretched out in front of the empty grate, 'What you need is a run,' and left the cottage with him.

They took a lane that led past the village, Nick disappeared under a hedge, she called him back, he came gambolling up to her as though they had been separated for a long time. Then he disappeared under a hedge again.

When they came back to the cottage she found Mawson on the sofa, smoking his pipe.

'I'll make you laugh,' she said. 'Osbert Hinley is coming down this weekend with a girl friend. Don't stare like that. He rang to tell met that she's bringing him down in her car. He wants us for drinks in the evening.'

'A girl friend,' said Mawson.

'Her name's Vivienne Long, if that's of any help.'

She enjoyed his discomfiture. She knew from ex-

56

perience that fundamentally he was a simple man. If anything interfered with his preconceived plans or ideas he was as bewildered as a child lost in a dark street.

'Never mind,' she laughed. 'I'll still manage to be your champion and see you're kept on.'

'You do put things bluntly,' he said, feeling better.

'I don't see why I shouldn't.'

'I'm going to the pub,' he said, getting up from the sofa. 'Are you coming?'

'Don't feel like it,' she said.

He called Nick, who wagged his tail but didn't budge. 'As you like,' he said to him, took his cane and left the cottage. Nick went to lie at Linda's feet.

How silly it all is, she thought, admitting that she wasn't exactly sure what she meant by all.

FOUR

'September,' said Vivienne, overtaking a coach filled
with old women, 'is the month of decadence. I've been
thinking of decadence ever since Simon spoke about
Byzantine art.'

'February?' asked Osbert.

'The enemy.'

She'll enjoy her weekend, said Osbert to himself. I
hope I'll enjoy it too. 'Turn to the left, then slow down
a bit because we're approaching the drive.'

'So this is the drive leading to your stately home,' she
said. 'Ought to be trees on both sides.'

'There ought to be lots of things.'

'Oh,' she exclaimed as the house loomed up. 'Never
seen anything so ugly before.'

'I agree.'

'It'll grow on you in time.'

Again he was struck by the narrow, small front door.
The house was the enemy of visitors, and wasn't he
only a visitor himself? Would Linda be there as on the
first day? Mrs Hackett came out through the front door,
grinning from ear to ear. She must have been waiting in
the hall, probably since lunch.

'Here you are Mr Hinley,' she said, her eyes on
Vivienne.

'This is Mrs Long who's spending the weekend
here,' he said. Vivienne returned Mrs Hackett's grin.
'Have you got the two bedrooms ready?'

'You're in porch room, the lady's in the room next to
it.'

'I want to see your Gothic chapel,' said Vivienne.

'Come this way,' said Osbert.

'So you know your way around,' laughed Vivienne.

In the drawing room her laughter soared to the high ceiling. The room was priceless, unbelievable and funny too. What did they have in mind when the house was built? And the stars. Did they want to feel in Heaven or what? She threw herself on a sofa to laugh better. 'Show me the rest,' she said after her laughter had subsided.

The dining room and the library she found acceptable though deplored the taste of those who had furnished it. Where was Linda? As if in answer to his wish she appeared as he took Vivienne into the unkempt garden. The sun was out, only a few clouds sailed in the breeze, and the park was innocent of cattle, thus looking even more desolate than on his first day.

Linda hadn't wanted to come before the evening, but Mawson insisted with such emphasis that she gave in simply not to hear the insistence in his voice. She had asked Mrs Hackett to ring her when Osbert and his guest arrived.

Osbert felt relieved at the sight of her. She's my strength here, he thought, smiling at her. Then he introduced the two women to each other, such contrasts what with Vivienne's smart worldly presence and Linda's almost solemn countenance. Vivienne wore a well cut grey skirt and jacket, her slimness and flat chest seemed to exaggerate Linda's broad shoulders, breasts and the simplicity of her blue jumper and brown tweed skirt.

'I got the drinks in,' said Linda. 'Mrs Hackett got the rooms ready.'

'She told me so,' said Osbert, wishing that Vivienne hadn't come. Wasn't it he who had asked her down?

'Where can I cook the dinner?' he asked. 'I brought down food from London.'

'There's a small kitchen at the end of the first floor passage,' said Linda. 'It was I who persuaded Miss Hinley to have it rigged up because the real kitchen is too far.'

'What flower is this?' asked Vivienne.

'Cow parsley,' said Linda. 'There shouldn't be any of it here, but Hackett says he hasn't the time to look after the garden.'

'But I like it,' said Vivienne.

Hackett was digging in his plot with his back to them. Linda and Osbert exchanged an amused look which Vivienne missed.

'Is all that yours too?' asked Vivienne, making a sweeping gesture that took in the park.

'Alas,' he laughed, sure that Linda didn't care for the alas. 'Where's Nick?'

'I left him in the cottage,' said Linda.

'Bring him in the evening,' said Osbert.

'Is that your child?' said Vivienne.

'My dog,' said Linda. 'We haven't any children.'

'I haven't either,' said Vivienne in an approving voice. 'I've no dog. Even a dog is too much of a responsibility.'

'I don't mind responsibility,' said Linda as if speaking to herself.

'I'd like to see my room,' said Vivienne.

They went upstairs, Vivienne laughed at the minstrels' gallery, and when Linda stopped in the passage to open a door she observed, 'You do know your way around here.'

'Not surprising after all the years,' said Linda.

The porch room and the room Mrs Hackett got ready for Vivienne were furnished with no taste whatever. 'Could be rooms in an oldfashioned boarding house,' Vivienne muttered. Then raising her voice and speaking with excessive politeness, 'Thank you so much for showing me round. I think I'm going to put my feet up for a few minutes. Always need it after a long drive. Call me in half an hour, Osbert. I understand,' that was for Linda again, 'we'll see you this evening.'

'I'll bring up your suitcase when I come back,' said Osbert.

'Hackett can do that,' said Linda.

'I don't want to disturb him,' laughed Osbert.

He followed Linda to the staircase, where she turned round, saying 'Jack and I will come at half past six. Is that all right?'

'Of course it is. See you down to your car.'

'Don't bother,' she said, and ran down the stairs. Though she was sure that he was watching her from the minstrels' gallery she went out of the house without looking back. She drove to the office, but Jack wasn't there. He had gone in the landrover to see one of the farmers, Rex Wheeler told her. She drove on to the cottage, and Mawson rang her an hour later. 'What is she like?' he asked.

'I can't tell you on the 'phone,' she said, 'though I can promise you a good laugh.'

'I'm coming back rightaway.'

If her woman's conceit had a blow, she thought, Jack's blow would be far more lethal.

'Well?' he said, striding into the room.

'You must have run. No car goes so fast.'

'What is she like?'

'She's a self-possessed domineering woman, one I couldn't cross swords with. Your great plan or scheme – call it by any name you want – has misfired, I can assure you.'

'What do you mean?'

'I feel like a village bumpkin in her presence. I don't think he needs anything from me with her around.'

To her surprise Mawson didn't seem surprised or upset.

'The game is up,' she said. Perhaps that would make him twig.

'I can't see what you're fussing about,' he said. 'I never for a moment thought that we ...'

'You mean me.'

'... that you should bother about his London life. That woman surely belongs to his London life. What I thought was that you should influence him, I mean be nice to him, here in Maidwood. This woman won't come down every weekend, but he will live here, I'm sure of that, and it's here and nowhere else that your influence, his friendship for you will matter. What does she care who's the estate manager or who'll be the next tenant of the Home Farm? Linda, I'm nobody's fool. It's here we want him to listen to you. What they do in London is no business of ours.'

'You're a simpleton.'

'I don't think so for the moment.' He jumped up from the armchair. 'If it comes to the worst we can get rid of the Hacketts. Then he won't have anybody to fall back on except you.'

The dungheap Machiavelli, she muttered to herself. 'We're going there at half past six,' she said. 'I won't put on my best dress because it'll look cheap beside the dress she's sure to wear. I'll go in this lousy skirt and like it.'

He grunted, then filled his pipe. He wanted to say that with all her intelligence and poise she was no better than the rest of the women who trod the earth. Vanity and conceit, bothered only by trifles, and seeing in every other woman a competitor even if she didn't compete. However, he knew that he wouldn't say that because that would start an argument, and they had given up arguing long ago. 'If a woman wants a man to do something,' he said instead, 'she can always achieve it.'

'If he isn't tied to another woman.'

There you are, he said to himself.

She didn't even bother to put on a new makeup when they set out with Nick at a quarter past six. Vivienne's car was in the same spot in front of the entrance. Very symbolic, thought Linda. They entered the hall, and saw the drawing room door open. Osbert appeared, saying, 'Come in here. Vivienne has insisted on having drinks in the Gothic chapel, a new departure for Maidwood, don't you think?'

'Hullo,' said Vivienne, rising from a sofa. 'So you're the husband. What will you have?'

Linda and Mawson had gin and tonic. Vivienne and Osbert whisky and soda, and again Linda thought that it was very symbolic too, having drinks in the never used drawing room. Nick sat under a candelabra looking lost.

'Mrs Mawson knew my aunt very well,' said Osbert to make conversation.

'How interesting,' said Vivienne. 'She neglected this house, didn't she?'

'There was no room for the house in her thoughts,' said Linda. 'She lived in two rooms upstairs, and earthly matters didn't interest her beyond them.'

'Why didn't she get rid of it?'

'Because she wanted to leave it to her nephew,' said Linda who hadn't once glanced at Osbert though she felt his eyes on her.

'An excellent answer,' said Osbert, and Vivienne laughed her high pitched laugh.

'Glover, the accountant,' said Mawson, addressing Osbert, 'is coming over tomorrow morning. Shall I bring him here or are you coming to the office to meet him?'

'It'll have to be some other time,' said Osbert. 'I've got a guest to look after.'

'Surely your guest won't mind if you absent yourself for an hour,' said Mawson, ignoring Linda's warning look.

'Of course I won't,' said Vivienne. 'It's your duty, darling, to see the accountant. We live in an age of accountants, don't you agree?' The don't you agree was addressed to Linda.

'I wouldn't know,' she said.

'I'll come to the office,' said Osbert.

'Does that dog of yours never move?' asked Vivienne.

'He's overawed by this room,' said Linda.

'Aren't we all?' laughed Vivienne.

The conversation continued in that vein till Hackett made his entrance. He had come, he explained, on behalf of his wife who had gone into Banbury. At what time would Mr Hinley and his guest have breakfast? He beamed at them, then stared round him as though he hadn't seen the drawing room before, which, thought Osbert, was quite possible. Osbert wanted tea and boiled egg, Vivienne only tea and toast. 'No hearty country breakfasts for me,' she laughed. Hackett laughed with her because he liked her laughter.

'You have a drink with us,' said Osbert.

'A tot of Scotch, thank you ever so much,' said Hackett.

He drank the whisky in one gulp, accepted a cigarette from Osbert, and when it was lit he wished them good night, and scuttled from the room.

'If I may say so,' said Mawson whose cheeks had turned purple, 'you shouldn't have offered him a drink.'

'Why not?'

'Because it'll spoil him and give him ideas.'

'Above his station?' smiled Osbert.

'It's like that in the country,' said Mawson.

'Jack's very old fashioned,' said Linda.

'I know the people,' snapped Mawson.

'We ought to be going,' said Linda. 'I've got to put the chicken to bed.'

Osbert saw them to the door, and Linda took care not to meet his eyes. For hers had nothing to say to him.

'Hell,' said Vivienne as Osbert returned to the drawing room. 'What I mean is they're sheer hell.'

'He's the man who runs the place, and her I rather like.'

'She's a scheming woman, the two of them work together like a couple of thieves. I guessed at once what they're after.'

'Come off it, they're after nothing that could harm me.'

'So you say,' she said, lying back on the sofa, 'because you choose to be an innocent because that's less of an effort. He has run the estate for eight years, and she sucked up to your aunt. Sharing the effort, I call that. With you they're going to share the effort again, he doing on the estate as he pleases, she sucking up to you, but, my dear, you suck up differently to a man in his prime than to a desiccated old maid.'

'Nonsense,' said Osbert, helping himself to whisky. Had Linda's devotion to his aunt been calculated? Was reading Pascal part of the scheme? He refused to believe it. 'More whisky?'

'Yes, please, but don't sidestep the issue. I watched her carefully. She looked at you whenever your eyes were turned away. They were the eyes of the scheming woman. You heard the catch in her voice when she spoke of your aunt? A normal, healthy person hasn't a catch in his or her voice when speaking of a dead woman who died of old age. All that is part and parcel of the big act.'

'What's the big act?'

'The big act,' said Vivienne, sitting up, 'sticks out like a telegraph pole in a desert.' She liked that, so she repeated, 'Like a telegraph pole in a desert.'

'I've never been in a desert.'

'You're a funny dear. The big act is to keep things as they were in Miss Methuselah's time. He does what he wants while she keeps you sweet. I bet she'd go to bed with you if she thought it necessary.'

'You're going too far.'

'I know where I'm going. When your aunt died and they heard that an unknown man, who's neither old nor an eccentric, has inherited the place they were frightened out of their wits. Their rule might be over, the new owner may want to change things. The husband looks bright enough to understand that no one is irreplaceable. You could, if you wanted, find a hundred who'd be only too happy to become the estate manager. To stop that the wife has to step in.' She jumped up from the sofa, and pointed a long forefinger at him. 'You felt the same even if you refused to admit it. Why did you ask me down? Because you had your own suspicions.'

'It isn't that at all,' he said in a discouraged voice, for he couldn't explain to Vivienne that he had invited her in his fear of the almost uncanny intimacy Linda inspired in him. How could he say to her that in Linda's presence he felt as though they had been lovers all their lives? 'I don't believe a word of it. For me he's irreplaceable, and he knows as well as I that I want him to carry on as he carried on in my aunt's time.'

'She left in a huff because she thinks there's something still between us.'

That, he thought, was better to leave unanswered.

She looked out through the french window: darkness had set in, obliterating the trees in the park, and light rain fell soundlessly, the wet gravel shining in the light of the candelabras the only proof.

'I'm sick of this room,' she said. 'I tire quickly of stage sets. Is there a more human room in this house?'

'We'll go to my aunt's study. Take the glasses, I'll take the bottles.'

He closed the french windows before they left the room. Vivienne went up the stairs in front of him, and he couldn't help saying to himself that her figure was still as splendid as it had been in the days of their love. That made him think of Linda whose figure wasn't so splendid, yet he would have given a lot to have her mounting the stairs in front of him instead of Vivienne. Hadn't he asked Vivienne to Maidwood to stop him having such thoughts?

'This is my aunt's study,' he said, throwing the door open.

'Nothing feminine about it,' said Vivienne.

'There probably was nothing feminine about her, poor woman. Why poor woman? Linda told me that she was serene and happy as only those can be who fear not death. She would call us poor.'

'Linda,' said Vivienne with relish. 'I can see Linda sitting at the old woman's feet.' He wished he hadn't spoken of Linda. 'Not your serene and happy old woman: her husband's boss, the source of their income. Linda's eyes sparkle with faked devotion as the old boss dissertates on her bowels. They didn't open as well today as they opened yesterday, and Linda drinks it all in with her faked devotion.'

'You're disgusting,' he said. 'Better have a whisky.'

After the third whisky they went to the kitchen, where they drank claret he had brought from London while he prepared the meal. 'Like old times,' she said.

'We'll eat here in the kitchen,' he said. 'The study's too far.'

He unwrapped the steaks he had bought in the morning.

'I love watching you cook,' Vivienne said. 'I love this Château de Sales.'

She seemed to love everything, and forgot scheming

Linda and her scheming husband in the course of dinner. After dinner they went back to the study. 'How chilly it is here,' she said. He switched on the electric heater. She remembered that she had brought him a present, went to her room to fetch it, and when she came back she held out a bottle of brandy like a trophy. 'I want to get pissed,' she laughed. 'This house asks for it.'

'If you do,' he said, 'you'll be the first person to get pissed here these last hundred years.'

'How do you know that your aunt didn't tipple in secret?'

'I wish she did. She'd seem more human to me if I could believe that.'

'You know nothing about her. You told me so before you met the Linda woman. Now she's a sort of saint because to remember her as a saint is part of Linda's act.'

'Forget Linda.'

'I don't know what's wrong with me tonight,' she said after the third brandy, 'but I seem to like you again as a man. Funny that.'

'Don't. You'll hate yourself for it tomorrow.'

'Fuck tomorrow. When we're together we refuse the past, have no present, and don't care a rap about the future. So why should I care now? You say I'll regret it. Let me regret it. Come here and kiss me.'

He stood up obediently. Drink had made him cold and more level headed than usual. They would both regret it in the morning, and it might even jeopardise their friendship. Besides, he hadn't asked her to Maidwood for that. He bent over her, hoping that a light kiss would bring her to her senses. However, her tongue forced its way into his mouth, her arms came round his neck, and the kiss was of such vigour that he nearly reeled. So his arms went round her shoulders. When he drew back at last regaining his balance she said like one giving an order, 'I'm coming to your room right now before either of us can change his mind. Anyway, I refuse to sleep alone in this ghost packed house.'

She held on to his arm on their way to porch room. She began to undress the moment he switched on the light. Down came the skirt, showing her long thighs and legs, up went the silk jumper and her small breasts with tiny pale nipples appeared, and when she was naked his eyes fell on her rust coloured pubic hairs. There had been a time when he thought that rust coloured pubic hairs were the finest sight he could imagine.

They got into bed, the sheets were cold, and she trembled while his hands tried to warm her body. She trembled even more as he penetrated her. Then she let out a cry of pleasure, and ruffled his hair as of old as their bodies moved together. It seemed to him that two Osberts were making love to her, the Osbert of the past who had come back for this brief moment, and the Osbert he was today, the Osbert who had no business to be inside her. The first Osbert loved it, the second was sure that Linda's breasts would be more ample under him, and he would feel fewer bones. The act was finished by the first Osbert.

'I loved it,' Vivienne mumbled. 'I feel such peace now. What a large bed. Don't let me sleep alone, touch me now and then.'

She turned on her side to fall immediately asleep, he switched off the light, but sleep held back. This must have been, he mused, the first time anybody made love in Maidwood since Mr Curtis fell off his horse. The spirit of the house was dissatisfied with him, and rightly so because it went against its very essence. He had demolished a hundred years of purity. What would the consequences be? None, where Vivienne was concerned, and he dreaded her awakening. To conjure up the past should be a matter of reverie: to make love on a bed of dry leaves was killing the past outright. They wouldn't be able to speak of their halcyon days again since they would too much be reminded of tonight. He cursed the weakness of the flesh, and cursing it he fell asleep. 'It's cold next door,' said the little old man in the doorway. True enough it was cold as he woke with the grey light filtering into the room halfheartedly. He didn't have to look or put out his hand, for he knew that he was alone in the bed.

Her clothes were gone too. His watch said it was seven in the morning, so he had slept longer than he thought. He got up, put on his dressing gown and went to the window. The drive stretched towards the road that the trees hid from him. A little boy and a girl were moving along the drive with their backs to him, the girl holding the boy's hand. A strange sight in Maidwood, he thought, not the place for children. Perhaps they had come to explore, and now sick of the ugliness were returning to the road. Soon the trees hid them.

When he was a small boy and expected punishment he pretended to himself that no punishment was due. That used to last till he heard the first grown-up voice. Instead of a grown up voice he heard the bedroom door open, and he became as frightened as he had been as a child. What would Vivienne's reaction be? He continued to stare out through the window while she approached him.

'We made proper fools of ourselves last night,' she said, and he turned round because her voice reassured him. 'For God's sake don't let us make a song and dance about it.'

'Then why did you steal out in the night?'

'I was too shy to face you in bed in the morning.'

'Ha ha,' he laughed. 'Frankly, I'm relieved.'

She wore a navy blue dressing gown with white

lapels, and nothing under it. With one movement of his hand he could open it, and see her bony body. His hand wasn't willing, proof that Linda mattered more to him than he had been ready to admit. What it all amounted to was that asking down Vivienne had misfired completely.

'The only snag is,' Vivienne said, 'that I'm going back to London tonight.'

'Why?'

'You've no imagination, Osbert darling. Can you see us in your aunt's study as night falls and brandy follows whisky, both of us pretending noisily that last night didn't happen, and both of us hoping the other was thinking the same? It would be too ghastly for words. I'm leaving after tea.'

'I think I've enough imagination not to hold you back.'

'I'm pleased. I'd better dress before I meet your Mrs Hackett.'

Mrs Hackett wasn't talkative despite Osbert trying to make her talk. Was it because Vivienne's presence awed her?

'Tomorrow being Sunday,' she said as she was making for the door, 'I won't be able to come if you don't mind. I'll get some eggs in for you, and there's plenty of bread left.'

'That's perfectly all right by me,' said Osbert.

'I was afraid you'd mind,' said Mrs Hackett.

'Not at all,' said Osbert.

'I wish you both a happy weekend,' said Mrs Hackett, and the door closed on her.

'These people will do with you whatever they want,' said Vivienne. 'I'm truly worried about you. The Mawsons scheme, this woman doesn't make breakfast on Sundays – maybe Tuesdays or Wednesdays don't suit her either – and you've no idea what her official position is. Do you pay her for it?'

'I don't know.'

'There you are. She and her husband live in the house. Why? You told me last night he has a vegetable patch. Who gave it to him? And why does the garden look like nothing on earth?'

'He says he has too much work to do as handyman.'

'He says that. Is there anybody to clean the house? Answer.'

'I don't know.'

'And you don't know what Mawson does with the estate. In short, you know nothing. Osbert, you must either move down here and be the boss or go to the solicitor and tell him Maidwood is for sale lock, stock and barrel.'

'I've been thinking of it. I'm too fond of my London life and too ignorant of country life to move in here as the boss. As long as this place keeps itself and brings in a little money I don't see why I shouldn't go on the way I do.'

'Let's forget the estate,' said Vivienne, pushing her cup away. 'Take this house. Did you notice the dust in the drawing room? And on the stairs? Your aunt had two servants. You ought to have at least one person to look after the place.'

'The Hacketts.'

'You make me laugh. They do as they like, and if you try to pin them down they'll walk out on you, or, knowing you, they'll tell you to mind your own business.' She threw back her head to laugh better.

'What's the answer?'

'I've got it. Should have thought of it before. Mrs Hickson.'

'You mean the painter's widow who accepts only cheques?'

'Exactly. She lives somewhere in Kennington in a pretty poor way, and I think she'd be only too glad to get out into the country. Engage her as your house-

72

keeper, let her run the house, take on a daily woman or two if necessary, and the house won't look like a cowshed with her here.'

'It hasn't struck me as a cowshed.'

'It struck me. I'll ring her on Monday, a perfect solution, and this house is large enough for the two of you without you having to see her when you don't want to. I did a bit of exploring when I left your bed. On the other side of the minstrels' gallery there are five rooms along another passage. There's some furniture in them too. You could plant her there, tell Mrs Hackett that the housekeeper will run the place, so her altruistic help isn't needed any more. I'll ring Mrs Hickson first thing Monday morning. How clever of you to have asked me down.'

'More tea?'

She didn't want any more tea, and while she drew him a colourful picture of a revived, well run Maidwood he coudn't help thinking that his aunt would have done much better if she had left the place to Vivienne of whom she hadn't ever heard. Vivienne was born to boss, the bossy woman she was. Listening to her he forgot last night, and he was sure that she had forgotten it too.

However, he remembered last night as on his way to the office to meet the accountant he heard a car braking behind him and Linda's voice calling to him. The rain had ceased, the clouds remained dark, and Nick, who sat beside her, growled at him.

'I'm on my way to Banbury,' Linda said.

'I'm on my way to the office.'

Could she guess that he had lain with another woman last night? What a stupid question since it had nothing to do with the estate manager's wife. Indeed a stupid question, yet looking into her grey eyes he went on repeating it to himself, for again he felt that closeness which was beyond facts or explanations.

'The accountant,' she said. 'The office is too near to give you a lift. Is everything all right in the house? Has Mrs Long slept well?'

Partly in my arms, he nearly said. 'Very well I think, but she must go back to London tonight.'

'What a pity.'

Why must they lie to each other? 'She doesn't care for the country. A bit like me.'

'Are you going back too?'

'I'll stay till Sunday night. Mrs Hackett says she doesn't come in on a Sunday. Never mind, I'll fend for myself.'

'I'll look in tomorrow morning to see if you need anything.'

'That'll be very kind of you.'

Then, as she drove off, Vivienne's words came back to him. Scheming Mawson and his scheming wife. She would look in on him tomorrow to see if he needed anything because that was part of their scheming. She would even go to bed with him if it suited her and her husband. Supposing Vivienne was right? He had, he was the first to admit, a great inclination to live in a fool's paradise. That sense of closeness and intimacy might simply be the fancy of a man who coveted a woman. Living in a fool's paradise he imagined that she shared that closeness and intimacy, and that their becoming lovers was as much her wish as his. It isn't imagination, he said half aloud, and opened the office door.

Glover, the accountant, had a grave countenance, his words sounded grave too. None the less, he let out a chuckle at the end of every sentence. He and Mawson got on fine, and were each other's yesmen. What one said the other agreed with, and all Osbert gathered during the hour he spent with them was that everything was perfect in the garden which was precisely what Osbert wanted to hear.

They came out together the three of them. It was raining again. Glover got into a large car after assuring Osbert that he was mighty glad to have met him. 'I'll run you back to Maidwood,' said Mawson. Osbert got into the landrover beside him.

'My assistant Rex Wheeler is leaving,' said Mawson as they turned into the drive. 'He's marrying a girl from Bicester, and his father-in-law, who's a land agent, wants him to work for him. But you don't have to worry. He's leaving only next month, and I'm sure I'll find some suitable chap to take his place.'

'I never worry,' said Osbert, thinking that even if Mawson were the scheming sort Linda certainly wasn't. Why was he so certain? Damn, Vivienne.

And he damned her for the rest of her stay. She forced him to go through the entire house, even opened cupboards and moaned loudly about the awful state of everything. 'Mrs Hickson is the answer,' she repeated. When she wanted to go up to the second floor he stopped her, saying that it was the Hacketts' domain.

'But there must be lots and lots of rooms up there.'

'I don't know. Hackett told me that they knocked several rooms together.'

'And who gave them permission?'

'Probably my aunt.'

'Probably,' she sneered.

They had reached the servants' staircase which was at the end of the passage beyond the minstrels' gallery. A man in a tweed jacket and flannel trousers was mounting the stairs, smoking.

'Excuse me, who are you?' asked Vivienne.

'Linch,' said the man. 'I'm dining with Mr and Mrs Hackett.'

'They're on the second floor,' said Osbert.

'I know my way, ta,' said Linch, and climbed on.

'There you are,' said Vivienne.

'You're not going to tell me that the Hacketts can't receive guests.'

'You know what I mean. People come and go here as they like, and they treat you as if you didn't exist.'

'Possibly,' said Osbert. Now he was sure that he had thought only of Linda while he made love to Vivienne.

She turned away from the staircase, they were face to face, and he said to himself that last night couldn't have happened if Linda hadn't entered his life. Illogical yet it was true.

'Don't look so worried,' said Vivienne. 'Mrs Hickson will solve everything.'

She repeated that before she left, and when she was gone he made a wry face at the prospect of spending a rainy evening and night alone in Maidwood. As if to prove to himself how alone he would be he saw the Hacketts driving off in their car. There surely was a pub in the village, but having no car it was out of reach. He could ring for a taxi. He shrugged his shoulders because he couldn't be bothered to look in the directory, then dial a number, and he felt certain that the house wouldn't approve of it. This house approves of nothing, he thought. Last night it had been screwing Vivienne, today it was taking a cab to the local. 'We won't get on,' he said in a loud voice. If he had Mrs Hickson on the premises he could go to her suite and have a chat with her. However, that might be even more deadly than being alone. He had never exchanged a word with Mrs Hickson who, as the cheque business showed, was a pretentious woman. He forgot Mrs Hickson as an awful thought came to him. Last night had given Vivienne a new entry into his life, the last thing he wanted. Last night had entitled her to run Maidwood even if only from a distance. He climbed the stairs to the study.

Later he went down to the library, and as he took a book down from a shelf a cloud of dust came with it.

He put back the book, and went to the downstairs cloak room to wash his hands. Of course, there was no soap, so he had to climb the stairs again. Were he in London he could spend an agreeable evening alone or with friends. He would ring for a taxi to take him to the station. He remembered that Linda was coming in the morning, and he sat down in the study to read the life of St Jerome. When he tired of it he read a book on the Curé d'Ars.

He had brought down ham from London, so he made a ham omelette followed by bread and cheese, and before turning in he finished the brandy of last night. He heard an owl in the night, and wished he could ask it in.

The sun came out in the morning, lighting up his (according to Vivienne) boarding house bedroom. At what time was Linda coming? All she had said was that she would look in in the morning. He couldn't go even into the garden because he wouldn't hear the doorbell. The doorbell? He hadn't locked the front door last night. What would Vivienne say? That made him smile.

He was in the porch room as the Ford turned into the drive. He watched it advancing towards the house so fascinated that he forgot to run downstairs to meet her. He left the porch room only when the car had stopped. He was in the minstrels' gallery on his way to the staircase as she entered the house. What would Vivienne say? She ran up the stairs, and they met on top of the staircase. She wore corduroy trousers and a tight fitting rollneck sweater. Vivienne's tiny breasts seemed to float by. If he touched Linda's would Linda understand? She certainly would, one of the many reasons not to touch them.

'Come into the study,' he said.

'This was the usual time of my calling on your aunt in this room,' Linda said. What did Vivienne say about sucking up to the aunt? He bade Linda to sit down, then he sat down facing her. 'Has Mrs Long left?'

'Yesterday afternoon. She suggested I take a house-keeper. What do you think of it?'

'The Hacketts would leave.'

'Would that be such a calamity?'

'I don't know,' she said, frowning a little. 'If they leave you must find a new gardener-handyman. I for one believe in the devil you know.'

'But I don't know any of the local devils.' Was Vivienne inspiring him from London? 'What I mean is that I'm not accustomed enough to the Hacketts to miss them if they go.'

'I understand,' said Linda.

'There's no hurry. Let's talk of more amusing matters.'

'The reason I came is to find out if you need any-thing.'

'Your company,' he said, immediately regretting his words.

'You're kind,' she said, the grey eyes solemnly fixed on him, 'but I'm not very good company, especially in this room.'

'Because of my aunt?' he asked, glad that the subject had changed. If it hadn't he couldn't have restrained himself from jumping up and throwing his arms round her. She wouldn't have resisted, for how could she the way they both felt? Call it an electric current or give it any other name, yet the fact was that he knew that she felt the same.

'Because of my memories of her. Try to understand my feelings when I was in her presence. Like most people I live from day to day, busy only with small matters and even smaller ideas. You mentioned a housekeeper. That's food for thought for me. I'll debate it in my mind, weighing up the pros and cons.

Jack and I are lunching today at Bloxham with some people. When I woke up this morning I was wondering what to wear and what to say when they bring up their son who's become a virulent anarchist. Personally I don't care about the son whom I hardly know, yet he took up part of my first thoughts this morning. That's why I've said small matters and even smaller ideas. Your aunt didn't have a single small thought or small preoccupation.'

'She didn't live in this world.'

'And that's why I was devoted to her.'

'Linda,' he said, rising from the armchair. 'May I call you Linda? I'll call your husband Jack if he doesn't mind.' He found that so neat that he sat down. Safer like that in any case.

'Call me, Linda. I like the name Osbert.'

'Oh good.' Why must they go on acting? 'I was going to say that I think you're very intelligent.'

'My intelligence hasn't got me very far.'

'It could if you wanted it.'

'If you knew what I wanted,' she said, laughing, 'you'd be shocked.' To hell with it, he would kiss her, and to hell with the consequences. 'One of the reasons I came is to ask you whether you'd like me to drive you to Mass in Banbury. I've just time to do so. You'll have to take a taxi back.'

He felt like a pricked balloon. He hadn't thought of going to Mass, however as his aunt's nephew he couldn't say no. 'Awfully nice of you,' he said.

'Then let's go,' she said, rising.

As she went past him he put out his hand. It touched her shoulder just for a second. Though she pretended not to notice it he saw her cheeks turn red. Sufficient unto the day, he said to himself.

'When are you going back to London?' she asked in the car.

'This afternoon.'

'Then I won't see you before your next visit.'

'I'll ring you before I come.'

'And don't be in a hurry about a housekeeper. In my small brain I'll give it a lot of thought.'

'You're too good to me,' he said, and leaned over to kiss her cheek, a light kiss, and as he withdrew he mumbled, 'That was just to thank you.'

'Here's the church,' she said.

He got out, gave her a long look, she drove off, and in the driving glass saw him motionless outside the church, his head turned in the direction the car had taken.

Mawson wore his best grey suit, ready for the lunch in Bloxham.

'Well?' he said.

'He wants to call me Linda and you Jack,' she said.

'I'm all for it.'

'I know you are.'

'Sounds fine.'

'Mrs Long has persuaded him that he needs a house-keeper.'

'Why not?'

'With a housekeeper running the house I'll cease to be his guardian angel. Haven't you thought of that?'

'Linda, you're cleverer than I. You must dissuade him.'

FIVE

On Monday morning Osbert went to see Bone to sign some papers concerning the inheritance. He told the taxi driver to stop two doors away to give him a chance to walk past the little old man's house. To his disappointment nobody was in the doorway. However, the same unpleasant young woman sat behind the desk in Bone's office. She sent him to the empty waiting room.

He remembered the man and the woman who had sat in there on the day of his first visit. 'The question is do you or don't you love me?' He had been shocked at the time. Would he be today if he sat there with Linda and heard his voice asking the same question? She hadn't been out of his thoughts since she dropped him in front of the church. It wasn't that he wanted her, for that would be easy and understandable. What he felt in her presnece was that they both needed each other. The light kiss in the car had been such a puny token of their feelings that it was just derisory. The rest was bound to come, and what then? It was too frightening in its complications even to envisage it. Again he felt his fear of fear, and he wished Vivienne were right about the scheming wife and the scheming husband. How much simpler and uncomplicated that would be.

When he came out of the church he took a taxi to Maidwood. At the sight of the Crimean soldier he told the driver to wait, rushed upstairs, packed his bag, and asked to be driven straight to the station.

'Mr Bone is expecting you,' said the grey haired woman from the door.

'So we meet again,' said Bone, holding out his hand. 'How do you like Maidwood?'

'It'll take time to get accustomed to it. The little old man next door wasn't in the doorway.'

'Old Ramsbottom. Saw him the other day. He's completely dotty. "It's cold next door," he called to me, and the sun was shining.'

'I wish I could meet him and find out what he means.'

'He means nothing. Have you gone through the inventory?' Osbert shook his head. Just as I expected, said Bone to himself. 'As regards the death duties we've quite a bit of money thanks to Mawson's clever management, and we'll sell some of the houses in the village.'

'If I decided to sell the whole estate?' If he sold the estate Linda would cease to be his estate manager's wife.

'You mustn't think of it,' said Bone, lifting his hand. 'It's the worst possible moment to sell.'

'In my experience it's always the worst possible moment if one wants to sell.'

'There you are,' said Bone. The man's an unimaginative fool, said Osbert to himself. 'How do you get on with Mawson?'

'Fine.'

'I'm glad to hear that. He's an excellent man. Speaking of the inventory, you could, if you need money, sell the Stubbs.'

'Firstly, I don't need money, secondly it isn't a Stubbs.'

'How do you know that?'

'I've examined the picture, and I happen to know a little about china, pictures and furniture.' Knows a little, sneered Bone under his breath. Knowing a little summed up the man. 'There's nothing valuable in Maidwood, except a few pieces of Meissen, early nineteenth century.'

'I see,' said Bone who had no idea what Meissen was. 'Well, that'll be all for the moment. Come and see me whenever you want.'

Ramsbottom was invisible when Osbert went past his door.

In the taxi that took him to Bloomsbury he decided to face facts for once. Linda is his mistress, Linda can find any pretext to come to the house, but that means he can't engage Mrs Hickson who was bound to find out. He wouldn't be the first lover or she the first wife to face the husband with equanimity, and in time they would get so accustomed to their adultery that they wouldn't think of it in his presence. So far so good. However, with a woman like Linda and with his own sentiments which would be a hundredfold stronger once he was her lover there could be no half measures. What then? He told himself to stop facing facts that in any case weren't facts yet. His mind wouldn't let him. Linda is his mistress, he can't live without her which means that Mawson must be told or if he isn't he will soon find out. Then Mawson goes, the estate crashes to pieces, Linda comes to live with him, and he can't marry her because his Catholic conscience won't let him, permanent sin being unacceptable to it, an awful vista, and the only answer was to keep away from Linda, that is from Maidwood. Mawson didn't need him on the estate, the estate could carry on without him. If only Vivienne were right, if only Linda were just the scheming wife how easily he could cope with that.

As he alighted from the taxi a tall bearded man in his late thirties accosted him. 'You don't recognise me with this beard,' said the man.

'Tony,' said Osbert. 'I thought you were abroad.'

'I've been ill, Osbert,' said Tony Howells, and when he said he had been ill Osbert knew that it meant that he was down and out.

'Come upstairs,' said Osbert.

Tony Howells had been a young man of promise at Oxford. He shed all promise in time, even a rich marriage hadn't managed to make him keep the only promise a marriage entails. So the wife left him. He was always willing to tackle anything in order to make a mess of it then he regretted it more than they whom he let down. He climbed the stairs in front of Osbert. The movements of a leopard, said Osbert to himself.

'I rang your bell, no answer, so in the hope that you might come back I loitered in the street,' said Tony.

That meant that he hadn't enough money to go to the nearest pub.

He waited for Osbert on the landing, smiling diffidently, then followed him into the sitting room. He wore a T-Shirt that needed washing, a long sleeved pullover and jeans. His suede shoes were in a lamentable state. 'Got a cigarette?' he asked.

'What's wrong this time?' Osbert asked, handing him a packet of cigarettes.

Frowning Tony selected a cigarette before answering. 'I'd some sort of malignant fever in Singapore. Was in hospital for two months.' Osbert didn't believe a word of it. 'The only answer was to come back.'

'And your job out there?'

'A total fiasco. What else could I expect?'

He had chosen to sit on a small chair so as to look uncomfortable as proof of his wretched state. He smoked like one who had been kept from smoking for a long time.

'When did you get back?' asked Osbert.

'Three weeks ago.'

'Saw your brother?'

'You know my brother. I can't count on him.'

84

His brother was an MP and sat on the boards of several companies. He had helped Tony for years, then put his foot down.

'What do you intend to do?' asked Osbert. 'First have a drink.'

On the Day of Judgment, thought Osbert while getting the drinks, my only defence will be that I looked after Tony whenever he was in need.

'I don't know,' sighed Tony after he had emptied his glass. 'I'm sick and tired of the life I lead.' Osbert had heard that before. 'I want to get away from the hell I've got accustomed to. I've become modest, if you get my meaning. Nothing hectic for me any more. I'm through with all that. Don't laugh, old boy, but what I should like is a quiet, peaceful life away from the cesspools I used to wallow in. The only happy time was my childhood. And why? Because we lived in the country, in the depth of Shropshire, and it's only in the lap of Nature, to use a cliché, that I feel really contented. How could I get a job, however humble, in the country? You know so many people. I wouldn't even mind being a cowman or just an ordinary farm labourer.'

The hangover of the man who hasn't a bean in his pocket, smiled Osbert to himself. Yet wasn't looking after Tony his only redeeming quality? His smile broadened.

'I think I can help you,' he said.

'God bless you,' said Tony in a fervent voice.

'I've inherited an estate in North Oxfordshire ...'

'Lucky man. I always say that luck is something that comes to others.'

'The assistant estate manager is leaving in a month's time. To help you I'm willing to give you his job.' Tony's eyes shone. 'But I can assure you it won't be a cushy job. Mawson, the estate manager for whom you will be working, is, I'm sure, a hard boss.'

'All I want is work. I'll never let you down.'

'I won't have anything to do with it, and Mawson will sack you if you don't do your job. I can give it to you, but I can't keep you on if Mawson isn't satisfied with you.'

'Of course, I quite understand that. Have no fear on that score. What's he like?'

A difficult question, thought Osbert. What was Linda's husband like? 'He's about our age, he's devoted to his job, he ran the estate for eight years without any one interfering, and he's run it remarkably well. He's a hard worker.' What else or more could he say? Speaking about him without mentioning Linda Mawson had become a nebulous figure. 'I repeat I can put you in, but I can't do more.'

'I understand. You'll see he'll be satisfied with me. I'm dying to work hard, and I pick up things very quickly.'

The telephone bell rang. 'Excuse me,' said Osbert.

'I spoke to Mrs Hickson,' said Vivienne's bright voice. 'She says she's ready to consider it, but can't take a decision in a hurry. The lady all the way. We agreed on her coming to see you, then if she still likes the idea she's willing to go down for the day to look at Maidwood and see what it's like. When can she come to see you?'

'Not this week,' said Osbert, remembering that Linda was thinking it over. 'Tuesday next. Is that all right? Anyway, I'm not going down this weekend.' That was the fruit of facing facts in a taxi.

'I don't blame you,' laughed Vivienne. 'I hope the Hacketts won't make a bonfire of the furniture in the meantime.' Then after a little pause. 'I hope you've forgotten the meaningless error of Friday night.'

'As much as you,' said Osbert pleased with himself.

'In that case come and dine Thursday night.'

His eyes were on Tony while he spoke to Vivienne. Colour had come into his cheeks, he moved to a more comfortable chair, and he looked as though he had stopped believing that he had been ill and lain in a hospital.

'I'm writing to Mawson this afternoon,' said Osbert.

'Osbert, you're a real friend. Does accommodation go with the job?'

'I'll find out next time I go down, though that won't be before the end of next week. Keep in touch.'

'I'll keep in touch. By the way, I'm not alone. That's why I'm so interested in accommodation.'

'Who's the lucky girl?'

'You don't know her. She's French. We met on my way back from Singapore. She's in Paris at the moment, but she'll come over once I've got a job.'

'If you take her to Maidwood you'll have to say she's your wife.'

'Anyhow, I intend to marry her.' Poor girl, Osbert couldn't help saying to himself. 'I'm sure you'll like her.'

'Where are you staying in London?'

'In a wretched flat off Sloane Square.' He didn't think it necessary to mention that his brother was paying for the flat. 'Osbert, I haven't a sou. Do you think you could let me have something on account? You'll take it off my salary.'

'Not an unreasonable request,' said Osbert who had been expecting it. 'I give you a cheque for a hundred pounds.' He wanted to say fifty, but remembered the Day of Judgment. 'I'll make it out right now.'

'Open it, please,' said Tony as Osbert wrote out the cheque. 'Do you want a receipt for it?'

'Unnecessary. I'll tell Mawson that I advanced you that sum. More gin?'

'Very kind of you, but I must be going.'

The cheque, thought Osbert, was burning a hole in his pocket.

'Osbert, you saved me,' said Tony from the door. 'I came here a miserable creature, I'm leaving with hope reborn.'

'The least one can do for a friend if one has the chance.'

A Miss While came three afternoons a week to attend to Osbert's correspondence and files. All Osbert knew about Miss While was that she was short, had black hair and a pale complexion. She came, worked, and went. Whether it snowed or rained she made no allusion to the weather or anything else. He was certain that if the third world war broke out she wouldn't mention it and her impersonal manner would remain the same.

She arrived that afternoon at three o'clock sharp. She carried a brief case which she put on the table. Then she pulled out the typewriter from a drawer, put it on a small table, sat down on a stool and waited. Osbert dictated several letters which she took down in short-hand. The letter to Mawson came last. He addressed him as Dear Jack. In a few lines he told him that an old friend, whom he had known all his life, would take the job as assistant manager when Rex Wheeler left. He would explain all about him when he came down to Maidwood which wouldn't be before the end of next week. The reason for this letter was to stop him from looking for somebody else. The old friend was well aware that he would have to earn Jack's satisfaction with his work, and do as Jack told him. In the meantime could he tell the Hacketts that he wouldn't be down at the weekend. (He could have said, ask Linda to tell the Hacketts, but, somehow he didn't want to pronounce her name in front of Miss While.)

When he had finished dictating he went to the dining room because the noise of the typewriter coupled with Miss While's lack of expression he found too much to bear. When she had typed the letters, she knocked on the door, he called 'Come in,' and she appeared with them. He signed the letters. 'I've a business appointment,' he said. 'I'm going out. If anybody phones take the message.'

'There's the correspondence with New York to be filed.'

'You do that. See you on Wednesday.'

He left the flat. Now that she was alone she lit a cigarette. She chain-smoked till six o'clock, her time to leave. She carried the ashtray to the lavatory, emptied the stubs into it, pulled the chain, and as some remained in the bowl she waited till the tank filled to flush the water again. She wiped the ashtray and put it back on the table. She pushed the letters into the pillarbox at the corner, then boarded a bus that took her to Islington, where she lived in two rooms with separate entrance which she rented from an old Italian widow. She took off her skirt and blouse, brushed her thick black hair, put on a crimson dressing gown, and waited. Had Osbert seen her reclining on the divan-bed he wouldn't have recognised the Miss While who worked for him. She looked like a heroine in a silent film who with her poise and gestures imparts to the audience that she is waiting for her lover.

She didn't have to wait long. The door burst open and a giant with ginger hair nearly fell into the room as though he too were acting in the same silent film. 'I haven't got much time,' he said, taking his jacket off.

She got off the divan-bed, threw off the dressing gown, and there she was naked with dark nipples and a coal black bush. He had stripped too, forgetting in his hurry to pull off his socks. He was as hairy as an ape, but Miss While loved that. He jumped on her, they made love violently, then he dressed without uttering a word. Once he was dressed he said, 'I forgot to buy cigarettes. Got one?' She opened her bag, and saw that she hadn't posted Osbert's letter to Mawson. 'I'm coming down with you,' she said. 'Got to post this letter.'

'Better not,' he said. 'One never knows whom one might run into. I'll post it for you.'

'You're the sweetest person I know,' she gushed.

'I must rush. Same time tomorrow, okay?'

'Okay,' she breathed.

In his hurry to get back to the wife and kiddies the giant forgot to post the letter. Next day as he was cutting salami for a client he suddenly remembered it. He took it from his pocket, and sent his assistant to post it.

'What a greasy envelope,' said Mawson disapprovingly as Wheeler brought in the mail two mornings later.

To show his disapproval he left the letter to the last. When he opened it his expression changed. It was signed by Osbert, but why did Osbert write to him? Wasn't it simpler to telephone? Having read the letter his expression changed again.

'What's wrong?' asked Wheeler.

'Hinley has found a new assistant manager to take your place. One of his pals, of course.'

'Stands to reason doesn't it?' said Wheeler who had never cared much for his boss, and now that he was going could afford to care for him even less. 'He's the master, and naturally he wants to help his own friends. I don't see anything out of the ordinary in that.'

'You wouldn't, but I'm the one who'll have to work with the fellow.'

'If I may say so be very careful when the friend arrives.'

'What do you mean?'

'He'll have Hinley's ear. I don't have to say more.'

'I've got to go out,' said Mawson, jumping up. 'If I may say so keep your advice to yourself in future.'

The future here is less than a month, Wheeler felt like saying. Instead he grinned at Mawson's back.

Linda was in the cottage garden, cutting dahlias; Nick sat in a flower-bed, his eyes full of pathos.

'Read this,' said Mawson.

She straightened herself, took the letter and read it. Nick left the flower-bed, and came up to her as if to give her moral support.

'He sent it in a greasy envelope,' growled Mawson.

'What's wrong with this letter?' Linda asked.

'Don't pretend. You know what's wrong with it. He has chosen my assistant all on his own.'

'He says he's a life long friend.'

'Don't speak like that fool of a Rex. What did I say when Bone told us that she left Maidwood to her nephew?'

'You said we were in for trouble.'

Now they would speak about it for hours, she sighed.

'We're in the thick of it,' he said.

She put the dahlias into the basket she carried, then started for the cottage. He followed her with Nick bringing up the rear. 'I want to put these dahlias into the big vase,' she said.

'They can wait.'

She took the empty vase and the basket into the kitchen. He paced the room till she came back, with the vase full of dahlias.

'This is his first move,' said Mawson, lighting his pipe. 'I'm nobody's fool, so I can see what he's after. He doesn't say a word about his friend's qualifications or experience. That means the man knows absolutely nothing about estate management.'

'That isn't certain,' said Linda, sitting down on the sofa.

'Anyhow, the man will be his spy.'

'Jack, you can take it from me that Osbert isn't

the sort that employs spies. He's far too uninterested in the estate to employ a spy.'

'Listen, Linda,' he said, stopping in front of the sofa, 'We can't take risks. You know what erosion of power means?' She nodded. 'He wants to erode my power. For the moment he needs me, but if he puts in his own man he might need me less later on. Under that bland manner of his I immediately sensed that he's the scheming, cunning sort.' She shook her head. 'I repeat the scheming, cunning sort. Why does he want to put this man here?'

'Probably to help him.'

'That's what you think. He's too clever by half. I'm going to teach this man all the intricacies of estate management, and when he knows all they think he needs to know he'll be able to get rid of me, or reduce me to nothing. And what about the Home Farm? Answer me.'

'I've no answer to give you because I don't believe that Osbert is the scheming sort.'

He strode to the end of the room as if wanting to go through the wall. He turned round like one who remembers he has forgotten something.

'Maybe he isn't a schemer,' he said, 'but Mrs Long is. You can smell it from a mile. And how do we know that this man Howells isn't one. He might easily be Mrs Long's selection. How do we know? And what about a housekeeper? Inside the house, and inside the office. Not bad for a start, is it?'

'If you look at it like that ...'

'The only way to look at it. Linda, I seldom bring it up, but you know why I had to leave the family farm, and why I grabbed this job. We can't afford to lose it. It's the new life we started together, and you can't say I didn't make a success of it.'

'What do you want me to do?' she asked, playing with Nick's ears.

'He says in his letter he won't be down before the end of next week. By then it might be too late.'

'Too late for what?'

'Too late to know where we stand.'

'I repeat, what do you want me to do?'

'As he isn't coming down it's for you to go to London to see him.'

'And if he isn't in?'

'He told me he's in every afternoon.'

'And what do I do when I see him?'

'You find out what's behind all this, what's at the back of his mind.'

'My going to him is playing with fire, I warn you.'

'You know how to look after yourself.'

He wouldn't mind, she thought, if I went to bed with Osbert if that helped him. Besides, why should he mind? But I might mind, and what about Mrs Long? She was surprised by the violent hatred she suddenly felt for Vivienne. 'I'm not the hating sort,' she said to the room as if to apologise. Mawson didn't hear it.

'Anyhow, I ought to go up to see Jenny,' he said. Linda chuckled. 'Haven't seen her for six months. I could drive you up, I mean we could drive up together. We could go tomorrow. I'll come back in the afternoon, you take a train when you finished sounding him. Forewarned is forearmed. We need to be forearmed.'

'If I don't find him in?'

'You don't seem to listen. I've told you that he's at home every afternoon. His flat is his office too.'

'And who'll look after Nick? I don't want to leave him locked up here the whole day.'

'Take him with you.'

'You'll chaperon me, Nick,' she laughed, and Nick wagged his tail.

'You'll easily find out what's at the back of his mind. You've the brain for it. Don't forget there are moments when a woman can do much more than a man.'

'You don't have to apologise or explain. You reminded me of my duty. I'll do my duty.'

'Thank you, Linda.'

As he couldn't think of anything else to say he nodded and smiled, then left the cottage to drive back to the office, for he had a score to settle with Rex Wheeler whom he found reading a newspaper behind his desk.

'I want you to go to the village,' Mawson said, 'and see Miss Wetherell. The rent is overdue, and you don't bloody well leave her cottage without a cheque.'

'But she frightens the wits out of me that awful old spinster.'

'Whether she does or doesn't,' said Mawson, smiling grimly, 'you bring back that cheque. Off you go.'

Wheeler left the office, preparing a little speech for formidable Miss Wetherell who lived in her cottage with seven cats and a parrot that shouted, 'Heil Hitler.' Miss Wetherell said that it shouted Heil Hitler before it came to her, but the villagers were convinced that it was she who had taught him. Wheeler would say that he came strictly on Mawson's behalf, it had nothing to do with him, and if she got too aggressive he would tell her that she could always stop the cheque as long as she doesn't say that the suggestion came from him.

Mawson dialled a number in Hammersmith.

'Is that you, Jenny?'

'Hullo, Jack.'

'I'm in town tomorrow on business. I'll look in on you after lunch.'

'What is it about?'

'Nothing in particular, just to see you.'

'I'll be in,' she said, and rang off.

Mawson filled his pipe, then opened a ledger, forgetting to light the pipe.

SIX

They said little to each other while they drove to London. When they arrived they went to lunch in an Italian restaurant in Kensington, practically the only restaurant Mawson knew in London.

'I ought to call him,' said Linda towards the end of the meal.

'It's better to surprise him.'

'Perhaps you're right.'

'If you want the car I can take a taxi,' he said as they came out of the restaurant.

'You keep the car.'

'Good luck.'

'I don't have to wish you good luck.'

'As long as you bring me good news.'

'I'll do my best,' she said, and went off with Nick.

He drove the car to Hammersmith, pulled up in front of a house that looked ready for the demolition gang. A strong smell of fried onions rose from the basement as he climbed the six steps to the front door which was open. He rang a bell on the second floor.

It was opened by a woman as tall as Linda and about the same age. She had a flat face and a straight nose, her hair was flaxen, and her chest flat. Both belly and behind stuck out, and the legs were thick. She spoke with a Norfolk accent. And this, he thought, had been the most desirable girl of his youth.

'I hope you didn't come to bring up the old story again,' she said.

'May I come in?'

She took him into the small living room with a high ceiling. It's stuffy in here, he said to himself as he sat down in an armchair that had once been his. 'How are you keeping?' he asked.

'I'm all right,' she said grudgingly. 'Why shouldn't I be?' She let out a little laugh. 'You're like the criminal who comes back to the scene of his crime.'

'You say that every time I call on you. It's so old a story that I can't conjure up enough strength to answer it.'

'I asked for no answer. You used to say I don't discuss, I just state facts.'

'Your facts.'

'They can't be anybody else's can they?'

'That's true,' he said, trying to smile. He was bitterly regretting that he had come; he regretted it bitterly every time he called on her; yet he knew he would come again in six or seven months' time. Perhaps she was right about the criminal and the scene of his crime. And it wasn't even a crime any more, he sighed to himself. 'Still enjoying your work?'

'It gives me much pleasure,' she said. 'I'm doing tapestry for six armchairs in some French style. I forget the name, but it's in a book I've got here.' She got up, and fetched a large book on tapestry. How could that once slim girl bother so little about her figure? 'Aubusson,' she called putting the book back on the shelf, then she sat down heavily. 'That with your monthly cheque keeps the wolf from the door.'

'Good,' he said. 'No sweetheart on the horizon or nearer?'

'Once bitten twice shy. You won't catch me out, Mr Jonathan Mawson.'

'The last thing I want to do.'

'How's the great lady?'

'She's very well.'

'Now it's my turn to say good. Do you want tea?'

'Thank you, Jenny, but I'm on my way back, have a long drive before me.'

'I saw in the papers that your Miss Hinley has died.' She loved reading births, marriages and deaths. 'Does that affect you?'

'Not for the time being. The estate belongs now to her nephew, and we get on fine.' Linda must be in Osbert's flat by now. 'We get on perfectly.'

'I'm glad,' said Jenny. 'Your father and your brother always said you're a born farmer.'

'Well, Jenny, it was nice to see you.'

'I don't mind seeing you,' she laughed, 'though not too often.'

'No fear of that,' he said, leaned forward to give her a friendly goodbye kiss.

'None of that,' she said, pushing him away.

She saw him to the door, and as he reached his car he wished he could hear what Osbert and Linda were saying to each other.

They weren't saying anything yet because Linda took her time, partly because frightened by London traffic and crowds Nick sat down after every few steps and she had to drag him on the lead, chiefly because her heart wasn't in it since she was honest enough with herself to admit that the visit to Osbert could turn out very differently from what Mawson expected from her. Thus it was nearly four o'clock when she rang the doorbell.

Osbert heard it above the noise of the typewriter next door. He went to the window, looked out, and his jaw nearly dropped as he saw Linda and Nick on the doorstep. Without bothering to ask himself why she had come he burst from the flat, and chased down to the front door.

'What a pleasant surprise,' he said. 'Come upstairs. What brings you to London?'

'I came up to lunch with an old school chum, and as I didn't want to catch the first train back I thought I'd look you up.'

'An excellent thought,' he said, bending down to pat Nick. The dog growled at him.

'He's a fish out of water in the turmoil of London,' she said.

'Poor chap. Let me lead the way.'

He had done what he could, that is to say he had resolved to keep away from her for twelve days at least to give himself time to digest the facts he had faced on Monday in the taxi. She had come, he hadn't asked her to come, hence the responsibility for the disaster wasn't his any more. He heard his voice saying that they had better enter the flat through the kitchen as his secretary was working in the sitting room. His voice was calm, and dammit he was man enough to control himself. He would take her into the dining room.

'What a well appointed kitchen,' Linda observed.

'Does Nick want water?'

'Yes, please.'

'Go in there,' he said, opening the dining room door, 'and I'll get him water.'

When he appeared in the dining room, carrying a saucer he found her standing in front of a glass case admiring some of his collection of Blue Sèvres.

'Very lovely,' she said.

'Sit down at the table,' he said. 'It would be more comfortable in the sitting room. Let him off the leash.'

She sat down on a chair with her back to the window, so he chose the chair that faced it. A whole table was between them, frankly he couldn't be safer. 'Can I get you a drink? I've some very good mirabelle. Or would you prefer tea, though it's a bit early for it?' The perfect host.

'A drink,' she said, adding to herself I need one.

The scheming wife, he reminded himself, Please God let her be just the scheming wife of my scheming estate manager. He poured out two glasses, then sat down at the other end of the table. Nick had collapsed at Linda's feet without having bothered to sniff round the room.

'I'm delighted to see you,' said Osbert. She was, he noticed, wearing the jersey dress she wore when she came to fetch him to dinner on his first night at Maidwood. 'How's Jack?' Those breasts, he sighed.

'He's very well. He's received your letter about the new assistant. Why aren't you coming down this weekend?' She shouldn't have asked that.

'I can't. I'm expecting somebody from New York, a business connection, and he'd be so disappointed if I were away.'

'I see. How's Mrs Long?'

'I dined with her last night.'

'Has she got over the awfulness of Maidwood?' She could have boxed her ears.

'She didn't think it so awful.' He nearly shouted the words to fend off so to speak that warmth that was oozing from her. It would envelope him. Why wasn't the table any longer?

'I told the Hacketts you weren't coming this weekend.'

'Thank you. I'm sure they'll manage to get through the weekend without me.' He should laugh: he laughed. 'Have you given the housekeeper idea any thought?'

'Frankly, I haven't yet. If you take a housekeeper you must change everything in the house.'

'What do you mean by everything?'

'I don't really know. Told you I haven't thought about it. How good this drink is.'

'Like some more?' he asked. She was as confused as he. Why hadn't they the courage to throw off all this pretension?

'I don't want to get tiddly. How hard your secretary works. The typewriter never seems to stop.'

'That reminds me,' he said, got up, and went into the sitting room, closing the door behind him. Miss While didn't look up.

'I'm in conference,' he said, 'so I can't be disturbed. If anybody rings say I'm out and take the message. When you finish just leave the letters on the table. I'll sign them when I'm free.'

'Who'll post them?'

'I will.'

'Okay.'

'See you on Monday.'

'Okay.'

He returned to the dining room. Linda has pushed her chair back a little so as to cross her legs. She held out the glass for the light to catch it, and Nick sat up to gaze mournfully at Osbert, not sure whether to bark at him.

'Excuse me,' said Osbert in a thick voice, 'but I had to give my secretary some instructions.'

'It's I who barged in on you,' she said.

'Not at all, it's a pleasure to see you. Won't you change your mind about a drink? This mirabelle is really excellent.'

'It is excellent.'

He took her glass, their hands touched. He filled the glass, and pushed it across the table. None the less, their hands touched again.

'So Jack received my letter about Tony Howells,' he said, Tony Howells being neutral ground.

'He received it yesterday. My poor Nick, how thirsty you are. He's lapped up all the water.'

'Does he want more?'

'In a few minutes. I couldn't live in London because of my poor bewildered dog.'

Why haven't we any courage? he asked himself.

'Tony Howells is a life long friend, but that's no recommendation to Jack. I made it clear to Tony that if Jack isn't satisfied with him he'll have to go.'

'I see,' said Linda, her grey eyes fixed on him.

It's no good trying to look away, he thought. 'I'll bring him down myself before Wheeler leaves so that he should get the knack of things. He'll be on probation, and it's for Jack to judge him.' She didn't seem to be interested. 'Have you been to the house since I left?'

'I'd no reason to go.'

'Quite,' he said, and stood up. 'Doesn't the dog want water? He's panting like mad.'

'He's just tired.' She rose too. 'I can fetch him water.'

'You mustn't.'

He was willing to swear afterwards that the only reason he advanced was to take the saucer. As he reached her he uttered a little cry like one who is no longer responsible for his actions, and his arms went round her broad shoulders. He faintly heard her putting the saucer on the table before his face reached hers. Her mouth was open, and as he kissed her he felt precisely what he had expected since the day he had met her, namely that their kiss would be as natural for them as breathing. It was a long kiss, both of them loath to end it. She rubbed herself against him, letting him feel the strength of her breasts. Nick had risen, and was wagging his tail. Miss While continued to bang on the typewriter in the sitting room.

When he drew back he looked into her eyes which appeared to turn from grey to blue. As deep as the sea, he thought, smiling at her, hoping that his eyes conveyed his delight. 'Again,' she said.

They separated when the typewriter stopped. Nick had changed his mind, and let out a shrill bark.

'Silence,' said Linda.

The telephone bell rang in the sitting room, Miss While answered it. 'He isn't in. Can I take a message?' they heard her say.

Osbert touched her right breast. Despite dress and bra he could feel the hard nipple. She shuddered, then said, 'Hanged for a lamb, hanged for a sheep. Where's your bedroom?'

That was natural too, his sole regret that it wasn't he who suggested the bedroom first. 'On the other side of the sitting room,' he said. 'We'll go through the kitchen, then cross the landing, and there we are. Can we leave him here?'

'He'll bark the house down,' said Linda.

When they came out on the landing Nick started down the stairs. She called him in a hushed voice, and he climbed back, looking reproachfully at her. Osbert put his finger to his lips as they entered the passage no larger than a cubbyhole that lead to his bedroom which was filled with the afternoon sun.

'I like this room,' said Linda.

Nick sat in front of her while she undressed, watching every movement she made. Osbert was with his back to them, undressing too, but in the wardrobe glass he could see her stepping out of her dress, then sitting down on a chair to take her tights off. She was naked when she rose. Her breasts were as he had seen them in his daydreams; the bush was as thick as her hair, the same colour too, and her thighs were as well shaped as her legs. There's no nonsense about her body, he said to himself, not quite certain what he meant by that. When she got on the bed Nick let out a sigh, lay down under the chair she had sat on and closed his eyes. Osbert joined her on the bed.

'I haven't been with a man for four years,' she said. 'I feel like a virgin.' She let out a little laugh. 'That shouldn't stop you.' Having said that she pulled him on top of her.

Their love making was like the meeting of two bodies that know from long experience how to move in unison. There was nothing new for him in the contact, and he was sure that there was nothing new for her either in it. No fumbling, no trying to find out what the other liked: they knew, hence they didn't feel like strangers sharing it for the first time, no need to think that it would be better at the next occasion. Hadn't eternity no beginning and no end? In the distance the telephone bell rang again.

'Ours is a miracle,' he said. 'Linda, I've been waiting for this all my life, yet I feel no different than on the day I met you. I wanted you on that first afternoon, but I can't call it wanting. I felt we'd been together before we ever set eyes on each other.'

'I was drawn to you from the start, though that wasn't altogether my doing.'

'What do you mean?'

'I don't feel like confessing today. I enjoyed it far too much for that.'

'I don't follow you.'

'You go through life like a sailing ship in a smooth sea with a fair wind. I'm an old tramp in a choppy sea with hardly any coal in the bunker. Don't let me dramatise myself. Don't let us spoil the beauty of this afternoon.'

She pulled him to her, and Nick growled in his sleep because the bed shook too loudly.

'It's nearly six,' she exclaimed as they lay smoking. 'I must catch a train back.'

'Can't you stay a little longer?' he pleaded.

'Honest, I can't. I'll see you when you come down next time, Osbert. I'll be thinking of you all the time.'

'Can't you come up one day next week, my darling Linda?'

'I've no excuse,' she said, getting up, and he thought that she moved with the same calm purpose when she was naked as when she was dressed. 'It's too wonderful to spoil it.'

'What do you mean?' he asked.

'Jack. We don't want to bring him into this, do we?' She waited, but he remained silent. 'He's a heap of suspicion.'

'But you don't go to bed with him any more. You said so.'

'Nothing to do with it. I don't want him to get the upper hand, and he would if I started absenting myself. Osbert, I implore you to think only of this and of nothing beyond it. When you come down next time we'll manage to snatch a few minutes together, so forget about a housekeeper. If there's one we won't be able to.'

'Housekeeper is out.'

'Where's the bathroom?'

'I'll show you.'

If Jack is a heap of suspicion, she said to the glass in the bathroom, I'm a pack of lies. She glared at her reflection, then returned to the bedroom.

'Perhaps I'll manage to come down before next weekend,' he said.

'I wish you would.'

'My darling.'

'Is your secretary still here?'

'I heard her leave while you were in the bathroom.'

'So I won't have to tiptoe. Come on, Nick.'

'Can I ring for a taxi?'

'I'll find one.'

He saw her down, and remained in the street till she and Nick vanished round the corner.

She found a taxi in Russell Square, and sat stroking Nick all the way to Paddington, repeating several times, 'I hadn't reckoned on this.'

The train was crowded, she sat hemmed in by a man with a brief case in his lap, and a large woman with several parcels. When it wasn't the brief case it was a parcel that hit her with the rocking of the train. After a time the large woman tried to pat Nick who shrunk from her. Suddenly the man rose, raising the hope that he would get off at the next station. He came back with a cup of tea, so she received a few drops of it on her dress. She kept her mind a blank, and if it became impossible she muttered, 'I hadn't reckoned on this.' Reckoning or not reckoning every lurch of the train brought her nearer to Jack. What, or rather how much, should she tell him?

The man and the large woman got off in Oxford. Immediately their places were taken by two young Americans who carried on an animated chat, to which she didn't bother to listen, till the train pulled up in Banbury. 'Now for it, Nick,' she said as they came out of the station.

The mirabelle and the love making had parched her mouth. She asked the taxi driver to stop at the first pub. She went in, had a gin and tonic, and was hailed by Rex Wheeler before she reached the door.

'Had a nice day in town?' he asked.

'Too many people for Nick.'

'Only twenty-seven days left.'

'I don't follow you.'

'In twenty-seven days time I'll be bowing myself out of Maidwood.'

'Are you glad, Rex?'

'Very glad, Linda. You were the only person who'd any consideration for me.'

'Jack liked you a lot.'

'It wasn't what I call liking. Don't repeat it to him.'

'I'm not the repeating sort. I must rush, got a taxi outside.'

'Can't I drive you back?'

'I can't let down the taxi man,' she laughed.

The last thing she wanted was to listen to Rex or anybody else while she tried to make her mind up. It remained blank during the journey to Maidwood, and when she went into the house she hadn't the faintest idea how much she would tell Mawson. He sat in an armchair, his legs stretched out, reading a farmers' weekly, the picture of self-satisfaction. I won't ask any questions, he said to himself, putting on a smile which, she knew from experience, was to conceal his anguish.

'You don't have to worry,' she said, letting Nick off the lead.

'What do you mean?'

'He's known the man all his life, they were at the same college in Oxford, and the man is on his uppers, so out of sheer kindness he's going to give him a chance. It'll be for you to decide whether he's the right man for the job.' Osbert had told her about his relationship with Tony Howells, as they lay side by side after their second bout. She wished she could put her hand out as she had done then to touch him. 'You can't ask for more.'

'Sounds satisfactory,' he said. 'Thank you, Linda.'

'And there won't be any housekeeper.'

'Why not?'

'Because I don't want one.' Her eyes shone while she waited for him to speak.

First he filled his pipe to show her that the housekeeper was no concern of his. 'Why don't you want her?'

'I prefer to deal with Osbert alone when he comes down. I don't need a housekeeper as a witness.' Surely he would ask her what she meant. A witness to what? she expected him to say.

'I've enough with the estate,' he said. 'I leave the house entirely to you.'

Fundamentally we understand each other better than we pretend, she said to herself.

'Would you like to come to the pub for a drink?' he asked.

'Why not? There are two things I want to tell you first.' She mustn't raise her voice. 'The first is that you shouldn't have focussed my attention on Osbert even before I met him.'

'You know my reasons. My keeping my job and continuing to run the estate to the best of my abilities was and is as much your concern as mine. You've no other future in view either. Don't you agree?'

'Perhaps I do. All other solutions could only lead to turmoil and exposure.'

'We agree,' he said. 'What's the second?'

'We ought to stop sleeping in the same room,' she said in a tense voice.

'That's for you to decide, Linda.'

Good God, she thought, I could have said that years ago. The fool I had been not to. 'I'll move tonight to the guest room.'

'I'll move to the guest room. Fair is fair.'

'I prefer to move. The guest room's nearer to the bathroom.' The guest room had nothing to do with him and their joint past. In their bedroom he would leave his presence behind.

'You'll do as you like,' he said. 'Let's go to the pub, and as we both had a long day we'll have something to eat there.'

Considerate, grateful Jack, she said to herself.

The sky was innocent of clouds, and the moon shone down on the thatched roofs. They walked side by side to the pub with Nick trotting in front of them. A Gordon setter came out of a garden, and ran off in the hope that Nick would join the game. Nick trotted on as though the setter didn't exist. The setter barked: Nick ignored it. The setter came back, then ran off again. Nick turned his head to see whether Linda was still behind him. Satisfied he trotted on in the same leisurely fashion, while disgusted the setter returned to the garden.

The pub wasn't the sort of pub you expect and hope for in a village of thatched roofs. Wall brackets with pink shades sent their discreet light on the red carpet and the Finnish tables and chairs. Gregson, the publican, was a tall youngish man with fairly long hair, Janet, his wife, wore a dress with Chinese patterns down to her ankles. You waited for her to trip up whenever she moved. The record player played the kind of music you cease listening to after a few minutes.

'Well Mr Mawson,' said Gregson, 'had a successful day?' He had been barman in a bar in Maidenhead, where film people gathered.

'Was in town,' said Mawson.

'Janet and I always say we never want to go back to London.'

'Idyllic country life,' said Janet.

'London's very tiring,' said Mawson, thinking of Jenny for the first time since he had left her. 'Have you anything to eat?'

'Canard à l'orange or Spanish omelette,' said Gregson. 'I recommend the canard à l'orange.'

'The Spanish omelette will do me fine,' said Linda, thinking of the guest room, where she could dream of Osbert unmolested.

'I'll have sausage and mash if you've such a thing,' said Mawson.

'Most certainly, Mr Mawson,' said Janet with a chuckle that implied that it was a pity that Mawson understood nothing about gastronomy.

'Would you like a bottle of chianti or beaujolais?' asked Gregson.

'I'll have a large whisky,' said Mawson.

'I'll have one too,' said Linda.

There were only two other customers, a vet who lived in the village and a commercial traveller, both at the bar, talking politics in which neither seemed much interested.

'Simpson of the Home Farm looked in on me shortly before you arrived,' said Mawson when they had sat down at a table farthest from the bar. 'He spoke about the new lease. I managed to put the fear of God into him.'

'How did you do that?' Linda asked, wondering what Osbert was doing at the moment. Of one thing she was happily certain: he hadn't the strength left to make love to that horrible Mrs Long. None the less, she felt a pang of jealousy. Like an embryo kicking inside the mother, she said to herself.

'I told him about all the repairs we'd insist on, also that the new lease would be far higher. He said he might not want it renewed. I'd prefer it if it came from him.'

'Do you want me to speak to Osbert about it?' she asked.

'Not yet,' said the man on whom irony was wasted.

The Spanish omelette arrived and she felt sorry for the Spaniards if they really made their omelettes like that. Mawson ate the sausages and mash with relish. A new customer appeared, evidently a friend of the Gregsons, and they had such a lot to say to each other that the customers were forgotten. Mawson and Linda sat in front of their dirty plates till they rose to go back to the cottage.

'I'm going up to make the bed in the guest room,' said Linda.

Life was easier than one expected, thought Mawson, stretching his legs. He wouldn't have dared to suggest they sleep in separate rooms because he feared an unpleasant scene with a lot of recrimination. One should worry less, he said to himself, smiling broadly. Then he nearly jumped with pleasure, for now he could go to bed the instant he felt like it. In order to profit from his new found liberty he took the farmers' weekly, and called to her from the first floor landing that town having tired him out he was going to bed. 'Sleep well, Linda.'

'You too,' she called.

When she had undressed in the somewhat Spartan guest room she planted herself in front of the wardrobe glass, her body no longer a stranger to her, and it wasn't difficult to imagine Osbert's hands caressing it. In her teens her mother, who had been a smart WREN officer, often said that she acted as if tomorrow or consequences didn't exist. She had acted like that eight years ago; was she doing the same? She shrugged her broad shoulders because she had suffered enough after that venture to be entitled to suffer again. That made her laugh a little. Would she have noticed Osbert if Jack hadn't pinpointed him as it were? Perhaps it would have taken longer, but what did it matter now that it had happened and every particle of her had loved it? No tomorrow, no consequences, and on that she went to bed, alone at last, though not really alone because her thoughts and body longed for Osbert. How did he spend his evening after she had gone? Nick curled up on the only chair in the room.

After she and Nick had turned the corner Osbert went upstairs, then into the sitting room to look at the letters Miss While had typed. Only when he had finished reading them did he allow his mind to fill with Linda again. It had been grand, it had been as perfect as he had dreamt it. He should leave it at that, and wait impatiently till their next meeting. However, his fear of fear lurked in the back of his mind, and within a few seconds it pushed the delight of Linda's body out of it, that is to say fear filled it completely.

He had been to bed with his estate manager's wife, not only to bed, but had fallen in love with her, no good denying that since he would have to reckon with it henceforth. It wasn't the kind of love he could handle, say, as he had handled his affair with Vivienne. If he and Vivienne couldn't meet for a week or even a fort-night he went about his business in a normal way. He couldn't remember thinking of her while he examined a piece of china or gave his learned opinion on some complicated matter, whereas while he had read the letters Miss While had typed he couldn't made any sense of them because there was Linda.

Nothing was wrong with falling in love with a woman as desirable as Linda. To go on making love to her was sheer delight. (He could do it at that very moment.) However, Linda was a married woman, and he couldn't say to hell with her husband as the husband was his estate manager. If Vivienne were right and they were just a scheming couple it could all work smoothly. No scheming woman gave herself as Linda had given her-self to him, so scheming was out. She had given herself wholeheartedly, he could still feel that in his groin. What a stupid expression giving yourself was, he couldn't help smiling. She had given herself to him for two hours, but because she had to leave she took herself back. The expression should be used only if it meant for life, and that was the cause of his fear of fear, for he feared precisely the complications and im-possible situations that love for life would entail. If they couldn't live without each other Jack would have to be told since he would see it even if he weren't. To marry Linda was out of the question. To marry her in a registry office, and be barred from going to communion would kill their love. Besides, what would happen to Maidwood and Jack? He with Linda in the house and Jack a couple of hundred yards away in the office would be a more intolerable situation than even his fear of fear could conjure up. Or they don't go the whole hog, and he and Linda snatch a few hours of bliss every week. He shook his head because with her you could only go the whole hog. No half measures with those grey eyes. I am caught, he said to the room, caught by myself.

He went into the dining room: the two glasses were still on the table. He took them to the kitchen to put them into the sink. On his return to the dining room he sat down on the chair she had sat on. He could lie to himself as well as any one he knew, but this evening he wasn't in the mood for lies. Perhaps the reason was that he had enjoyed too much his two hours with Linda. He was born a Catholic, brought up as one, and went through life accepting the Church as the mystical bride of Christ, never letting doubt creep in. Even if certain aspects of Vatican II didn't please him, such as the new Mass in lieu of the Mass of St Pius V, his answer was *ubi Petrus ibi Ecclesia*, and continued worshipping as before. He confessed about twice a year, then took communion. While it had lasted with Vivienne he kept away from the confessional which didn't upset him too much since their affair was bound to end sooner or later. In brief, he was like many other Catholics, no saint, yet not too bad a sinner either. If Linda entered too deeply his life the peace of his conscience would be shattered, and knowing himself that would be fatal for him. As a man of few principles he clung to the few like a poor man to the little he had. He shifted in the chair.

Wasn't he going too far with his fear? Not every cup asked to be emptied. A love affair on the side might easily have no dramatic significance for Linda. She and Jack hadn't had sexual intercourse for four years. She had told him that, and in such circumstances a lover on the side must seem the normal solution to a woman starved of sex and probably of affection too. The other night he had heard somebody creeping up the stairs. Immediately he thought it was a burglar, and saw himself kneeling in front of him, imploring him to take all he had as long as he spared his life. And he would be ashamed of his cowardice for the rest of his existence. The creeping footsteps stopped on the landing, then continued up to the second floor, the high ranking executive coming back sloshed from some late party. Wasn't his present fear similar to that one? Painting the devil on the wall when no devil was to be found. Reassured he took a stiff whisky to the sitting room.

Before he could sit down to glance through the newspapers he had bought in the morning his doorbell rang. Had Linda come back because she couldn't face the night without him? As he leaned out through the window he recognised Vivienne's car. As he leaned out more he saw her on the doorstep. She stepped back to call to him, 'Can I come up?' The last person I want to see this evening, he muttered to himself on his way down.

'I've been to a deadly cocktail party not far from here, so I couldn't resist stopping here on my way.'

'Come in and have a drink.'

She wore a dark green cocktail dress and a lot of jewellery. The late Long had hung on his wife as much jewellery as he could for shareholders and other mortals to see that he was doing well. All Linda seemed to have was her wedding ring.

'The party was given by the Hilliers whom I don't think you know,' Vivienne chatted. 'He's an economist which isn't excuse enough to be as dull as he. His wife Madge is just as dull, and because they're dull they talk only about themselves which forces the guests to talk only about themselves too. Dialogues des sourds as the French call it. "I spent three weeks in Tunis," says one person. "My son got eight A levels," says another. "That's why my tan lasts so long," says the one who's been to Tunis.'

'I'm glad you're here,' said Osbert who wasn't listening. 'I've decided not to engage a housekeeper. Tell Mrs Hickson that it's off.'

'I wouldn't dare to. She's too frightening a woman. Besides, I think you're making a great mistake. Your life will be hell in Maidwood without a competent woman looking after the house.'

'I hate and fear competent women.'

'Maidwood needs one. Being a man you've no idea how filthy and neglected that house is.'

'If a new broom arrives the Hacketts will go.'

'Which will be all to the good.'

'Listen, Vivienne. I don't want Maidwood to become a cause of fuss and bother. I didn't want it, I didn't ask my aunt to leave it to me, but now that it's mine I want to be involved with it as little as possible.' He could have laughed at himself. 'The Hacketts are there, let them stay, far less trouble than looking for new people who might even be worse. How do I know.'

'Mrs Hickson will look after all that.'

'And whenever I go down I'll have Mrs Hickson breathing down my neck.'

Vivienne rose, stubbed out her cigarette, had a sip of whisky, then came and stood over him. The scent she used seemed to float round him.

'Has Mrs Mawson put you against the idea of Mrs Hickson?'

Osbert thought that over, that is asked himself how much he should say. 'I don't think she's interested one way or the other.'

'Don't trust appearances,' said Vivienne, still standing close to him. 'She's a woman with a very strong will, and as I've told you she's a schemer too. Mrs Hickson would be in her way, that's why she doesn't want her. Beware of her, Osbert. To further her and her husband's interests I'm sure she'd be ready to go to bed with you. I hope she doesn't attract you.'

He shook his head, smiling, while he said to himself

that he must be a straight descendant of Judas. 'Not in the slightest.'

'I'm dining with Simon,' said Vivienne, stepping back. 'I'm late, so must rush.'

'Give me Mrs Hickson's telephone number.'

'Haven't got it on me. I'll ring you in the morning. Thank you for my drink. Don't bother to see me down.'

She went, leaving her words about Linda and the cloud of scent behind.

So Linda would go to bed with him if it suited her and her husband's interests. Linda had been to bed with him. He wished Vivienne hadn't looked in, but that was no answer to the problem. Which problem? Supposing Vivienne was right and Linda was a schemer? You can't be a schemer with those grey eyes. Hadn't scores of men been duped by women before him? Damn Vivienne for touching him on such a raw spot. That spot hadn't been raw before she touched it. Damn her again for the awful night he would have.

Afraid of it he went to bed early, and like two legions of demons her words and the memory of his afternoon with Linda fought each other most of the night. There is only one thing to do, he said to himself when he got up in the morning. At nine o'clock he dialled the Mawsons' number. It was Linda who picked up the receiver, and when he heard her voice Vivienne's words vanished as though they hadn't been uttered.

'Osbert speaking.'

'Yes, Osbert.'

'My American isn't coming this weekend, so I'll spend it at Maidwood.'

'Osbert, I'm so glad.'

'I'll be arriving at twelve. Could you pick me up at Banbury station?'

'I'll be there. Wait.' He heard her say, 'I want the Ford to fetch Osbert at the station at twelve.' He faintly heard Mawson saying that it was all right. Then she spoke into the receiver. 'I'll fetch you in the Ford.'

There was, he said to himself, nothing wrong in her speaking in such a warm voice to him with Jack in the room. Curse Vivienne.

In the train he went to the buffet car to have a drink, not that he really wanted one: it was to kill time which seemed moving exceedingly slowly. He would look into her eyes the moment he alighted. Those eyes would tell him whether she was a schemer or not. But why did he have to wait so long to meet those eyes?

'For once we're running on time,' said the steward.

Linda was waiting for him on the platform. She wore trousers and a jumper, and his eyes took in the shape of her breasts before they met hers.

'I'm so pleased,' she said. 'I've been to the house to see that your rooms are ready. I had a village woman in during the week to clean the downstairs rooms.' He remembered the dust in the library. 'I should have told you yesterday, but it went clean out of my mind.' Her smile he found ravishing. 'I've told Jack that you asked me to lunch with you. We can have a sandwich somewhere, then go straight to the house. I've told Mrs Hackett that you've a lot of work to do so not to disturb you before the evening. We'll have all the afternoon to ourselves.'

They came out of the station, got into the car, and he pressed her hand before saying, 'Tell me, Linda, do you like me?'

'Can't you feel it?'

'I fear I'm falling in love with you.'

'Why fear? I don't fear.'

'I was born to fear.'

'Not I. If I love let the whole world crash round me. It happened once, but we've nothing to fear. Here's the pub.'

To make it quicker they had sandwiches at the counter, unaware of the Saturday crowd round them.

They didn't speak because of their impatience. Then they drove to Maidwood, and watching her profile he remembered that his first reaction on the first day when she had come down the stairs was that she wasn't his type. How wrong you can be, for looking at her was a joy in itself.

It was a cloudy day with intermittent sunshine. The sun chose to shine through the clouds as the car came down the drive.

'It's not so ugly,' he said, pointing at the house.

'I never thought it ugly,' said Linda. 'It was my oasis. I mean my morning visits. Oh dear, what will she think?'

'Who?'

'Your aunt.'

'Think about what?'

'You and me.'

'Not within her terms of reference,' he laughed.

'She can't mind,' she said more to herself than to him. 'It's no fault of ours because it had to happen.'

They went up the stairs, and he didn't consider the minstrels' gallery as ridiculous as before. He asked where Nick was. She had left him with Mawson who would take him for a walk.

'The test,' she said as they entered the study.

'What test?'

'Kiss me, Osbert.'

Had she qualms too while they were separated?

'It's all right,' she said after their long kiss. 'I wanted to know whether I could kiss you in front of the chair your aunt used to sit in. I could which means she understands.'

'You're a quaint, sweet girl,' he said, moved. A person like that could never be a schemer.

They went into the bedroom and looking at the bed he remembered his night with Vivienne in it. Linda began to undress, and he forgot the night with

Vivienne. This is the first time, he thought while they made love, that I experience peace with ecstasy.

'You begin to mean more to me,' she said when they should have been too exhausted to speak, 'than I imagined or thought even yesterday.'

'I can't speak about my feelings. They're too deep.'

She put her head on his shoulder, and they lay shrouded in silence as if words had become unnecessary. He stroked her body, and she trembled with pleasure. It should always be like this, he said to himself, no words, no explanations, no trying to peer into the future, and no fear. Her firm body and the pleasure he took in it should be all that mattered. It was a pity that she was his estate manager's wife. How much simpler and easier it would be if the husband were unknown to him. He shook his head, upbraiding himself for worrying again. In bed with her no husband, no outside world existed.

'That's the landrover,' she said, jumping up, her elbow knocking his chest. 'What does he want?'

Osbert scrambled out of bed. So they were schemers, the husband had come to catch him out with the consent of his wife.

'Dress,' she said, starting to dress herself. 'We'll go into the park, so you can say you didn't hear the bell. He's no business to come here.'

They were dressed when the front door bell rang. When it rang a second time they were on their way down a spiral staircase at the end of the double L-shaped passage. 'I didn't know this staircase existed,' he said. The staircase led to the servants' hall which he hadn't seen before. She pushed a door open, and they were in the garden a little beyond Hackett's vegetable patch. 'A narrow shave,' said Osbert.

'I can't understand why he's come here,' she said. 'What does my face look like?'

'Perfect,' he said, bitterly regretting his thoughts as they flew out of bed.

'You're sweet,' she said, taking her lipstick from her bag. 'He's spoilt everything.'

The trees sighed in the wind, Simpson's cattle and sheep were all over the park, and walking at her side he felt deeply depressed. For it was useless pretending that the outside world didn't exist in Maidwood. Maidwood was the outside world in every sense. He wouldn't come down again, let the house rot and crumble. Only a few minutes ago it had been joy and peace, and now here he was in the desolate park with his unquenched desire, frustrated as he had never been before because the estate manager had suddenly decided to see him on some stupid estate business. Or had he found out? (He no longer believed that Linda and Jack had schemed together, her own frustration proof of it.) He may have come to say, You're my wife's lover, what are you going to do about it? I don't want her back, from now on she's your responsibility. What would he answer? Sorry, old boy, but my Catholic conscience doesn't let me go beyond a little love making now and then.

'Don't be angry with me,' said Linda. 'I'm just as furious as you.'

'I could never be angry with you, Linda. Do you think we could go back to the house? It's dismal out here.'

'There he is,' she said. 'He's come in through the gate next to the horse pond.'

The landrover loomed up in the narrow lane, dispersing the cattle. It pulled up near Osbert and Linda. Nick was the first to appear, jumped up on Linda, and whimpered, the whimpers ending with a shrill bark. Mawson climbed out, smiling.

'I thought you'd be in the park,' he said.

If he knows, he dissimulates well, thought Osbert.

'What is it?' asked Linda in a gruff voice.

'I wanted to see Osbert,' said Mawson. 'Rex would like to leave us earlier than we agreed on. In a fortnight instead of a month, something to do with his future father-in-law. So nothing stops your friend from coming down and starting on the job. Rex will explain everything to him before he leaves.'

'I don't know where he hangs out,' said Osbert, 'but I'll get in touch with his brother when I go back tomorrow. I'll ring you early in the week.'

'Fine,' said Mawson. 'Do you think, Linda, that we should ask round Osbert for a bite tonight?'

'Do you want to?' asked Linda, looking at Osbert, the grey eyes telling him to say yes.

'I should like to very much,' he said.

'I'm going home,' said Mawson. 'I've got a lot of home work to do.' He laughed as if that were a huge, original joke. 'When are you coming, Linda?'

'I want to take Osbert round the park first,' she said.

'Fine,' said Mawson. 'You must begin to get acquainted with the estate.'

That too was a huge joke, and still laughing he got into the landrover. Nick, who had hid behind Linda in fear of being taken back by Mawson, came out, wagging his tail, then trotted off in the direction of the cattle. She called him.

'We'll explore the park some other time,' she said. 'We'll go to what used to be the ornamental garden long before my time.'

She strode out, Osbert and Nick followed her.

'So there was nothing to fear,' said Osbert as he caught up with her.

'Don't think of fear all the time,' she said. 'We've better things to do.'

The ornamental garden looked as if a horde of Barbarians had camped there for years, the cracked ponds, the yew hedges and empty flower beds all proof of their sojourn. Cow parsley abounded where roses had

bloomed, and the emaciated poplars behind a crumbling wall seemed like sentries the occupiers had left
behind. To the right of the wall was a gazebo with
a turret that was ready to collapse. 'Come in here,' she
said.

A chipped looking glass faced the door, reflecting the
decay of the ornamental garden. A wooden bench was
against the wall, and at the other end lay a rusty old
lawn mower. 'This,' said Linda, closing the door, 'had
once been elegantly furnished, the sisters told me. Look
at it now, but here nobody will ring the bell. There isn't
one.'

She undressed while Nick sniffed the lawn mower. In
the half light her body appeared as white as the lillies
had been in the garden.

SEVEN

Osbert came back from Maidwood dissatisfied with himself, Linda, and even with Tony whom he would try to find next day because Tony too would belong to the Maidwood crew. After they had left the gazebo he asked Linda why she didn't go to bed with Mawson any more. 'Too long a story,' was her reply. 'I'll tell you some other day.' A little later she added, 'Anyway, it's of no importance to us.' Thinking it over her answer seemed unsatisfactory. Looking back on his weekend he found that apart from their love making all had been annoyingly unsatisfactory. The dinner in the Mawsons' cottage had been a heavy affair what with Mawson talking nineteen to the dozen and Linda impassive as though her presence were unnecessary. He had hated poor Nick because she spent the whole evening patting him and playing with his ears. And half the time she was out of the room. Was Mawson acting? He was unable to reach a conclusion. Could he and his wife spend all their days and nights just chatting like a couple of chums? One moment he believed it, the next he didn't. When she drove him back she came to his bedroom and they made love. If it could only be love making all the time. Before she went she said, 'You should beware of me, my love. I'm more than you bargained for.'

'What did you mean?' he asked her next morning in the study filled with sunshine. It was ten o'clock, and she had just arrived.

'One says a lot of stupid things at night,' she smiled. 'I say so much I don't mean. I've come to drive you to Mass.'

'I don't think I want to go.'

'You must go, you owe it to your aunt.'

She was an unfathomable creature. After Mass he took a taxi, rang the cottage from the house, and told Mawson who answered that he was returning right away to London. 'I don't know,' he said when Mawson inquired when he was coming down again. In the train he regretted his leaving so quickly, for had he stayed Linda might have come to him in the afternoon.

He was less dissatisfied on Monday morning. His trouble was that he liked imagining foul weather even if the sky were cloudless. He could have Linda whenever he created the opportunity, so what was he grousing about? If Linda and Mawson had given up going to bed together he the lover could have no cause for fear. But how long could it last and how would it end? If you don't answer it the question ceases to exist, strange logic, yet it should be his in the circumstances. I must stick to that, he said to himself several times.

He telephoned Tony's brother in his office.

'I hope you haven't changed your mind,' said the brother in a frightened voice. 'Poor Tony is counting so much on the job.'

'Don't worry. I want to get in touch with him because his job will start earlier than we thought.'

'I'll send him to you this very afternoon,' said the brother relieved.

Tony came while Osbert dictated to Miss While. Tony had one look at her and lost interest. He had shaved off his beard, and he was better dressed than at his first visit. When Osbert had explained why he wanted to see him, 'Have you arranged about the accommodation?' he asked.

'Till Wheeler leaves you'll stay at the pub. They've

got several rooms they let. Once Wheeler's gone you'll move into his cottage.'

'Is there any furniture?' Osbert didn't think so. 'With a job one can always buy on credit. When do you want me to go down?'

'In the course of the week.'

'I'll go down on Wednesday. I've got quite a lot to do before I leave. Can I look in on you early Wednesday morning?'

'Have breakfast with me.'

'Jolly decent of you.'

Osbert accompanied him to the landing.

'I wouldn't have a secretary with such a plain face for anything on earth,' observed Tony, taking leave of him.

If they hadn't had any sex the last four years her going to bed with him couldn't mean a damn to Jack, thought Osbert. He dialled the cottage number: the telephone rang but nobody answered. Where was she? He put down the receiver, and felt disheartened again, for it stood to reason that Jack would make him pay the price of his connivance. He couldn't get rid of him as long as he remained Linda's lover. Why should he want to get rid of the man who ran Maidwood so efficiently? Because he, the boss, was his wife's lover. Truly, he was going round in circles.

Back in the sitting room he sat at the writing table next to Miss While, he studying a document, she reading a paperback, waiting for him to dictate. At such moments they were completely unaware of each other. 'The door bell,' she said, raising her head.

He looked out through the window: a woman in a tweed skirt and jacket stood in the doorway. He had no idea who she was, so he pulled back from the window. The bell rang again. He wished his landlord would keep the promise he renewed every year, namely to put in a system for the tenants to be able to open the front door from their flats. Pending that there was only one thing he could do, which he did by going downstairs and opening the front door.

'Mr Hinley?' asked the woman. 'I'm Mrs Hickson.'

He had clean forgotten her with all his other worries, so he didn't ring Vivienne to get her number. Facing that stern looking woman he hadn't the courage to say that he had changed his mind, and needed no housekeeper.

'Come upstairs,' he said. 'My secretary's working in the sitting room, we'll go to the dining room.'

He motioned her to the chair Linda had sat in. Though he had seen her for brief instances in Vivienne's flat this was his first occasion to examine her at leisure. She wore her grey hair in a bun, was between fifty and fifty-five, on her right arm dangled a lot of cheap bracelets. She drummed on the table with her long fingers.

'I understand from Mrs Long,' she drawled, 'that you're looking for a housekeeper for your country house. I'm the widow of Frank Hickson as you surely know, and acting as housekeeper has never entered my mind before, but in my present circumstances I'm quite willing to consider it. After all I never cooked for anybody except my own guests while Frank was alive; nowadays I cook for other people's guests. So I could run somebody else's house. My doing that would uproot me. I must, therefore, know what's expected from me, and see your country house before I make up my mind. Mrs Long told me on the 'phone that she was willing to run me down.' No mention of wages because she was too much of a lady for that. Her surprisingly large dark eyes said that she hoped that he appreciated that.

He held out a packet of cigarettes.

'I don't smoke,' she said.

'The point is,' he said after short reflection, 'that it's

too early for the job I've in mind for you. There's still a lot to be settled as I inherited the place only recently, but perhaps in a month or two we could discuss it again if you haven't anything better in view.'

'It isn't a matter of having anything better in view. Mrs Long made the suggestion which under certain conditions seemed acceptable. One of them is to see the house.'

He heard the telephone ring, then Miss While answering.

'Very fair,' he said. 'I hope to see you again at a later date. Give me your telephone number, and I'll give you a ring in a month or two, or it might be earlier.'

'I'm generally in till ten in the morning,' she said, rising.

Coming into the flat she hadn't bothered to glance at the kitchen. Now on her way out she stopped to look round.

'Not much cooking is done here,' she said in a scathing voice. 'Don't bother to see me down.'

'I'll be in touch with you.'

He returned to the dining room, sat down heavily like one who had run many miles, and asked himself why he hadn't told her that he was in no need of a house-keeper. Hadn't he promised Linda not to take one? He hadn't the courage to send that formidable woman packing; he was too timid or polite to say bluntly no; and he knew that he was lying to himself. With an effort he admitted that in an underhand manner he wanted to keep Mrs Hickson up his sleeve. He admitted too that one side of him continued to fear imminent trouble, and if that trouble came and everything, meaning his affair with Linda, collapsed because of Mawson of some other reason, a housekeeper in Maid-wood might be useful to him. I seem to trust nobody, he thought, because I don't trust myself. He went into the sitting room.

'A Mrs Mawson has telephoned from Maidwood,' said Miss While. 'I told her you were in conference. She wants you to ring her back.'

He dialled her number.

'Why did you go back yesterday so early?' she asked.

'I felt depressed.' Miss While had picked up her paperback, and he was sure she didn't bother to listen. 'I felt depressed as I wouldn't see you in the afternoon.'

'Oh my darling, how sweet you are. I've told Jack that I'm going to London tonight.' Instead of crying out with joy he asked what excuse she gave him. 'I've an old aunt who lives in Bayswater. You're not the only one with an aunt, my love.' She laughed into the mouthpiece. 'So that's all right. I'll be at Paddington at seven, then will take a taxi straight to your flat.'

'I'll meet you at Paddington at seven.'

Paddington was heavy with commuters, and the taxi queue seemed to extend beyond the station. And there blew a special wind which, he had noticed long ago, you met only at stations. Despite the many lights there was a special sort of darkness too. Linda towered above the other passengers as they were vomited out of the train. She spotted him at once, and came towards him, her smile smothering any qualms he had left though he knew they would return.

'I went to the house yesterday after lunch,' she said, 'certain that you were in. I roamed all over it, no Osbert. I then decided that I must see you today.'

'Jack suspects nothing?'

'I didn't ask him.'

He was ashamed of himself, but he was getting accustomed to that. 'I'm afraid of there being some snag to our happiness,' he said lamely. 'Perhaps because I'm not worthy of it. We won't join the queue. I'm too much in a hurry. We'll take the Tube. I really ought to buy a car.'

'If you do I won't have an excuse to drive you to Mass.'

How could he ever have doubted her? He took her suitcase, and they went down into the Tube station. The train was so crowded that they could hardly exchange a word. However, their eyes spoke enough.

'This is where I lost my second virginity,' she said, entering his bedroom.

Here was the opportunity to insist on her telling him why she and Mawson had given up intercourse. However, she was already undressing, so all he could do was to follow suit.

The telephone rang when they were ready to go out to dine.

'Mrs Hickson just called me,' said Vivienne. 'She says you told her that you don't need a housekeeper for another month or two.'

'That's it,' said Osbert.

Linda stood in the doorway, the grey eyes watching him.

'What's come over you, Osbert? Why did you change your mind? Is the Mawson woman behind it?'

Linda stepped forward as if she had guessed what Vivienne was saying.

'Oh no,' said Osbert. 'The simple reason is that I want to wait a bit. I've a dinner engagement, am late as usual, call you tomorrow.'

'Was that Mrs Long?' asked Linda.

'It wasn't,' he said. 'Why do you think it was Vivienne? We call each other very rarely.'

'Then why did you bring her down?'

'Because she wanted to see the place to which she's entitled as an old friend.'

'Don't bring her down again. When you're there I want you to be only mine.'

He kissed her, and if she insisted he knew he would take her back to the bedroom.

They went to a restaurant in Soho which served food of Piedmont with French names. From a table at the other end of the room a bald headed man waved to him. Linda sat with her back to him. Because they both had the same thoughts they didn't linger over their food, and left well before the bald headed man and his party.

'I begin to feel that we can't live without each other,' said Linda as they fell into bed.

Her words seemed to dance in front of him while they made love. When she lay with her head on his chest, her hair tickling his chin he said as a belated answer to those words, 'But how can we manage it?'

'Manage what, my love?'

'You said that you begin to feel that we can't live without each other.'

She sighed before saying, 'Can't we leave it to the future? The future knows how to look after itself. When I was beginning to teach the headmistress, a woman I much admired, said to me — I can't remember à propos of what — as there is no nothing nothing never happens, one more reason why we can trust the future.'

'If it were only you and me, but there's Jack.'

'I've told you we haven't been lovers for the past four years, so don't bother about him.'

'He's in the picture.'

'A shadow in the background, that's all.'

'But he's your husband and my estate manager.'

'Do you want to spoil our night? Darling, I don't want to think of it till I'm forced to. Isn't it perfect as it is? What more can we want than being here together in each other's arms.'

'You're right, darling. I'm an old fusspot, forgive me.'

'You're forgiven,' she laughed.

In the morning he remembered that his charwoman was coming at ten. The old fusspot again, he said to himself. Linda looked a ravishing sight even in the pale light that entered the bedroom willy nilly. 'At nine,' she said, sitting up, 'I'll leave you, that is tear myself away.'

'Why so early? The charwoman's coming only at ten.'

'Charwomen don't frighten me. When I love nobody frightens me. I'm seeing my aunt at ten, then I catch a train back.'

'Couldn't you wait till the afternoon?'

'I don't want to leave Nick alone too long.'

'Jack looks after him.'

'He refuses to take him to the office.'

When she left he ran to the window, and leaned out despite the rain that was falling from a gloomy sky. How erect she carries herself, he thought. Only a woman who hasn't a worry in the world can walk like that. The telephone bell rang.

'Christopher Coote speaking,' said a deep voice.

Coote was the bald headed man who had waved to him in the Soho restaurant.

'Saw you last night,' said Osbert.

'Which reminded me that we haven't seen each other for ages. Is it too much of a sudden shock to ask you to lunch with me?' Coote's laugh was as deep as his voice.

Vivienne was coming to lunch, he didn't look forward to it because of all the questions she would put about his not engaging Mrs Hickson, so this was a Godsent opportunity to put her off. 'With the greatest pleasure,' he said.

They arranged to meet in a restaurant off Covent Garden.

Coote was connected with a brewery, and as far as Osbert knew all he had to do was to take whisky or gin with the brewery's tenants, then ask them if they were satisfied with the beer. He dressed in an old fashioned manner, always looked spick and span, and his gold watch chain seemed to contain his whole personality. Also he was a fast talker, laughing at everything he said.

He ordered the lunch with gusto and discernment, the wine waiter listening with abject deference while he chose the wine. With the fish he spoke about himself, with the grouse he entertained Osbert with stories about his customers. When the cheese arrived he said, 'I was surprised to see you dining with Linda Hattrell. Haven't seen her for eight years.'

'Linda Hattrell? She's Linda Mawson.'

'So she married him in the end.'

'They live in Oxfordshire,' said Osbert, his heart sinking, certain that nothing good would come from this.

'Do you know her well?' asked Coote.

'I met them recently. She was up in London, so I took her out to dinner.'

'Quite,' said Coote who wasn't the listening sort. 'It's a most amusing story, I might even say tragic story, but isn't amusing and tragic often the same?'

It was Osbert's turn to say 'Quite.'

'I've relations near Norwich, close relations with whom I often stayed. That's how I met Jack Mawson. His father had an enormous farm near my relations' house. He ran it with his two sons, Jack the younger of the two. Beyond the village was a girls' boarding school. They had a new mistress who was no other than Linda Hattrell. So far so good, but afterwards it wasn't so good. Linda used to come on Sundays to my relations' house as her mother was a friend of theirs ... My dear fellow, you don't drink anything, and this mercurey goes very well with cheese.'

Osbert took a gulp.

'That's better. As a matter of fact, I was present when she met Jack Mawson. It was love at first sight. However, there was one snag: Mawson had a wife.'

'What?'

'A wife,' said Coote, pleased with himself. 'The young lady didn't consider a wife a snag, a wife being no obstacle to her. Jack found her irresistible. The result was that she broke up his marriage, and his father kicked him out. It was a great local scandal, believe me. Linda and Jack went off together, and we didn't hear any more of them, and I didn't set eyes on her till I saw her with you last night. So she and Jack are still together and married too?' Osbert nodded. 'So she had her way, good luck to her, though I don't approve of women who wilfully break up a marriage. When Jack's father died he didn't leave him a penny. Do you see a lot of them?'

'I spend some of my weekends not far from them,' said Osbert who for nothing on earth would have told Coote that Mawson managed the estate he had recently inherited.

'If you see them give them my best regards,' said Coote. 'After all, I'm no judge of other people's morals. Frankly, I admired her the way she set about it. There was no holding her, and my relations told me that in the end it was she who went to the wife to tell her that she and her husband loved each other and would go off together. A tough girl who knows her mind. What does he do?'

'He manages an estate.'

'I'm sure he's very good at it, a very capable chap.'

'What was the wife like?'

'A hard mousy woman whom nobody much liked. Nevertheless, she and Jack got on well till Linda appeared on the scene. A brandy?'

'No, thank you. I've an appointment at three at the other end of London.'

132

All Osbert wanted was to be alone with his thoughts, and when he left he walked down to the Strand as if there were more scope for them. Then he forgot that he was in the Strand. So Linda was a wilful woman who broke up marriages. That was stupid since she had broken up only one, but isn't one a precedent for breaking up another, namely her own? He shook his head because now that she was eight years older she surely wasn't as headstrong and wilful as she had been at the time. He shook his head again as that wasn't a basis for argument even if he argued only with himself.

'So sorry,' he said, barging into a man carrying a large parcel. 'Look where you're going,' grumbled the man.

I wish I could, Osbert felt like saying.

He must see Linda as soon as possible. That depended on him alone. He could take the next train to Banbury, be there before her, and ring her on some pretext in the evening. Nothing could be simpler, yet he continued ambling along the Strand like one who wanted to kill time. If Linda were still the Linda of eight years ago she would break up her marriage with Jack if she really cared for him. Wasn't last night proof of her caring for him? His male vanity was of course flattered, but what about his Catholic conscience? Jack married her after his divorce, he couldn't do that however, out of the question, the quicker she grasped it the better for both of them. He had reached Fleet Street.

He saw a free taxi. He should hail it, go home, keep it waiting, pack a few things and then go on to Paddington. He continued walking. Wasn't he exaggerating again? He had made it clear to Linda how complicated their affair was on account of Jack being his employee. If she broke up their marriage, and came to live with him Jack would have to go. That stood to reason. On the other hand, they had ceased having sexual relations four years ago, which was only four

133

years after her breaking up his first marriage. The great passion hadn't lasted long. Perhaps Jack would say now, Let her go, do with her what you want as long as I keep my job. He had given up everything for her when he left his father and brother, no reason to do that again after having stopped loving her or she loving him. He wouldn't go down, it was too complicated. Let it ride though a fat lot of good that would do him.

He took a taxi near St Paul. That night he dined with friends who thought he was in great form. His hostess asked what his house near Banbury was like. 'A house to be avoided,' he said, and they all laughed. He took a sleeping pill before he turned in.

He was still under its influence when Tony arrived as fresh as a country rose (so thought Tony). He wore a tweed jacket and smart corduroy trousers.

'You've no idea how pleased my tailor is since I've got a job.'

'So you're off today?'

'Straight after breakfast.'

'Haven't you breakfasted yet?'

'My dear Osbert, you invited me to breakfast.'

'How remiss of me. Of course I have. What would you like?'

'As a countryman I need a heavy breakfast, eggs, bacon and sausages.'

'I'll see what I can do. If you excuse me I'll have only strong tea. Got a bad headache.'

'Poor fellow.'

Osbert hurried to the kitchen.

'No sausages,' he said, coming from the kitchen. 'Bacon and eggs. Have six rashers.'

'Country air is good for the appetite,' said Tony, sitting down. 'Brief me.'

'Jack Mawson will do all the briefing you need. I want to impress on you that your future depends on his approval, that is his being satisfied with your work. I won't interfere because I refuse to have anything to do with the estate management. Firstly, because I know absolutely nothing about it, secondly, because I like a peaceful life.' He could have laughed.

'I'll get on with him, don't worry, Osbert.'

'It's your worry, not mine.'

'Do I go first to his office?'

'Naturally.'

'And then to the pub?'

'Tony, you're not a baby. It's for you to find your way around.'

'Sure,' laughed Tony. 'When are you coming down?'

'No idea.'

After the six rashers and three eggs Tony announced that he was leaving at once. 'There might be a lot of traffic on the road.'

So he has a car, thought Osbert.

It was a brand new car which Tony had bought on credit. He enjoyed his drive down with the radio blaring the whole way. He had taken some money off his brother, so he stopped at several pubs, and had a good luch near Bicester. He arrived at the office soon after three o'clock.

Mawson sat behind his desk, Rex at a smaller desk not far from his. Rex felt like chatting, but got no encouragement from Mawson.

'Whom do you want to see?' asked Mawson as Tony appeared.

'Mr Mawson. I pressume you're Mr Mawson, ha ha. My name's Tony Howells.'

'I see,' said Mawson who didn't like the chuckle and the too new clothes. 'Pull up a chair.'

'I breakfasted with Osbert this morning,' said Tony to show how near to the boss he was.

'When is he coming down?'

'He told me he'll let us know.' The us, he thought, was clever.

'I don't want you to start right now,' said Mawson, 'as you must be tired after the journey. Which train did you take?'

'I came by car. It's outside.'

'Rex, take him to the pub. I booked a room. You'll start tomorrow at eight. As you're taking on Rex's job he'll initiate you. When he leaves you'll work on your own, under me, of course.'

Tony wondered whether he should ask for an advance on his salary; he decided to wait till tomorrow.

'Come in tonight for a drink,' said Mawson. 'They'll tell you at the pub how to get to my cottage.'

Mawson lit his pipe, and the two young men departed. Mawson shook his head, then took the land-rover to see a builder with whom he spent the rest of the afternoon, arguing over an estimate.

'You shouldn't be so fierce,' said the builder after he had given in. 'Maidwood isn't your property, the money you save isn't for yourself but for your new land-lord.'

'If I work for somebody it's like working for myself.'

One day the landlord will get rid of him, thought the builder, and he'll bitterly regret the money I'd have given him if he'd accepted the estimate.

When he got to the cottage Mawson found Linda, seated in an armchair, a book in her lap, Nick at her feet. 'What's wrong?' he asked.

'Nothing's wrong,' she said. She had tried to ring Osbert several times without getting an answer.

'You don't look very happy.'

'It's not for us to discuss each other's happiness.'

To answer that would take them too far, so he told her that Tony was coming for a drink, then he sat down and switched on the television set.

'What is he like?' she asked.

'You'll see for yourself. I for one don't like chaps

who're nearly forty and try to look as if they were twenty.'

'Can't you switch the bloody noise off?'

'Your nerves,' he muttered, switching the set off. 'I'll make myself tea.'

He reappeared only when he heard the door bell.

Tony looked round the living room, saying to himself that it was exactly as he had expected. However, Linda wasn't as he had expected the estate manager's wife to look. She was the sort of woman who appealed to him on sight. She must be a stunner in bed.

'It's very kind of you to have asked me in,' he said.

'Osbert tells me you've had some farming experience,' said Mawson.

'Quite a lot,' said Tony, trying to catch Linda's eye.

'Your job here will be mostly an administrative job, but farming experience will come in useful.'

'I worked in offices too,' said Tony, and smiled because Linda looked at him. It wouldn't be too difficult to seduce her. Wives of heavy husbands interested only in their work were an easy catch for a man of his experience.

'Osbert told us that you've known each other almost all your lives,' she said.

'We were real chums already in our toddlers' days,' laughed Tony. 'Mind you, he wasn't like most toddlers. He had begun his career as an egotist when he was three.'

'He hasn't struck me as an egotist,' said Linda.

'Wait till you know him better. He's friendly, charitable, loyal and everything twice as long as you don't ruffle him.'

'What do you mean by ruffling him?' asked Linda.

This is in very bad taste, said Mawson to himself.

'Interfering with his fads,' said Tony, staring at his empty glass. 'I'm sure that's the reason why he never married. You can't trust a woman not to interfere with your fads. I knew a man who was very keen on his garden which I admit was a very fine garden. He didn't get on with his wife, in fact hated her guts. One day I said to him, "Why don't you leave her?" Do you know what was his answer? He said that it would be too much bother to lay out a new garden. Well, our Osbert is like that, the only difference that he hasn't a wife. He's just rooted in his garden.'

He lifted his empty glass to his lips. Linda came over, took the glass, and poured gin and tonic water into it. My sort, thought Tony.

'I thought, and so did many of his other friends,' said Tony, 'that he would marry Vivienne Long when her husband died.'

'She came down here the other day,' said Linda.

'Perhaps they're still lovers,' said Tony, 'I wouldn't know as I've been overseas for a time, but rest assured he wouldn't marry her, too much of a responsibility though she's an independent woman, rich, clever, well organised, in short the ideal wife, but the word wife is a responsibility in itself. Before her husband died I said to him, "Why don't you persuade her to leave her husband and get a divorce?" His answer was that as a Catholic he couldn't marry a divorced woman. He remembers he's a Catholic whenever it suits him.' As he was speaking to Linda and his eyes were focussed on her he couldn't see Mawson's scowl. (If he had it wouldn't have bothered him.) 'He began to see less of her after the husband died.'

'They seemed to be very close friends,' said Linda, and Mawson made an impatient gesture, which she decided to ignore.

'He likes his friends,' said Tony. 'Friendship is his great activity. You can love your friends without causing yourself too much inconvenience. He shrinks from any form of inconvenience. He's never gone out into the world. His father, whom I knew well, used to

138

say that Osbert was a perfectly balanced person, therefore nothing exciting would ever happen to him. He said that with regret.'

'Are you all right in the pub?' asked Mawson in a heavy voice.

'Like it,' said Tony. 'Take this estate. I thought when I heard about his inheritance from my brother that here was at last an incentive for him. Nothing of the sort. He said at breakfast this morning that he shirks any sort of responsibility, all he wants is a peaceful life. Isn't he lucky to have you Mr Mawson.'

'I ran the estate for the aunt, so I can run it for the nephew too,' said Mawson, rising.

Regretfully Tony rose too.

'Come and see us again,' said Linda.

Hardly had the door closed on Tony that Mawson turned on her as if it were all her fault.

'An abject swine,' he growled. 'How dares he speak like that about a man who's helped him and employs him? I've a good mind to ring Osbert, and tell him to kick him out.'

'I found what he said most interesting,' said Linda, helping herself to gin. 'He said nothing really disloyal about Osbert. If he's like that why shouldn't his friends be allowed to speak about it? I repeat I found it most interesting.'

'He's his employer now.'

'Come off it, Jack. At least we know now much more about him.'

'I don't need that sort of knowledge.'

'What kind of knowledge do you need? I could supply you with some.' Her cheeks were flushed with anger, and she knew that she couldn't hold herself back. The telephone bell rang before she could blurt out that she had spent the other night with Osbert.

Mawson lifted the receiver.

'Oh, Osbert,' he said. 'Yes, he's arrived. Just left us

... We'll see, I haven't had time yet ... What? You're down here ... I'll call her.'

Linda went slowly to the telephone.

'Can he hear us?' asked Osbert almost in a whisper.

'No,' said Linda, looking at Mawson who had sat down with his back to her.

'I've come down because I must see you,' said Osbert. 'Can you think up some excuse to come over?'

'I don't have to. I'll be over in a jiffy.'

What did she mean with 'I don't have to,' Osbert asked himself anxiously. Had she told Jack? If all Coote had said was true, and there was no reason to doubt it, she was quite capable of doing so. He shouldn't have come down, yet he couldn't have done differently. Another night with sleeping pills and another day with his thoughts going round in circles were more than he could face. And what would she say to him? A stupid question since he had come down to find out though he had no precise idea in his head. Deny that she broke up Mawson's first marriage? She would probably say that was no business of his, and in a way she would be right. Why not admit that he had come down to be with her? He went out to wait for her in front of the door.

A carpet of clouds hung above him; he walked up and down like a prisoner in a cell. There was light in two of the second floor windows. He should have told the Hacketts that he had arrived, but surely they had heard the taxi and him coming into the house. He smiled because seven o'clock was after working hours for them. Were Mrs Hickson on the premises she would now be trotting round him, asking what he wanted for dinner and seeing that his bed was made. He had her up his sleeve, a comforting thought. Then he forgot Mrs Hickson and his sleeve, for he saw the headlights of the Ford turning into the drive.

'Hullo,' she said as she got out of the car. 'I rang your number four times yesterday afternoon before I came back. Four times this afternoon.'

'Come in,' he said. The Hacketts might be at the window, their excuse that a car had stopped in front of the house.

'Afraid of the Hacketts hearing us,' said Linda. 'Do they know you're here?'

'If they do they're too discreet to let me know it.'

'But mine was a second car. I take it you took a taxi.'

'As you don't want me to buy a car.'

They had reached the first floor landing, the minstrels' gallery on each side of them. There ought to be minstrels, he wished, making an awful racket to drown his thoughts. He took her into the study, switched on the light, and saw at once that the room hadn't been cleaned since his last visit. 'How dirty this is,' he said, pointing at an ashtray full of cigarette stubs.

'They didn't expect you down before the weekend,' said Linda.

'Sit down,' he said. 'I want to talk to you.'

'Don't you want to kiss me first?' she said, coming up to him.

I'm lost, he said to himself as her arms went round him, bringing the peace that she alone could give him. I'm lost, he repeated as her mouth opened, waiting for the kiss. 'Come to the bedroom,' he whispered after he had kissed her.

'First I want to hear what you've to say,' she said, sitting down. 'This is your aunt's armchair. I feel a different person sitting in it. Beware, Osbert, I might suddenly become a saint, and go where your aunt wasn't allowed to go.' She laughed loud, and he didn't care for her laugh.

'Go where?'

'Into a nunnery, and that'll save you from all responsibility. You'll be able to stay in your first garden, you won't have to lay out a new one.'

'I frankly don't understand what you mean?'

'Perhaps I don't either,' she said. 'Give me a cigarette, then fire away.'

'I'll get you a drink first.'

'It can wait.'

He sat down, and gazing at her Coote's story seemed insipid and no concern of his. He would kill the peace she gave him if he spoke about it.

'Do you know a man called Christopher Coote?' he heard himself asking.

'I used to know him a little. Haven't seen him for ages. Why?'

'He saw us in the Soho restaurant the other night. Yesterday he rang me soon after you left and asked me to lunch. We lunched together.' She was smiling as though she knew what would come next. The grey eyes remained unperturbed, there being no lipstick on her lips she looked younger though not defenceless. 'He spoke about you and Jack, and about his first marriage.'

'Which ended because Jack and I fell for each other,' she said in a serene voice that irritated him.

'The expression he used was that you broke up his marriage,' he said.

'Can you break up something that has ceased to exist?' she asked in the same voice. Then she leaned forward. 'Can you hear it?'

'Hear what?'

'The little owl. The other night just at sunset I looked at one with Jack's field glasses, a delightful sight, so innocent yet so wise.'

'I can't hear it.'

'You would if you were a field mouse,' she laughed. 'My darling, don't look so solemn.'

You can't break up something that has ceased to exist, he was repeating to himself. Nothing existed between her and Jack any more, hence in her eyes he and she weren't breaking up Jack's marriage.

'What Coote said was that it was you who went to see Jack's wife to tell her that Jack was your lover and you would go off with him.' Had Coote really used those words? Anyhow, that was what happened. She straightened herself, still smiling.

'So you think I'm a horrible hussy,' she said. 'Give me a cigarette. I came out without any in my hurry to be with you.'

He stood up, crossed over to his aunt's favourite armchair, and while he lit her cigarette he felt warmth and peace oozing from her. He wished he hadn't brought up Jack's first marriage. They could be in each other's arms instead of speaking about things that happened eight years ago, and which were no concern of his. 'Oh, no,' he said aloud, for it concerned him in every sense.

'I take it that oh no means that I'm not a horrible hussy,' she said.

'You broke up the marriage, and look where it landed you.' He didn't want to say that. He was ready to swear that he didn't want to.

'In your arms,' she said, 'so neither of us can complain.'

He would get nowhere with her if they went on like that. 'What I want to know is why did you break up his marriage? I wouldn't ask if I didn't love you.'

'The little owl again.'

'Blast the little owl.'

'Poor little owl. I well understand that if one loves one wants to know everything about the loved one. I ought to be flattered on your insisting on it. I'll tell you everything, but promise not to interrupt.'

'I promise.'

She got up, went up to him, gave him a swift kiss, then before he could throw his arms round her she retreated to the aunt's chair. As she spoke she joined her hands as if in prayer. She saw herself in the only looking glass in the room, and was satisfied with what she saw.

'I must start a long way back. My father was a sickly man, my mother burst with health. When the war came my mother joined up, my father wasn't wanted because he was an invalid. My father died, and my mother became pregnant. I've no idea who my real father is because my mother never spoke about him. Besides, I worked out the dates, I mean my father's death and my birth only when I grew up. After the war my mother became an upright woman, one who wouldn't stoop to sin, and who despised sinners. When her metamorphosis was complete she married a local solicitor, and became a pillar of society in Norwich.'

'Is she alive?'

'You promised not to interrupt.'

'Sorry.'

'She is alive, but we haven't seen each other since I left with Jack. She's, as I've told you, an upright woman. I did very well at school, got my degree at Cambridge, and then taught English literature at a boarding school near Norwich. I think I told you that.' Osbert nodded. 'After two years at the boarding school I met Jack. I was still a virgin, yet I think it was I who did all the seducing. Osbert, I'm speaking about a person who's become a stranger to me. When I look at Jack nowadays I just can't understand what that stranger saw in him. I suppose all women who've fallen out of love feel like that, but I can speak only about myself.' She shook her head. 'I anticipate. So there was Jack, I fell head over ears in love with him, a consuming love. I burned when I was with him, I was ash when I wasn't with him. I forced him to make love to me, forced him because he was a cautious, circumspect man, and had lived in the shadow of a grim Quaker father and brother and an equally grim Quaker wife. What did I see in him? The first man. I don't want to call it calf love, though, frankly, I just can't see any more what I saw in him.'

'You'll say the same about me some day,' he couldn't help saying.

'You're not the first man, my love, and today I burn with a different flame, a steadier flame, therefore a lasting one. But we're speaking about Jack and me. He fell in love with me, probably because he hadn't met a person like me before.'

'I well believe that.'

'You're interrupting again. Naturally, I loved him romantically, that is I wanted him all to myself, never to be away from him, our love should never end, but there was Jenny, his wife. He couldn't leave her, he moaned, and what would his father say? We went on like that for three months, meeting in secret, now and again making love behind a hedge or in his car in a dark lane.' Osbert winced. 'I was too much in love to let it go on like that. I wanted my man completely to myself. So one morning without saying a word to anybody I went to see Jenny. I'd guts in those days.' She smiled reminiscently. 'I told her Jack and I loved each other. She said she didn't believe me. "Do you want proof?" I asked, and showed her his love letters.'

'I can't see Jack writing love letters.'

'I can't see myself loving Jack either. She was pale with rage. They lived in any ugly brick house in the village. Jack should be back to lunch in about half an hour. I went on speaking to her, begging her to let Jack go, at the same time threatening her that I would take him away, the whole time listening, waiting for Jack to arrive. He came, and there was a terrible scene. They both lost their heads in their anger. I didn't lose mine. Jenny said she would never let him go, he said

145

he loved me, she said he'd get over his infatuation. She loved the word infatuation, and hurled it at him like a stone … I hear footsteps.'

The footsteps slowly approached, then stopped in front of the door, and two heavy knocks followed.

'Come in,' said Osbert.

'Excuse me,' said Hackett, opening the door, 'I just wanted to see if you're all right.' He was wearing a red sweater over his striped pyjamas, his boots were unlaced. 'I see you're here, Mrs Mawson, so I'm sure everything's all right. The wife wants to know what you want for breakfast.'

'Tea and a boiled egg.'

'As usual,' said Hackett. 'Staying for some time?'

'Don't know yet.'

'You'll tell the wife at breakfast,' said Hackett. 'I wish you good night, sir. Good night, Mrs Mawson.'

He stamped away.

'They heard two voices,' said Linda, 'so they thought you brought down some woman from London again, but now that he saw that the second voice belongs to Mrs Mawson, who's above suspicion, he left disappointed. So there we were the three of us, and to put a stop to her reproaches and his trying to explain what he felt about me, I declared that I would never look at him again if he didn't go off with me.'

'And he went off with you.'

'And he went off with me. I lost my job, he lost his with his father, there was nothing to stop us. We rented a cottage in Bury because it was far enough from them, he advertised for a job in the farmers' papers, and landed this one. The estate was in a mess, and within a year he got it out of the mess, and now, as you know, it makes good money.' She stood up. 'That's the end of hussy's story, my love.'

'It isn't,' he said. 'Why did your great love end?'

'Tear and wear,' she laughed. 'The real trouble was

that after a time we'd nothing to say to each other. When we'd stopped saying "I love you," we'd nothing more to say. He's fundamentally a cold man, and he returned to his coldness once passion was spent. He was and is still ready to continue the joint cold existence for the rest of his life. We made love less and less, we talked less and less, but there was something else too.'

'What was it?'

'My admiration for your aunt. With her one didn't speak about boundaries, ditching, fencing and the rest of it. Hers was a pure soul, and I bathed in her purity. My hour with her every morning was sheer joy and lifted me above myself, then I had to go back to the bleak humdrum life with Jack. It was really she who awakened me.'

'Why didn't you leave him?'

'I was waiting for you.'

He threw his arms round her, saying, 'Come to the bedroom. I can't wait any longer.'

'Nor can I.'

The bed was unmade, the window open, and the trees groaned angrily as if wanting to burst into the room. He closed the window, and when he turned round he saw that she was undressing. He had thought so much of her and her body the last two days that he gazed at her incredulously. Surely those breasts, belly and the triangle weren't waiting for him. She threw herself on the crumpled sheets, her arms and legs opened, her mouth too, and the grey eyes were focussed on him while he undressed. 'I'm yours more than you imagine,' she said in a loud voice as he got on the bed. Had she said the same to Jack in the beginning? Entering her he forgot Jack.

They made love as though it were their last chance to find happiness, peace and contentment.

'What more can we ask for?' she said.

'What more,' he muttered.

'If only we could spend the night together,' she said when she was dressing. 'Alas, I can't go that far yet.'

'What will you say when you go back?'

'He'll be asleep, and I'll go to my room which used to be the guest room, lie down and think of you.'

'My darling.'

'You're not leaving in the morning, I hope,' she said on their way downstairs. 'I want to see you in the morning. I'll be here at nine. Don't get cold feet and rush off before I arrive. It's very difficult to tame an egotist.'

'I'm not an egotist.'

'We all say that about ourselves, but take it from me that you are one. Why shouldn't you be?'

'Anyway, I won't run away.' That, he thought, was proof of his not being an egotist. 'I'll be expecting you at nine.'

'A very important question,' she laughed. 'Why do you want a boiled egg for breakfast? In your flat you'd have a fried egg.'

'I wouldn't dare to ask Mrs Hackett to fry me an egg. She might think it's too much work.'

'I see,' she said, letting in the clutch. Nobody and nothing should ruffle him. 'I'll be here at nine.'

He watched the rear light till it disappeared. He looked up: the carpet of clouds was lower, and no light shone from the Hackett's windows. He lit a cigarette.

Fundamentally she had told him nothing new, that is added nothing to what Coote had said. She broke up Jack's marriage because she had fallen for him, but that he had already gathered from Coote. She had spoken of no qualms, no remorse, in fact considered it the logical consequence of her wanting to be with Jack. The wife's feelings, the father disinheriting him seemed not to have mattered to her. Yet she called him an egotist. He heard the little owl this time.

She was ruthless in her fashion, and he should beware of her. 'I'm saying all this because I'm not with her,' he said to the night. A blast of cold, wet air was the night's reply. He stamped out the cigarette, and went indoors.

He switched off the light in the study before going to the bedroom. He took the ashtray to the lavatory, emptied its contents, then returned to the bedroom. He lay down on the crumpled sheets. She was ready to break up another marriage, namely her own if she truly loved him as she said and as her body proved every time he lay with her. You'll get sick of me as you got sick of Jack, he would say if she spoke about it. I'm much older, and I love you differently would be her answer. There was only one thing to do. He must explain to her that as a Catholic he couldn't marry a divorced woman. He had enough sins on his conscience without adding to them an irreversible sin. As she had admired his aunt she would surely understand. The aunt was the right line, and on that he fell asleep. In his dream he saw Linda tossing her head which meant that she was making love with him.

EIGHT

Nick received Linda as if she had come back from the dead.

'Quiet,' she said, patting him. 'We don't want to wake him.'

When she had left Osbert she had thought of waking Jack to tell him that she was in love with Osbert and Osbert with her. It would be one bit of hypocrisy less. She had told Osbert about herself and Jack, so why shouldn't she tell Jack about herself and Osbert? However, by the time she had reached the cottage all she wanted was to sleep and wait for the morning. She went upstairs with Nick in her wake. As she passed Jack's door she heard him snoring which made her smile. Poor Jack, she had nothing against him. Why poor Jack? He lived the life he loved, the only life that suited him. He should get Simpson's farm to fill his cup of happiness.

She lay down in the guest room, switched off the light, and Nick tried to climb into the bed. She pushed him down, he waited till he heard her breathing regularly, then he got into the bed, and curled up believing that he would be less conspicuous like that. Eventually she pushed him down, but by then the room was full of daylight. She heard the village girl in the kitchen.

'You stayed with him a long time last night,' said Jack as they sat down to breakfast. 'I didn't wait up.'

'I noticed that. Do you remember how it all began?'

'What began.'

'Osbert, you and me. When you got over your disappointment after Miss Hinley's death you became petrified by the unknown nephew. Between us we worked out a nasty, little plan, didn't we?'

'Nasty?' he said, putting down his knife and fork.

'Now it seems nasty to me, at the time I thought it might be a huge joke, and a slight change in my humdrum life.'

'You fell for the idea, and if I remember rightly it came from you.'

'I won't deny it. Besides, we'd no idea what the heir would be like. We imagined him as some busybody full of beans, a new broom that might sweep us away.' She shook her head. 'What a wrong picture. The point is that you pointed him out to me. If we hadn't concocted our clever plan and if it hadn't been decided that I should vamp him ...'

'I never used that word.'

'That's possible, but that's what it amounted to. If I could make him like me, befriend me, turn me into his confidante we could guide the busybody so that no harm should come to the estate manager.'

'Why are you bringing this up?'

'Because everything has changed. I am in love with him. Do you think that I spent three hours with him last night just to praise the estate manager?'

'I don't want to think about it, that's all, Linda. If I thought about it we would start on recriminations that would never end.' He started stuffing his pipe, leaving a shimmering egg untouched on his plate. 'We'd gain nothing.'

'I don't want recriminations either because nothing is left to recriminate about. I'm telling you about my feelings so that you know where I stand.'

'Where you stand? Where do I stand I who lost everything because of you?'

'I lost my job because of you,' she said, flushing. 'Mutual sacrifice.'

'Told you two years ago to try and get a job at that girls' boarding school over there.' With his pipe he pointed at the window. 'You said you didn't want to work. You said you were waiting for something better.'

'The better has come.'

'Where's that?'

'You're dense. Anyway it's a waste of time to start recriminating about the past.'

'I'm not as dense as I look,' he said, putting the pipe on the table.

'This is really a useless argument. I'm in love with Osbert, and I'm pretty sure he's in love with me. I mean as much as he's capable of being in love.'

'And you?'

'You know best, Jack. Why do I tell you that I'm in love with Osbert? Firstly, because I don't want you to tell me that I'm in love with him, secondly because I want to make it plain to you that I'd do nothing to harm you, my fellow conspirator. We started on Osbert together so to speak.'

'I'm sure you wouldn't do anything to harm me. You've no cause for it. If I did you any harm you did me twice as much.' She lifted her hand. 'It isn't recriminating, it's stating a fact. All I ask you is not to speak to me about it again, I don't mind how much time you spend with him and what you two do together. I find it very distasteful for you to discuss such things with me. Better tell him that I'm not the ridiculous conniving husband, so he should mind his steps in my presence. You tell him that.'

And this man was my great love, she said to herself. 'I repeat I won't do you any harm. I'm always very conscious of your having lost your delightful Jenny because of me.'

'Leave her out of this.'

'One can't even joke with you any more,' she sighed theatrically. 'I think we've cleared the air for the time being at any rate. I'm seeing him at nine, he'll probably come to the office. Rest assured that I won't repeat our little breakfast chat to him. Do you want me to speak about the Home Farm lease?'

'Not yet. I might have different plans, don't know yet.'

'Man of mystery.'

'This egg is cold. Give it to the dog.'

'The dog doesn't like cold eggs.'

'Will you be in for lunch?'

'Don't know yet.'

'Let the girl know when you do.'

He waved to her from the door without turning his head.

'Come, Nick,' she said as he closed the door, 'we're going to Osbert.'

When they arrived Nick went up the stairs in front of her, then made straight for the study. He's expecting to see Miss Hinley, she said to herself.

Osbert had eaten his boiled egg, and sat listening to Mrs Hackett who towered above him.

'The young man you engaged to take Mr Wheeler's place,' she was saying, 'looks a very pleasant gentleman. I looked into the pub last night just before supper, and Joe Gregson, that's the landlord, introduced us. Joe said to him that Hackett and me lived here. The young man ...'

'Not so young, he's my age.'

'Nobody would believe it. I'm sorry, I didn't mean it like that. You look young too, Mr Hinley, very young. He told me you were friends ever since your childhood.... Good morning, Mrs Mawson, I was just saying that I met the gentleman who's taking Mr Wheeler's job.'

'Good morning,' said Linda.

'Here's Nick,' said Mrs Hackett. 'Gets longer every day. Will you be here for lunch, Mr Hinley?'

'We're going out,' said Linda.

'And tonight?' asked Mrs Hackett.

'I'm returning to London,' said Osbert, keeping his eyes averted from Linda. 'I only came down to see how the young man fits in.'

'You liar,' said Linda when the door had closed on Mrs Hackett.

'Sit down, plenty of tea left.'

'No tea, thank you. I've had all the tea I'll ever want at breakfast. I told Jack that I'm in love with you.'

'Linda,' he nearly shouted, 'how could you?' So she was using the same tactics she had used with the first wife.

'Don't look like a frightened rabbit, my darling. Doesn't suit you. I told it to clear the air, that's all. It won't make any difference to his and my non-existent relationship.'

'I can't look him in the eyes again.'

'You can. I promised him not to tell you that I told him. I don't have to keep a promise I made him.'

'Why not?' Osbert couldn't help asking.

'Because you come first. He said he didn't mind one way or the other as long as we didn't behave like lovers in front of him, a fair request, don't you think?'

'I don't know what to say,' said Osbert. She was ruthless, she had put him against the wall. 'I never found myself in a more awkward situation before.'

'The egotist,' she smiled. 'There's nothing awkward as long as we don't start holding hands in front of him.' Nick barked for no reason whatsoever. 'Stop it. Can't you understand that I had to tell him? We're free now, my darling, we can be together as much as we want.'

'Free? I never felt less free in my life.'

'That's because you love me,' she said, putting her hands on his shoulders, and there was that sense of peace again to give his fears the lie. 'All you have to do, my love, is to behave in front of him as if nothing existed between us. No effort since we'll be very little in his presence.' She bent down and their lips met. 'If only Mrs Hackett weren't making the bed,' she sighed as she straightened herself. 'Now listen to me.' She sat down in the aunt's chair. 'I'll drop you at the office, you'll stay with Jack and the new chap for about half an hour, then walk back here, and I'll pick you up in about an hour. Jack knows that we're lunching together. I know a pub near Chipping Norton, where the food is good. We'll lunch there, and then we'll come back here.'

'You're running my life.'

'Our life. One kiss and we're off.'

The sky and the landscape sparkled in the autumn sunshine.

'Autumn for me is a woman past her prime,' said Linda, getting into the car. Nick wanted to sit beside her: she pushed him into the back. 'Will you go on loving me when I'm past my prime?'

'I can't see myself not loving you,' he said, surprised by the regret in his voice. A smile from her, and regret vanished.

Mawson sat behind his table, Wheeler and Tony stood in front of it. 'The most important thing in your dealings with the people in the village,' Jack was saying as Osbert opened the door. The window being closed the smell of pipe tobacco filled the room.

'Here's Osbert,' said Tony, wishing to be the first to welcome him.

'Hullo, Osbert,' said Mawson rising.

'Hullo,' said Osbert. Then with an effort, 'How are you, Jack?' Did his voice betray him? He forced himself to look at Mawson: he found to his surprise no change in his expression. The man was either a good actor or he truly didn't care one way or the other. 'I came down to see how Tony's fitting in.'

'He and I won't know that before a month,' said Mawson. 'Isn't that so?'

'I'll fit in,' said Tony. 'Osbert knows better than anybody how much I love country life.'

'I'm glad you're here,' said Mawson, taking a file from the drawer. 'It's about the death duties. Part of it will be paid from the money I managed to put aside for your aunt, the rest out of the money we'll make with the sale of some of the houses in the village. Here's the list of the houses. You should have a good look at it.'

'Give me the file,' said Osbert quickly. 'As I'm going back to London I'll study it, then see Bone. Can I ring him?'

Bone was in, and he was ready to see Osbert at four.

'Do you want me to drive you to the station in the landrover?' asked Mawson.

'Linda kindly promised to come to the house and drive me to the station,' said Osbert, looking steadily at Mawson.

'Good,' said Mawson, and Osbert understood that there was no reason whatever to look at Mawson steadily.

'Can you spare Tony for an hour? I want to show him the house.'

With Tony present Linda wouldn't be able to upbraid the fugitive he had become.

'Well?' he said to Tony on their way to the house.

'I love it,' said Tony. 'You really saved my life, old boy.'

'As long as it lasts. Is your French girl coming over?'

'I'm not so sure,' said Tony, thinking of Linda. 'Here I feel very far away from her. I can't see her in the landscape, if you get my meaning.'

'Sure,' said Osbert. With a roof above his head, an

assured salary Tony had no reason left to cling to a woman he had known before roof and salary were found.

'I'm fundamentally a bachelor like you,' said Tony.

When the house came into view Tony immediately said how ugly it was. Osbert took him into the drawing room which was full of sunlight. Tony craned his neck to look at the star studded walls and ceiling. 'The Sainte-Chapelle,' he said.

'I said the same when I saw it for the first time. It's like two people who look alike, but when you come to know the second well you don't see any resemblance any more.'

'How right you are. In Malaya I met a man who looked like you a bit. When I came to know him all resemblance went. He was a foul fiend whereas you're a lamb.'

Osbert heard the car pull up in front of the house.

'We're here,' he called as Linda came in through the front door which he had left open. She frowned slightly as she saw Tony who had put on his best smile for her. Osbert waved the file Mawson had given him. 'I must take this up to London to Bone, the solicitor. Can you drive me to the station? My appointment is at four.'

'I'll drive you to the station,' said Linda. Then she burst out laughing.

'What's so funny?' he asked.

'Everything. Come along, you might miss your train. Haven't you got to pack first?'

'I'm leaving here the few things I brought down. Come with us, Tony. Linda will be so kind as to drive you back to the office.'

'You sit beside me,' said Linda to Tony, 'so Osbert will be able to jump out when we reach the station.' As Osbert got in she whispered, 'Poor egotist.' Then in a loud voice, 'Give him room, Nick.'

After a while Nick put his head on Osbert's lap. Linda talked animatedly to Tony who became convinced that chatting her up would be no waste of his time. The French girl was receding fast.

'Run for it,' said Linda as they reached the station. 'You don't want to miss the next train.'

He waved to her: she didn't wave back.

He had to wait twenty minutes for the train. On the platform stood the man he had addressed as Mr Mawson on his first visit to Maidwood. The man seemed to be still bearing him a grudge, for whenever he walked past he glowered at him. He got into the train too, so Osbert chose another carriage.

He sat smoking and upbraiding himself for having run from the only woman whose company was the greatest joy he knew. Every pore of his longed for her, and if he hadn't been a coward he could be with her that very moment and all the hours to come. His fear of fear had made him bolt from her. He shook his head because it wasn't that any more. It was fear itself that had driven him away. She had told Mawson that she loved him, and that could only mean she was ready to leave Mawson for him. What then? It was a fearful vista, he saw it like a tunnel that lengthened as you advanced in it, the endless tunnel that he had feared in his nightmares. That tunnel had been waiting for him all his life. Now Linda had pushed him into it.

There was, of course, a more cynical way of looking at it. Mawson wanted to keep his job, Mawson and Linda had ceased to care for each other, consequently he could carry on with her as long as he paid her husband's salary. I'm no cynic, I'm not made for that, he said to himself. What was he made for? Well, not for that. However, that got his thoughts nowhere.

An enormously fat woman sat on the opposite seat, her legs like the Pillars of Hercules. Now and then she sneezed, her body shook, she took a handkerchief from her bag, wiped her nose, put back the handkerchief and sneezed again.

Perhaps Linda hadn't told Mawson, perhaps it was just a lie. No man could have looked less like the conniving husband. That was stupid since he had no idea what conniving husbands looked like. If he hadn't run from her he would be lunching with her, both of them waiting to go to his bed. He shook himself, then went to the buffet car to have a sandwich.

She had proved that she could be ruthless when she had broken up Mawson's first marriage. She would be as ruthless now if she were given the reins. It was up to him not to give them. He could go abroad for a while, he had always wanted to go to Morocco, here was his chance, and in Casablanca or Marrakesh he would long for her peace in vain. After a while everything ceases including longing. Man's limitations could be helpful at times. A tea drinker pushed him aside, and he returned to his compartment. The fat woman had got out at Reading.

If only she weren't married how easy it would be. No, it wouldn't be easy either for him who wasn't the marrying sort. You don't reach the age of thirty-eight unmarried if marriage has any meaning for you. She had called him an egotist, maybe she was right, and the last thing an egotist should do was to live with a woman since give and take weren't for him. He for one preferred giving to taking. With her he would have to take a lot, for he was sure that when she loved she was the giving kind. Hadn't she showed it unmistakably every time they made love? Even the grey eyes gave more than was good for an egotist. He sighed with relief as the train entered Paddington station.

First he went to his flat, Miss While had arrived already, he read through his mail, and dictated a few letters before he took a taxi to Bone. His eyes lit up as he alighted: old Ramsbottom stood in his doorway, looking exactly as he remembered him, the ash on his waistcoat just the same.

'It's cold next door,' Ramsbottom called.

'What did you say?' asked Osbert with a huge smile.

'Sir, I wasn't speaking to you,' said Ramsbottom, turning his back on him.

'Sorry,' said Osbert, and went in through Bone's door feeling stupidly disappointed.

A new, slightly more civil young woman sat behind the reception desk. A fidgety old man lifted one old magazine after the other in the waiting room only to drop it back on the table. The grey haired secretary beckoned to Osbert.

He always looks as if he came direct from a Turkish bath, thought Osbert entering the office.

'What can I do you for?' guffawed Bone, disliking Osbert even more than on the last occasion.

'It's about the death duties,' said Osbert.

'We discussed that on your last visit. Take a pew, you're too tall for me.' And he guffawed again.

'What I was thinking is this: if you can find buyers for the houses in the village you can surely find a buyer for the whole estate.' Goodbye Jack and Linda.

'It's quite a different proposition,' said Bone. The man's really stupid, he thought. 'Of course, you can sell. I could sell this old paperweight too if I accepted one p for it. If you sell Maidwood your loss will be enormous.'

'I can't lose enormously since I never paid for it.'

'That's a strange way of looking at it,' said Bone, positively hating Osbert. 'It's your property, if you sell it at a loss it's your loss.'

'How long do you think would it take to sell the estate?'

'We might have to wait a year or two.'

'That's of no help,' said Osbert more to himself than to Bone. Even three months would suffice to turn him into Linda's loving slave. Morocco was a better alternative. 'In that case don't do anything yet. I'm thinking of going abroad for a while.'

'And your work?'

'Thanks to Maidwood I'd no holiday this year.'

'Poor Maidwood.'

'Poor me,' said Osbert, smiling broadly.

Leaving Bone he decided to ring Vivienne. He walked to the nearest call box, where he had to wait till a gesticulating red bearded man finished a long call. 'The phone's a bloody nuisance,' said the man as he came out of the box.

'If you want to see me come right now,' said Vivienne. 'Simon's fetching me at six. We're going to some party.'

'Always the party girl,' said Osbert, ringing off.

She opened the door for him, and glancing at the pictures and furniture which he had known for years and were somehow immovable in his memory he began to feel a little relieved, and the grip of his anguish was less painful. Her hair today was Scandinavian fair which he found attractive, and made her look slightly a stranger till she began to speak. She had been to *Aida* last night, and had been surprised, pleasantly of course, by the depth she hadn't suspected before. Then she explained what she meant by depth. She interrupted herself, observing, 'You don't look too pleased with yourself. Been to Maidwood?'

'Came back three hours ago.'

'We'll have a drink, then you'll confess everything to mum.'

His eyes followed her while she got the drinks, a reed compared with Linda, no ruthlessness about her, a woman who had signed her contract with life and kept to it. Linda had signed no contract, for she dominated instead of coming to terms.

'I take it's Mrs Mawson,' said Vivienne, pulling up

a chair. I'll sit close to you so as to hear your whispers.'

'You've strange notions about confession.'

'I may have but I know what's coming, which is more than most priests do. I told you she was after you, it stuck out a mile, and I did warn you against her, isn't that so?'

'The trouble is that it's mutual. I'm as much after her as she's after me.'

'My poor Osbert, can't you see that the woman's an adventuress? She and her husband worked it out together, concerted action, together they dug the hole, and you, poor man, fell right into it.'

'I don't believe that.'

'Because you don't want to. If you don't want to why not enjoy it while it lasts? She's attractive in her way, I bet she's good in bed, and you have the immense advantage of the husband not finding out since it has all been done with his help. You used to speak to me about your fear of fear which I never quite understood, but with the Mawsons there's no fear of fear or fear itself. He won't do anything to annoy you as long as you keep him on as the estate manager. You've no reason not to keep him on since he does his job very well. You're in clover.'

'It isn't that.'

'It's not the sort of triangle you like. It was so much simpler while my poor Justin was alive. You practically never saw him, so your conscience was at rest. The ever present Mr Mawson and your business relationship with him naturally don't suit your lily white soul. Drink up, and have some more.'

'Perhaps you're right where Mawson's concerned,' said Osbert, putting his glass down. 'I don't like my sins being watched from the inside. Justin was almost non-existent to me whereas Mawson exists very much. But I repeat it isn't quite like that.'

162

'You mean she's forcing the pace more than is good for your delicate soul.'

'Lily white and delicate,' he sighed. 'Your trouble is that you have rigid pictures like those of Epinal about other people.'

'We're not discussing my trouble, we're discussing yours.'

'I like her more than is good for my lily white delicate soul, and I fear that she likes me more than is good for either of us.'

'You fear that it's more serious than just a romp in bed.'

Should he tell her that Mawson had been married before and Linda broke up that marriage? He decided not to because he wouldn't hear the end of it, twice an adventuress, a woman without scruples, and God knows what else.

'Far more serious,' he said.

'You mean you really fear that she'll leave him for you? What a terrible vista you and she living in the big house while the ex-husband works for both of you in the estate office. But, my dear, you've a perfect answer to that.'

'A perfect answer?'

'The same you gave me when I was in love with you.' She laughed, then put a cigarette into a long holder. 'Don't you remember? Of course you remember. Justin was still alive when I told you in a moment of burning passion that I was ready to leave him, get a divorce to be able to marry you. And what did you answer? Your Catholic conscience doesn't let you marry a divorced woman.'

'When Justin died I asked you to marry me.'

'I said no because my heart wasn't in it any more, and yours wasn't either. It was a gesture which I appreciated, most noble and all that. If you could say that to me you can say it to Mrs Mawson too. Then she'll know that she can go so far and no farther. Between you and me I don't think she'll want to go as far as that.'

'Why don't you think so?'

'Because that would go against her husband's interests. He can stay with you only as long as the affair doesn't become public.' To his surprise she burst into loud laughter. 'What an old-fashioned fool I am. Today people no longer care a damn what other people think. He'll rely on your wife to keep his job. The quicker you tell her that your finicky Catholic soul doesn't let you marry her the better for you.'

'Lily white, delicate and now finicky.'

'All three. That's Simon.'

'I hope I'm not late,' said Simon as she opened the door for him.

'Osbert is here.'

'Osbert is leaving,' said Osbert who wanted to be alone with his thoughts.

'We should be leaving too,' said Simon. 'I'm still bewitched by *Aida*, and it was so well sung.'

'You spend a lot of time with him,' said Osbert in the doorway.

'Not jealous,' she laughed. 'Mrs Hickson's the best answer. Get hold of her as quick as you can.'

'Too late.'

'It's never too late. I repeat Mrs Hickson is the answer. In the meantime tell Mrs Mawson about your fastidious deeply religious soul.'

'I add fastidious to the other three. Ring you before the weekend.'

In order to be alone with his thoughts Osbert went into the first pub he saw. It was crowded with rush hour business men swallowing their whisky fast, glancing at their wrist watches, calculating whether there was time for another snifter before catching trains to their wives who were also consulting their watches.

Vivienne was right in that the quicker he told Linda that he couldn't marry her the easier their relations would become. However, that wasn't as simple as it looked, for nothing was simple when he was in her presence. Vivienne was the last person to understand the peace Linda gave him as Vivienne wasn't a woman of peace. If there were no Mawson he would do whatever she wanted, even if it included marriage. Was he so sure of that? It was one thing to love a woman quite another to be married to her. How relieved he had been when Vivienne turned him down after Justin's death. Anyhow, no comparison could be made, for dead or alive Justin had been a hazy figure, whereas Mawson was more than life size, and whatever the future held in store he and Linda couldn't escape him. Imagine it if she suddenly said that she was ready to leave Mawson to live with him, and hang marriage, let him divorce her or not she didn't care one way or the other. Didn't thousands of women live with men they weren't married to? Social conventions, he was certain, didn't matter to her. He remembered Vivienne's words, 'He'll rely on your wife to keep the job.' She, who could break up a marriage in face of her mother and everybody she knew, would have no qualms about living with him in the house while Mawson worked for them in the office. Mind you, for himself too. Fortified by a second whisky he decided to go down the next day to tell her that his lily white, delicate, finicky soul could never let him marry or live with her.

He looked round: the businessmen were gone. Time he left too.

He took a bus that stopped two streets away from his street. He lit a cigarette, and walked slowly, no hurry, he was his own master, tonight nobody could interfere with his habits. He would make himself a simple meal, then go to bed and read. He touched his door key that would lock out the world and his worries too.

As he entered his street he saw that the curtains of the flat were drawn. Good old Miss While who thought of everything. He entered the house, mounted the stairs, and his blood nearly froze as he heard a dog bark. The barking became frantic as he opened the kitchen door. It became ferocious as he reached the dining room. He threw the sitting room door open, and Nick rushed up as if ready to eat him.

'Stop it you ill-mannered dog,' called Linda, rising from the sofa. 'You don't bark at a person in his own house.' Nick wagged his tail, then trotted back to her, but couldn't resist a growl as he lay down. 'Are you surprised to see me?'

She was wearing the dress she wore on the day he met her. He couldn't help comparing it with the expensive dress Vivienne wore, and the comparison made him love Linda even more than he thought. Still, that was no excuse to come to his flat without letting him know.

'How did you get in?' he asked.

'I rang the bell, your secretary let me in, she said you weren't in, I said I'd wait for you, she asked whether you expected me, I said you expected me, she asked me to sit down, I sat down, and as it was nearly six o'clock she said she would be leaving.'

'When she left she let you stay?'

'I told her who I was.'

'What did you say?'

'My Osbert is frightened. All I said was that I was Mrs Mawson, the estate manager's wife. She found that a good enough reason to let me stay.'

Miss While, he thought, would be the key witness when Mawson started divorce proceedings. 'Why did you come up?'

'Because I wanted to be with you.'

'And if I stayed out till midnight?'

'You'd have found me in your bed waiting for you, and this fierce hound would probably have climbed into the bed while I waited for you. He never wanted to get into bed while I slept in the same bed with Jack, but since I don't sleep with him any more ...'

'What did you say to Jack?' he interrupted.

'After you left so abruptly I drove your protégé to the office – by the way, he seems rather keen on me, just the right moment – and told Jack I was coming up after lunch.'

'What did he say?'

'Who cares what he said,' said Linda in an impatient voice.

'I do.'

'He said all right or words to that effect, frankly can't remember. Tell me, why did you rush off so abruptly? Afraid again?'

'You know that ours is an impossible situation.'

'It can't be impossible since we're here together.'

What's the good of it? he muttered to himself as he embraced her and her irresistible warmth enveloped him. They made love on the sofa as if they hadn't time to go as far as the bedroom next door.

'How right I was to come up,' she said.

She sat on the edge of the sofa, not bothering to dress. He dressed quickly with his back to her as though shirt, jacket and trousers were his armour.

'Bring me my bag,' she said, stretching out her legs. 'I've got my cigarettes in it.'

He brought her the bag, now feeling ridiculous because he was dressed. As he held it out she took his free hand and kissed it. 'To thank you for having come into my life,' she said. 'You've no idea how drab it was before.'

'I love you,' he said. If you suffered from vertigo and leaned over a bridge all you wanted was to jump into the water, 'but that won't get us far.'

'Do you want to go any farther? Isn't this perfect as it is?'

'It's perfect as it is,' he said, regretting that he had dressed.

'So we've no cause to worry. Could I have a drink?' She called him back as he started for the dining room. 'Stop worrying, Osbert. Take it from me you've no reason to worry. One never has if one loves.'

'You're right,' he said, wishing he could believe it.

Anyhow, he thought, while he got the drinks, it would be all right tonight as the outer world couldn't intrude. He wouldn't answer the telephone or the door bell, and let tomorrow look after itself. He wouldn't take her out to dinner. Last time it had been Christopher Coote, who would it be this time? Probably nobody yet he refused to take the risk. He went into the kitchen: there were eggs, ham and cheese, no grand meal, but no intruders.

'I don't want to dress,' she said when he returned. 'Give me your dressing gown. We're the same height.'

They turned in early, she slept with an arm round his shoulder, her body practically stuck to his. Despite the peace and the warmth he saw Mawson laughing in his face the moment he closed his eyes. Mawson lifted his stick to belabour him, he cried out, and Linda shook him gently, saying, 'My poor darling, was it a nightmare?'

NINE

He began to long for her before she closed the front door, though it had been she who had wanted to stay and he who urged her to go, his excuse that he had a lot to do and many people to see. 'I could have stayed a week,' were her parting words. He promised he would go down the next day.

He sat down at his writing table to study a document on which he had been asked for his learned opinion. Instead of taking in what he was reading he lived through the night again, repeating every word she had said, and conjuring up her facial expression when she spoke. It was unsatisfactory in that she had said nothing that had any bearing on his predicament, if predicament it was. Twice he had brought up Mawson, first at dinner, then at breakfast. Now that she had told Mawson that she loved him how would Mawson behave? She laughed, saying that it was for them to behave and not for Mawson who would carry on as before as long as they didn't flaunt their love in front of him. In the morning he had asked, 'But can the three of us go on like this?'

'I see no reason why we can't,' was her answer.

Unsatisfactory in every sense, and he thought of Morocco. It would be pretty lonely there without her, he said half aloud. He heard the charwoman mounting the stairs, a silent woman who did her work rapidly, leaving plenty of dust behind. He tried to concentrate on his work. Linda appeared, sitting naked on the edge of the sofa. He shook his head sick and tired of himself. If only his aunt hadn't left him Maidwood. Two men were fighting in him and he was both of them. He would be the victor and the loser, thus no respite was in store for him. He looked at his diary, and was glad to see that he had a lunch engagement. So he hadn't lied to Linda altogether. The telephone bell rang as he reached the door ready to go out. He went back to answer it.

'Is that you, Osbert?' asked a deep voice.

'Andrew, I recognised your voice. How are you? How's Patricia?'

'We're fine. Haven't seen you for ages? Could you come down this weekend?'

His first reaction was to say he was sorry but he couldn't because he had inherited an estate in Oxfordshire and was forced to spend his weekends there. Instead he said, 'That's awfully kind of you. I don't know yet whether I'm free this weekend. Can I ring you back on Friday?' After all, Kent wasn't as far as Morocco. 'I'll try to be free.'

'You know how much we love seeing you,' said Andrew Somers.

He and his wife were old friends of whom Osbert used to see a lot before Maidwood had dropped out of the sky. Out of a dark sky, he corrected as he made for the door again.

After lunch he returned to his flat, the document his excuse, refusing to admit that he was hoping for Linda to ring him. She must have got back by one o'clock.

She rang at four.

'Why didn't you tell me about Mrs Long and the housekeeper?' she asked.

'Mrs Long and the housekeeper?'

'I went to the house to tell Mrs Hackett that you were coming down tomorrow. I found Mrs Long showing round a woman the sight of whom made me immediately see red, the spit of my mother and the same pretentious manners, always afraid of not being respected enough.'

'That must be Mrs Hickson, but why were they there? What cheek.'

'Mrs Long explained in a sneering voice ... did you say to her anything about us?'

'Not a word,' he lied.

'The way she spoke to me made me think that you have. Not that I care.'

'I never told Vivienne to take down Mrs Hickson. I don't want or need Mrs Hickson.'

'Mrs Long said that it was high time the house was taken in hand, Mrs Hickson, whom she knew well, was the ideal person for it, so she brought her down to have a look at it before she makes up her mind whether to accept the job or not.'

'All I told Mrs Hickson when she came to see me was that if I needed a housekeeper I'd get in touch with her. I'm furious with Vivienne. Anyway, I don't want Mrs Hickson at Maidwood or anywhere else.'

'Wait, I haven't finished. Mrs Hickson chimed in, saying she had never seen a house in a more disgusting state, a real pigsty, but she could turn it into a decent dwelling if she were given a free hand. All the time Mrs Hackett was listening in the minstrels' gallery.'

'Oh my God.'

'I told them that as far as I knew you didn't want a housekeeper. I also said that I didn't appreciate anyone calling Miss Hinley's house a pigsty. "It was surely in a better state in her time," said Mrs Long. "Hadn't she reliable servants?" I said I hadn't time to discuss the state of the house, and walked out. Half an hour later Mrs Hackett arrived at the cottage to tell me that she and Hackett would leave if that woman were engaged. I told her I'd ring you at once. Darling, I'm sure that your dear Vivienne brought down that woman only to spite and annoy me.'

'I'll give her a piece of my mind, and you tell Mrs Hackett that there's no question of my engaging a housekeeper.'

'You tell Mrs Hackett yourself. She might not believe me. There's a train at five-twenty. I'll pick you up at Banbury station. We've been separated too long.'

She rang off before he could find some excuse. He dialled Vivienne's number: she wasn't back.

He travelled down in a crowded train, saying to himself that he had never seen so many evening papers and cups of tea before. Linda was waiting for him on the station platform, and as he pushed his way through the crowd to reach her he had the strange sensation that he was doing something he had been doing for many years, the husband returning from work to his waiting wife. Like those businessmen in the pub yesterday, he tried to smile.

'We're going straight to Maidwood,' said Linda.

'Have they left?'

'They left before Mrs Hackett came to see me.'

They got out of the station and into the car. He was silent because he hadn't yet shaken off the strange sensation on the station platform.

'I can well understand,' Linda was chatting, 'that you can't see what I saw in Jack when I fell in love with him. I can understand even less what you saw in Mrs Long.'

'Ours was a far milder affair.'

'There's the landrover,' she said, pointing with her hand.

'You mean Jack's in Banbury?'

'He's got plenty of cronies here. Darling, are you absolutely sure that you never said anything to her about me? I mean about us two.'

'Nothing whatever.'

'She must have guessed, probably it isn't difficult to guess. Anybody can see that we're made for each other.'

He swallowed hard, before saying, 'That's exactly what we don't want.'

'Why don't we want it?'

'I'm thinking of Jack.'

'Forget him.'

'How can I?'

'Think of me, and you forget him,' she laughed.

How little she knows me, he muttered to himself.

'When I was with those two women,' she was saying, 'and heard Mrs Hackett moving about in the minstrels' gallery I thought only of you because thinking of you gave the self control I was ready to lose. Calling your aunt's house a pigsty.'

'It could be a little cleaner.'

'When you decide at last to live here I'll get a couple of women in every day if you want.'

'My work doesn't allow me to live down here.'

'A pity for both of us though I don't mind your flat I can assure you.' She laughed and touched his arm. This is what is called a sensuous laugh, he said to himself, wanting her badly. 'Be awfully nice to Mrs Hackett. Those two women really ruffled her. The nicer you are to her the quicker she'll leave us alone.' There was the sensuous laugh again.

They turned into the drive, Nick let out a yap as if to remind them of his presence, and the house appeared, dark among the swaying trees with light only in the study.

'She's waiting for us,' said Linda.

Mrs Hackett burst into speech before Osbert, who was behind Linda and Nick, entered the room. She had answered the doorbell at five to three. It was five to three because she had looked at her watch as the doorbell rang. It was a habit of hers to look at her watch whenever she heard the doorbell. The butcher, for instance, came in his van around eleven in the morning, the baker shortly after two, and the man who helped Hackett three times a week in the garden came around three. So she had taken to consulting her watch when the doorbell rang to know who rang it. Today wasn't the day of the man who helped Hackett in the garden. Curious because you never know what sort of riff raff might ring the bell she went downstairs to open the door. Two ladies were on the door step, one of them she thought she had seen before. 'This,' said the lady whom she thought she had seen before, 'is Mrs Hickson whom Mr Hinley has asked to come here as house-keeper.' Mrs Hackett's jaw dropped.

'Let me explain,' said Osbert. 'Mrs Hickson cooks now and again for Mrs Long, it was Mrs Long's idea that I might need a housekeeper. I repeat might. I saw Mrs Hickson, and told her I didn't need one, so I honestly don't understand why Mrs Long brought her down. Anyhow, rest assured I'm not going to have a housekeeper here. I'm very happy with you and your husband looking after the house.'

'Now you're satisfied, aren't you, Mrs Hackett?' said Linda.

'I'm satisfied, Mrs Mawson. When I heard her saying that I took it as a direct, personal offence, and it hurt because I thought that you were satisfied with me and my work, and looking after a big house like that is real work, and if you don't believe it, Mr Hinley, ask Mrs Mawson.'

'I don't have to ask anybody,' said Osbert. 'I can see it for myself.'

Mrs Hackett went on for another ten minutes, then left them, saying that Hackett would be satisfied too because he had also felt offended in a direct personal way.

'Well, that's settled,' said Linda. 'I thought she'd

never go, and I want so much to be alone with you, my darling.'

'Wait, I'm going to ring Vivienne to tell her what I think. She must be back by now.'

'I'll wait for you here. Don't be long.'

He went downstairs to dial Vivienne's number in the shadow of the staircase. What a silent house this was after a hundred years of female rule. Vivienne was in.

'I'm speaking from Maidwood,' he said. 'I'm furious with you, Vivienne. I never engaged the Hickson woman, so what right had you to bring her down?'

'The right of a friend who wants to help. With Mrs Hickson in the house you'll be able better to resist. Take her on, she's willing.'

'I'm not.'

'She'd be your mainstay. With her in the house Mrs Mawson couldn't establish herself in it.'

'I wish I hadn't said anything to you yesterday. Anyhow, Mrs Hickson is out, and please don't do that kind of thing again. I'll be truly angry.'

'I feel that you're inamorata isn't very far,' laughed Vivienne. 'I tried to help you, you refused my help, so I can't do more for you.'

She rang off. So she's the hurt one, he said to himself, starting up the stairs. He was stopped by the doorbell. Not for him to look at his watch since he didn't know the time table at Maidwood. Could it be Jack? He opened the door slowly, grudgingly like one who fears an intruder.

'Hullo, Osbert,' said Tony with a huge grin.

'What on earth are you doing here?'

'Jack told me you were coming down this evening, so I decided to look in on the friend of my youth.'

'Come upstairs, Linda Mawson is here, fetched me from the station.'

'She's quite wonderful,' said Tony.

Osbert pretended not to hear him.

Linda's face fell as he ushered in Tony who said, 'Your husband told me that Osbert is coming down.'

'Is there any drink left in the house?' said Osbert. 'I think I drank the little there was the other night.'

'What about going to the pub?' said Tony. 'Linda, you could drive us there.'

'No pubs for me tonight,' said Osbert. 'I brought down a lot of work from London. I'll come to the office tomorrow, then take you to the pub.'

'I can stay a few minutes with my old friend even without drinks,' said Tony, sitting down.

'I'm off,' said Linda. 'See me down, Osbert.'

'It isn't fair,' he said on their way down, 'leaving me like this.'

'I'll never leave you, my love. Never worry on that count. I only go for you to get rid of him. Say you've got your work to do. I'll be back in an hour.'

Tony sat in the study with his legs stretched out, his hands clasped behind his head, the picture of repose.

'She's a remarkable woman,' he said, 'and attractive too. Jack's a different sort of person altogether.'

'What do you make of him?' asked Osbert, longing for a drink.

'He's deep, you think there isn't much to him because of the surface. I, who knocked about a lot and met all sorts of people, can assure you there's a lot to him.'

'What do you mean by a lot?'

'Firstly, you can't fool him, secondly he's full of hidden passions.' I don't like the hidden passions, said Osbert to himself. 'I'm sure he cares for his work only because he thirsts for power. Those who thirst for power don't care a rap what sort of power it is. He would make a jail warder whom all prisoners fear. A warder is a power in a prison, isn't he? To us outside the prison he means fuck all. Well, Jack's relationship

176

with Maidwood is the same as a severe warder's with his prison.'

'You've got it a bit wrong,' said Osbert. 'He's a farmer's son, so his job's in his blood.'

'He does no farming here, he's no more than a sort of official, but it gives him power over the farmers and the people in the village. While your aunt lived it was supreme power, with you around it might not be. He's too deep for that. Take it from me he isn't the man who likes sharing power or anything else.'

Osbert didn't like that at all.

'With you he's waiting, armed neutrality. Men who love power can't understand those who don't. It'll take you a long time to convince him that you don't want to interfere with his rule, that is his power.'

'I couldn't have made it clearer to him.'

'I repeat it'll take you a long time to convince him. With me it's different. I started out by making it clear that I'm your life long friend, but I quickly saw I wasn't endearing myself with that. Poverty and misfortune have taught me to be quick on the uptake. From now on I'll be his humble disciple, and you'll see how well that's going to work.'

'I took him for a less complicated person.'

'He's far more complicated than you think. He can't squash you because you're his employer, but for the peace of your mind I urge you to keep your distance from the estate management because, I repeat, he isn't the man who believes in sharing.'

'Thank you for the advice,' said Osbert, rising. 'I must get down to my work, and I want to go early to bed. See you in the office in the morning. Can you find your way down?'

'I can find my way through any jungle,' laughed Tony.

Osbert sat down when he heard the front door close. So Mawson didn't like sharing. Though he had seen marriage only from the outside he was pretty well convinced that husbands believed they had power over their wives, and probably wives believed the same. Power loving Mawson surely had the same feelings about his wife as about his job, namely no sharing. Yet at the moment he was sharing Linda with him. Linda would say there was no sharing since all was over between her and Mawson. However, Mawson might think differently since Linda was his wife, and remained his wife whether they made love or not. Love making is the lover's first consideration; for a husband it is surely of secondary importance. And if Mawson loved power as Tony said, he wouldn't take lying down his loss of power over his wife. I'm in a real mess, he said to himself, whichever way I look at it. He heard the front door open: she would be upstairs in a moment and he would melt under the impact of the peace she gave him. Peace in the midst of turmoil. He stood up, and his face lit up as she reached the landing.

'I brought you a bottle of gin and a bottle of whisky,' she said, holding out the bottles.

'There's nobody like you,' he said.

'Wouldn't your Vivienne have brought you drink in the same circumstances?'

'She's ceased to be my Vivienne long ago. Besides, she wasn't really mine.'

'She doesn't look the woman who knows how to give herself. I do because I'm made like that. Let's have a drink. You see I'm not disinterested in my giving.'

When they had finished their drinks he said he wanted to have a look at the drawing room of which he was growing fond, so out of the ordinary.

'To see whether it's fit for pigs?' she laughed.

'The joke isn't worthy of you,' he said.

In the drawing room lit by the gloomy lights of the Dutch candelabra she stopped in front of the empty fire place, observing, 'Mrs Hackett has never lit a fire though I told her to light one once or twice a week.'

She's speaking as if she were my wife, he said to himself, as if she were responsible for the running of the house.

'Soon winter will come,' she went on, 'and if the chill isn't taken off we won't be able to come into this room or any other room downstairs.'

'We,' he said to himself. Then aloud, 'What do you think of Tony?'

'The sisters,' she continued, ignoring his question, 'lit a fire twice a week in this room, also in the library, yet your aunt never used them. You're not going to bury yourself in the flat upstairs. Anyway, I wouldn't let you, my darling.' She stroked his cheek.

'Why not?' he asked.

'Because there's an old side to you which shouldn't be encouraged.'

'An old side?'

'All egotists have an old side. Age is respected, the old are entitled to rely on others and ask for compassion. Nobody complains about their inactivity. Isn't it playing the old man to tell Jack every time you see him that you don't want to interfere with the running of the estate?'

'Playing the old man or not I don't want to interfere with the running of the estate. I didn't ask for the estate, so I'm entitled not to be saddled with it.'

'But I want you to show more interest,' she said, turning away from the fireplace.

'Isn't it enough to come down to be with you?'

'More than enough. Nevertheless, I don't want you to be just a passive onlooker. Sit down, darling, I'm going to make a fire. I know where the logs are kept. Let it be a lesson to Mrs Hackett.'

'Don't bother.'

She was already on the way to the door which she

left open. Her footsteps died away in the vastness of the house.

He chose an uncomfortable bergère, and sat straight because of the carved back. There was no getting away from her acting as though she possessed him altogether, and the trouble was that it appeared to him as natural as to her. Each day would bring them closer to each other, each new day would make leaving each other more difficult. Where would it lead them? He shivered because of the draught caused by the open door. He looked at the gold stars which seemed too artificial to have compassion. The old man, he smiled, was in need of compassion.

Linda arrived, with a basket filled with logs. Their weight must be considerable, yet she carried the basket as if it were as light as a feather.

'We'll have a huge, roaring fire,' she said.

'You shouldn't, Linda. Leave the logs here, we'll go upstairs, and switch on the central heating.'

'If I do a thing I do it,' she said.

He watched her make the fire, thinking she was desirable whatever she did. She had brought a couple of old newspapers with her.

'I think I ought to put in central heating,' he said.

'Don't. I want the house to remain as it was in your aunt's time. If it's too much work for Mrs Hackett I'll do it myself, not twice a week, but almost every day because you like this silly room.'

'I don't deserve you.'

'That's the old man speaking,' she laughed.

The logs began to hiss, but as the chimney hadn't been cleaned for ages the room slowly filled with smoke. 'Blast,' she said, and went to open a french window. Chilly air vied with the smoke. 'Awful,' she said.

'Sorry, darling, but it's intolerable in here,' he said, rising from his uncomfortable seat.

'I'll have the chimney cleaned tomorrow,' she said.
'Come upstairs.'

'Anyway, the fire's going out. I feel sadly defeated.
Tomorrow you'll have a beautiful fire.'

'Tomorrow I'm going to London.'

'Always running away from me. It'll have to stop.'

The fire was out, the logs looked as defeated as she,
and the chilly air remained in the room despite her
closing the french window. She leaned on him as they
mounted the stairs. This is bliss, he said to himself.

'I wanted to make love in front of the fireplace,' she
sighed.

Instead they made love in the bedroom, then had
scrambled eggs in the study. When they had finished he
said, 'Oughtn't you be going back?'

'Why should I? I feel happy and contented here with
my love.'

'Think of Jack, it's nearly eleven.'

'When I'm with you I don't want to think of him.
When I'm alone I don't want to think of him either.
And you shouldn't think of him. But as we're on the
subject I'm going to tell you what really happened,
and then you won't want to think of him, take it
from me. Give me your hand, I need strength to tell
you the disgusting story, disgusting in retrospect.'

'I'm not insisting on your telling it if you find it
disgusting,' he said. The fear of fear, he added to himself.

'It's my duty to you and to myself. It was a put-up
job,' she said, squeezing his hand.

'What was a put-up job?'

'Let me tell you. For absolutely no reason whatever
Jack was convinced that your aunt would leave the
estate to him, lock, stock and barrel.'

'The solicitor thought that too, one more reason to be
nice to him. In his eyes I'm the interloper.'

'Your aunt's nephew the interloper,' she snorted.

'When Jack heard that the unknown nephew was the heir he was properly frightened. He saw his kingdom collapse, his power going up in smoke. What would the nephew be like? What would happen to him? All he knew was that you were a bachelor and under forty. Jack is simple, therefore he's full of simple ideas, and goes straight to the obvious point because of his simple ideas, one of the reasons the farmers fear and respect him. So he got the very simple idea that I should make the conquest of you for his own purposes.'

'I can't believe it,' said Osbert, letting go of her hand.

'Give it back at once,' she said, grabbing it. 'I don't lie to you. Lying to you would be like lying to myself. In my empty, bored life I fell in with his suggestion.'

'You mean to say that all this . . .'

'Never, my darling. Do you think I love you because Jack ordered me to? Love can't be ordered. Send me a load of love at seven tonight. Doesn't exist. The day I met you I warned him that it might go much further than either he or I intended. He said I knew how to look after myself. The irony of fate is that it was he who pointed you out to me.'

'If he hadn't?'

'It might have taken me a few hours longer,' she laughed. 'I owed you this confession.'

'But why did you agree to his plan?'

'Because I was bored and because I wanted to help him. If you'd been an unpleasant, domineering boss – my poor Osbert how can one even imagine that of you? – I might have been of help to Jack. As things are I'd have kept out of it if I hadn't fallen in love with you.'

'I don't think any worse of Jack,' said Osbert after a short silence.

'Because it all worked out satisfactorily, but that isn't

due to him. In his simple manner he would have considered it my duty to make up to you even if I had found you repellent.'

'The whole thing is too complicated to blame Jack for it.'

'I do,' she said, rising. 'Are you really going up tomorrow?'

'Duty calls.'

'I'll come up tomorrow evening, expect me around seven. It's awful to tear myself away from you. Tomorrow night will be ours. Roll on tomorrow.'

He saw her down, they embraced, and he remained outside the house till the rear light disappeared.

Nick received her with loud barks. Mawson must have dined with his cronies in Banbury as nothing had been moved in the kitchen. She fell asleep, regretting the fire that didn't burn. When she and Nick came down in the morning Mawson was finishing his breakfast.

'I've changed my opinion about that Tony fellow,' he said. 'I think he'll do, though of course only on the lowest rung.'

'And you're on the top rung. By the way, I'm going up to London this afternoon. I'm becoming quite fond of my aunt.'

She looked at him steadily: he returning her gaze, saying, 'Do as you like.'

'Rest assured I'll never do anything against your interest. I'm loyal to the past in my fashion.'

'In my fashion I'm loyal to it too. By the way, you don't have to hurry back tomorrow as I'm going up for the day.'

'To see Jenny?'

'I haven't an aunt in London.'

'Heavy sarcasm. Osbert is coming to your office before he goes back to London.'

'I'm sure to be there before him.'

He got up from the table, filled his pipe, decided not to light it, and as the door closed on him she let out a little laugh.

Nick wagged his tail.

TEN

Miss While was absent minded. The loved one hadn't come last evening or the evening before. Perhaps she wouldn't see him again, and she had no recourse since she had no idea where he lived or worked. Had he tired of her? She heard Osbert speaking, shook herself and tried to listen.

'You can leave early today,' he was saying. 'I mean you can leave right now.'

'Thank you,' she said, rising from the little table impatient to go home to wait in vain.

Now why did I send her away? Osbert asked himself as the door closed on her. He had two long letters to dictate. He shrugged his shoulders because the two letters could wait like so much else, for he was in a sort of vacuum, floating in a river without stream or banks, no going back and no moving forward. On entering the office in the morning he felt like the interloper Jack had been afraid of at the time his aunt died. Rex and Tony were in the room, also one of the farmers whose name he couldn't remember. I remember nothing any more, he said to himself while Jack and the farmer continued their discussion about some barn that needed repair. I remember only Linda whose husband stands in front of me.

'I'm going up to London,' he interrupted them. 'I promised Tony to give him a drink. Do you mind, Jack, if I take him to the pub for half an hour? I promise to send him back in half an hour.' He could just as well have gone on his knees.

'Most certainly,' said Mawson. 'You can drive Osbert to the station afterwards.'

Gracious husband, thought Osbert gratefully. It was funny how little Linda's confession had affected him. If Mawson had plotted against him he plotted against Mawson every time he took his wife. He and Tony drove in Tony's car to a pub in Banbury, and in his fear of Tony starting off on Mawson's hatred of sharing he questioned him about his French girl.

'I lost interest in her,' said Tony. 'I can't concentrate on two things at the same time, that is on the past and the present. When I met her I was pretty lonely, here I don't feel lonely because I like it.'

'Admit you're a bit of a shit,' said Osbert in an envious voice.

'A realist,' smiled Tony.

Now pacing the sitting room Osbert said to himself and his collection of china in which he had lost interest since the coming of Linda into his life, that his trouble was that he was neither a dreamer nor a realist, only the river without stream or banks. It had been so easy with Vivienne and the nebulous Justin, no worries, no thought of the future, but with Linda it was impossible not to contemplate the future. He sat down firmly determined that he would look into the future whether he liked it or not, no blinking and no glancing aside. First he must get himself a whisky.

The future consisted of his loving Linda and she loving him, their passion overriding every other consideration. So far so good; when two people loved each other they were entitled to be together if they were free to do so. He and Linda weren't free because Linda was the wife of a man he employed. If Mawson had really thought it up, that is to say had laid a trap for him through his wife, he had a little more right to be with Linda since he was acting as Mawson had hoped he would. However, the little more right wasn't sufficient any longer as he and Linda wanted to be together more and more, each day bringing them closer, and above it all was the peace she gave him, peace only a woman who lives with you permanently can give. The logical end (he mustn't shirk the issue) would be her coming to live with him. He poured out a second whisky because that was impossible. He couldn't imagine anything more distasteful than being allowed to live with a woman with her husband's consent. Revolting was the word.

There was an alternative, namely her divorcing Mawson, he selling Maidwood, and then marrying her in a registry office. The way she spoke the night before gave him every reason to believe that she had that in mind, though not quite since she wouldn't want Mawson to lose his job which he would if Maidwood were sold. She was loyal to the past, no Tony she, and her loyalty deserved admiration. Not his because married to her or not his relationship with Mawson would remain just as perturbing for his finicky soul, as Vivienne called it.

His one answer was to break with Linda, but he couldn't do that, and even if he mustered the strength to break with her he would be miserable and would soon be crawling back to her. Thus there was no answer. All he could do was to lighten the burden without getting rid of it. He looked up and smiled at the window because he was certain that he had found the solution. They would limit their meetings, let them take place mostly in London, and so that she should have no wrong ideas he would explain why as a Catholic he couldn't contemplate the idea of marrying her. She had venerated his aunt, had sat at her feet imbibing her faith, hence she would understand his scruples. He could have congratulated himself for having found the solution and keeping the goat and the cabbage (as the French have it). He heard Nick yapping outside the front door.

She came into the flat like a lot of sunshine, put the large parcel she carried on the table, and waited to be kissed. He kissed her lightheartedly because of the solution, the best in the difficult circumstances.

'I brought you a duck,' she said, 'a duck from the estate. Jackson of Pond Farm has lots of them.' Jackson had been the farmer in the office. 'I'll roast it for you, so we don't have to go out.' The wife speaking, he said to himself. 'Do you know what I did after lunch? I went to the house and made a huge fire in the drawing room and the library. I got the chimneys cleaned in the morning.' The wife again. 'Mrs Hackett assisted, and when the fires were blazing I said, "You see how easy it is. You'll light them again for Mr Hinley when he comes down." So tomorrow night we'll be cozy among the stars.'

She went to undo the parcel, and took the duck to the kitchen. She's moving around, he thought, as only a wife does. Then she went out on the landing and came back with a small suitcase. 'My things for the night,' she explained, and took the suitcase to the bedroom.

She roasted the duck, laid the table in the dining room, chose a plate in the kitchen for Nick. 'I brought some meat for him.' They dined, Nick lay beside her chair, growling whenever a car went by, and she laughed, saying, 'He feels as much at home as I.' This was his opportunity.

'I've got somewhere a bottle of very good armagnac,' he said, rising from the table. 'I'm going to find it.' He knew perfectly where the bottle was.

'Don't be long,' she called as he went into the kitchen.

The bottle was in the small pantry next to the

kitchen. Let it wait till he had mustered his arguments. He would start with the present and the future, go on to their love and their desire to be continuously together, then bemoan their state of bondage, hers to her husband and his to conventions and his dislike of sharing her openly with him. Before she could bring up her usual arguments he would move on to his aunt and hold forth on the workings of his Catholic conscience which she surely understood owing to her admiration and reverence for the old woman who hadn't really lived. No, that was unfair. Anyhow, the old woman hadn't had awful problems like he. Now they would be solved, even if only compromise. He fetched the bottle from the pantry, screwed on a smile that he thought was soulful, and entered the dining room. Neither she nor Nick were there. Surely they couldn't have evaporated. He opened the sitting room door: Linda lay naked on the sofa, Nick had crawled under Miss While's chair. The chandelier shone down on her firm body, and her legs opened at the sight of him. It was like an erotic vision one conjured up in secret.

'I couldn't wait any longer,' she said in a matter of fact voice.

Again he experienced passion coupled with peace, an eternity that made them one, and the sense of eternity remained with him afterwards. She kills the animal in me, he thought as he rose regretfully from the sofa.

'I brought a dressing gown with me,' she said, going to the bathroom.

He followed her to fetch his own, a far more expensive affair then hers, and he wished he could buy her a smarter dressing gown, and smarter dresses, and she had no jewels, whereas in his bank were plenty inherited from his mother. But if he started giving presents the solution would dissolve like aspirin in water. She smiled at him, and touched his cheek as if to make sure he was there. The telephone bell rang in the sitting room.

'Your Vivienne,' she laughed.

'You've become a real home lover,' said Vivienne. 'I never thought you'd be in. I've been sent two tickets for a concert tomorrow night. I can't go, so would you like them? You could tell your Linda to come up. There's nothing like music when one loves. If I'd three the husband could come too, he he.'

'Very bad taste. Besides, I'm not free tomorrow night.'

'You can't say I don't think of you. I'm going away for the weekend. Ring me next week. I want to know how it all goes.'

'What did she want?' asked Linda who had come into the room.

'She wanted to pass me on some concert tickets for tomorrow night.'

'But you're coming down tomorrow night. Think of the fires waiting for you.'

'I told her I wasn't free tomorrow night. You heard me.'

'I wasn't listening because I was thinking of you. I can do that even in your presence.'

It wasn't the moment to dissertate on the unsatisfactory future.

They sat down in the sitting room, and slowly polished off the bottle of armagnac, she chatting about Maidwood and all that could be done to improve its appearance, especially the garden.

'I love gardening, and it'll be another valid excuse to spend my time with you when you come down.'

He didn't grab the opportunity. Besides, her dressing gown had opened, and warmed by the armagnac, her voice and the sight of her breasts he soon took her to bed, saying to himself everything in its own time. And it would make no difference if he spoke to her in the morning. At the moment only her presence mattered.

That's surely how married people get into bed, he thought, no hurry, no impatience, for the whole night and their whole lives belong to them. He regretted having to switch off the light because darkness obliterated her smile and shining grey eyes. The warmth of her body brought back the smile and the shining eyes.

His dreams were serene as though they were hers too. A loud row in the street woke them towards dawn, then the shouting voices sent them back to sleep.

It was a cloudy, rainy morning with little light to offer. He switched on the bedside lamp to look at his watch: seven o'clock, he needn't rise yet. Her eyelashes fluttered then she opened her eyes, and smiled at him. Her hair wasn't tousled, and as she used little make-up the face was the same he loved in day time, in short you didn't have to fear the morning with her. If they could have their way he would look at that face all his mornings. He edged away from her.

'You're not getting up,' she said. 'I don't want you to get up yet. I'm not going back before the evening.'

She pulled him back, her deft fingers caressed him with the result she expected. The heat of her body, her gift of giving herself wholeheartedly and the dull light gave him the sensation of rising to heights he hadn't imagined before. The stars, real stars this time, were nearer to him than the painted stars at Maidwood.

'I never thought it could be so good,' he said nearly with a groan.

'It'll be even better when we don't have to separate any more.'

Her words hurled him back to earth.

'You're not getting up,' she cried.

'I must, my darling. I've an appointment at ten.'

'I'll wait for you, I'll only take Nick down for his morning duties.'

In the bathroom he stared at his reflection while he lathered his face. The eyes reflected his agony, for it was akin to agony to admit to himself that nothing he wanted more or pleased him more than being with Linda, and she had been right when she said that it would be even better when they didn't have to separate any more. However, not to separate was out of the question. He wouldn't go over it again, he would speak to her at breakfast.

She cooked the breakfast which they took in the dining room, he dressed, she wearing her dressing gown which looked even cheaper in the grey morning.

'Do you still think of my aunt?' he asked, considering that a good departure.

'Every day. As I've told you we never discussed me, but now I wish she were here to be able to tell her how much I love you.'

'You're a darling. Remember how religious she was?'

'As if I could forget it. Faith was the very essence of her.'

'You know of course that marriage is a sacrament for us Catholics.' She nodded, her eyes asking what he was driving at. 'It's for life, that is to say the Church doesn't accept divorce, if a Catholic marries he's married for good.'

'Otherwise it wouldn't be a sacrament,' she said.

'Precisely.'

'More tea?'

'Yes, please.' She stood up to pour out tea, and patted his arm before she sat down. 'Thank you. So you know a Catholic's position where marriage is concerned.' She nodded. 'Good. You know I'm in love with you.'

'And I'm with you,' she said, leaning forward, no more questions in her eyes.

'There's nothing I want more than being always with you. Even breakfast is sheer bliss with you. But there's a terrible snag. My Catholic conscience wouldn't let me marry a woman who's been married before except if she's a widow which you aren't.'

'My darling, I've never been married in my life, so what you're saying doesn't apply to me.'

'What are you saying?' he said, half rising. 'You're married to Jack.'

'I'm not married to Jack, I'm married to nobody.'

'What are you saying?' he repeated.

'Sit down, you haven't finished your tea.'

'But you're Mrs Mawson,' he said, clinging to the last straw.

'We couldn't arrive in Maidwood introducing ourselves as Mr Mawson and Miss Hattrell,' she smiled. 'I don't think your aunt would have appreciated that.'

'Why didn't you marry him?' he asked in a choking voice. She must say she was married. God, make her say she's married.

'His wife refused to divorce him, and I didn't insist. I got my man, and that was all I wanted at the time.'

'Why didn't she want to divorce him?' As if that mattered.

'Because she's like that. Isn't it lucky for us.'

'Why didn't you tell me before?'

'Because I wanted to make sure.'

'Make sure of what?'

'That you love me as much as I love you, and frankly, when I'm with you I forget everything except our love.'

'I'm dumbfounded,' he said, getting up and going to the window.

The high ranking executive came down the stairs, whistling. Nick rushed to the door, barking harshly.

'Stop it,' said Linda.

'I must speak to him,' said Osbert, turning round. 'It's about the front door-bell. Excuse me.'

He rushed to the landing, the executive was out of sight already. Osbert didn't feel like calling him back, the door-bell could wait as it had waited for donkey's years. He remained on the landing to gather his thoughts painful though they were.

So she wasn't married, so he could put his Catholic scruples at rest, that is if he wanted to marry her. She said she was married to nobody, but he wanted to marry nobody. He had started on the wrong foot, for he should first have explained that he wasn't attracted by marriage, proof of it that he remained a bachelor, and only then spoken about the sacrament of marriage. He shook his head because that would have been ridiculous. I don't know whether I'm coming or going, he said to himself. I must gain time, time my only salvation. He returned to the flat through the dark passage. The dining room door was closed. He tiptoed to the telephone, and dialled Andrew Somers' number in Kent. Patricia answered.

'Osbert speaking. I can come down for the weekend.'

'I'm glad, Andrew will be glad too.'

'Can I come down this afternoon?'

'Of course, my dear. Which train are you catching to Tunbridge Wells? We'll fetch you at the station.'

'I'll ring you from the station.'

Now for Linda.

'You said you only think of our love when we're together,' he said, opening the dining room door. 'It's the same with me. I completely forgot that I've a weekend engagement, an invitation to old friends I've postponed many times. I can't get out of it this time.'

'Postpone it again.'

'I just rang them, impossible. My darling, don't wait for me because I'm going straight down to them after my business appointment.'

'I think that suits me,' she said with a little smile. 'When are you coming back?'

'Sunday evening.' That gave him over forty-eight hours.

'Good. I'll tell Mrs Hackett not to expect you. I'm going to dress.'

'There's no hurry,' he said pleased with her docility. 'Leave the flat whenever you want. No charwoman, no secretary today. Take your time, my love.'

'I'll have a bath before I go.'

'May I run it for you?' Anything, even cleaning her shoes as long as the subject wasn't brought up again.

'I'll run it myself,' she laughed.

He remained in the sitting room while she had her bath, repeating to himself so she wasn't married, she wasn't Mrs Jack Mawson but only Miss Linda Hattrell. Suddenly he became furious with Vivienne who suggested he speak to her about his Catholic conscience. If he hadn't spoken about it she wouldn't have told him that she wasn't married, and he could continue in blissful ignorance. Anyway, her not being married made no difference since Mawson remained her man whether they were married or not. They lived together and were considered in Maidwood as husband and wife. So really nothing had changed. He couldn't steal his estate manager's woman married or unmarried. They were married in other people's eyes; they should remain married in his eyes too.

How quickly his aunt would have kicked them out if she had known the truth. He felt grim satisfaction till he laughed at himself. He went to knock on the bedroom door.

'Come in,' she called. 'I'm making the bed.'

'That's sweet of you. I'm afraid I must go or I'll be late for my appointment.'

She was in her underwear, and he tried not to look at

her, for one thing leads to another. He deserved a
respite from her attraction.

'Go, darling.'

'I'm off. I'll be back on Sunday, but probably very
late.'

'Can you give me a spare key to the front door?'

'Certainly,' he said, fetching it. Had she said the
moon he would have brought it too.

'Kiss me,' she said, taking the key.

He pecked her on the cheek before saying, 'It was
very interesting.'

'What was very interesting?'

'That you and Jack aren't married.'

'Perhaps I ought to have told you before. Still, it's
better late than never, and it isn't late.'

'Yes, darling. I'm off.'

It isn't late, he muttered to himself as he ran down
the stairs. He shouldn't have given her the spare key,
but if he had refused she would have asked why and the
fat would have been in the fire.

Afterwards he didn't remember what he had said in
the office of the insurance company, where he had spent
two hours. The people he saw had been impressed by
him, so it must have been satisfactory. As he came out
of the building it struck him that if he hadn't brought
up the marriage business he could be on his way to the
flat to spend the rest of the day with her. He cursed
himself from every angle.

He didn't feel like lunching, had just a sandwich in
a pub, then made for Charing Cross. He chose an
empty compartment which immediately filled with men
who he was sure came from behind the Iron Curtain to
judge by their hats.

'I told Baker,' said one of them, 'that we won't pay
that exorbitant price again.'

'Well done. All this nonsense about no pheasants
before November.'

'Leaves are the best excuse I know,' said the third.

They were members of a shooting syndicate on their way to their Saturday shooting.

Mawson had told him that the shooting on the estate was let to a syndicate. Damn these men with dark hats for bringing back Mawson. Osbert opened an evening paper, and the first thing he saw was that an irate, jealous husband had shot dead his wife's lover. He shrugged his shoulders as husbands and wives were no concern of his.

At Tunbridge Wells station while he waited for Patricia to fetch him he touched his pockets to see if he had enough cigarettes on him. Though generous in every sense Patricia bought no cigarettes, so as to smoke less, she said, and immediately asked you for a cigarette and a light too as matches encouraged smoking. She arrived in her Daimler, a tall, greying woman, all legs and a long neck.

'At last,' she said as he got into the car. 'Have you a cigarette on you by any chance?'

She was the daughter of a shipowner, Andrew had been an MP till he got suddenly sick of politics, and didn't stand again to the disappointment of his rich father-in-law. He was now writing a history of the Black Death which he said would take him ten years. 'How can you waste your time like that?' sighed Patricia's father whose country house was four miles from theirs, naturally much larger.

'Why don't we see you?' asked Patricia, letting out a lot of smoke.

'I think I've told you that I inherited a house and estate in Oxfordshire.'

'But you're still in London.'

'I go down now and then.'

'You ought to live down there. London isn't any more the London of our youth. Of course you're about ten years younger than I, so perhaps you don't feel that as much as Andrew and I.'

'London's my bastion,' he said. 'In the country I feel defenceless.'

'With us it's the other way round. How good this cigarette is. Do you see Vivienne?'

'Quite often.'

'I'm not the interfering sort as you know, but I do think she'd make the perfect wife for you.'

'I'm not the marrying sort,' said Osbert.

'A pity.'

The Somers' house was late Georgian and kept in excellent repair. The garden looked spick and span, and the wood behind, he was sure, was trimmed once a week and the leaves were handpicked in the autumn. No armless warrior of the Crimea would be welcome here. The floors were polished, cleanliness reigned, and he thought of the dust at Maidwood as he followed Patricia into the morning room. The chintzes looked brand new.

'You must have a large staff,' he said.

'One maid, she's Portuguese, and a char four times a week. I do a lot of the work myself. Besides, it isn't a large house.'

'You could put a Concorde into mine.'

He described the reception rooms at Maidwood, and while he spoke of them he saw Linda walking through the rooms, Nick trotting in front of her.

'A change after your London flat,' said Patricia.

He saw the sitting room in his flat with Linda lying naked on the sofa. Would there ever be any respite for him? Had she killed distance?

Andrew came in, a bouncing little man with thick hair whose favourite story was that when he and Patricia walked side by side in a street people behind them thought mother was taking her son for a stroll. Patricia's invariable reply was that people who came towards them asked themselves how could such a short man have such a tall daughter.

'How's the Black Death?' asked Osbert.

'Doing its stuff,' laughed Andrew. 'Some witty Frenchman, Philippe Berthelot I think, said after the First World War that if a man dies he mourns him, if a million and a half die it's just statistics. I think of that as I struggle with the Black Death.'

These two are real, thought Osbert, because they don't live in a nightmare. A little voice within him said, You created the nightmare.

'I'll show you your room,' said Patricia.

The window looked out on the wood, the mahogany furniture shone, and the carpet wasn't threadbare as in his bedroom in Maidwood. He sat down on the bed, wondering whether Linda had left the flat. With the spare latchkey she could come and go as she liked. He shouldn't have told her that he was returning Sunday night, he ought to have said Monday morning, but what difference would it make? She wasn't married, he wasn't either, they loved each other, so nothing should keep them apart. By the way, Jack, Linda and I are getting married. That should make no difference to you. You'll hardly notice whether she spends her nights in the house instead of the cottage. All you have to do is to tell everybody that you weren't married, and everybody will understand, considering it meet and proper for you to run the estate while the woman who wasn't your wife becomes mine. You'll lunch with us every Sunday for the whole world to see how normal our relations are.

He let out a forced laugh which he was sure no hyaena would envy, and hurried downstairs. Andrew was alone in the morning room.

'My father-in-law is coming to dinner,' said Andrew. 'You know him.' Osbert nodded. 'He's a study in wealth, catapulted from the reign of Edward VII. He still believes you can't run the country without money. There's only one thing he and I have in common: dislike which we both try to overcome.'

The father-in-law arrived shortly after seven, as tall as his daughter, as thin too. For his pleasure and profit he bred Ayrshire cattle. A cow had died that day, and he spoke of her like one who has lost a dear friend. He's thinking of her price, said Osbert to himself.

'I've a house in Bermuda,' said the father-in-law, addressing Osbert. 'I'm getting tired of it. I wasn't brought up to ignore the seasons. In my native Montgomeryshire we had seasons.'

'There are seasons in Kent too,' said Patricia.

'One of the reasons I live here,' said her father.

'Seasons were more like seasons in the Middle Ages,' said Andrew, smiling at Osbert. 'Rivers inundated, so there was more ice, forests were immense, so there were more Christmas trees. Wolves came out in the winter season to eat babies. What I mean is that people were more conscious of the seasons than today. Except you.' He bowed to his father-in-law.

'Central heating kills the winter season,' said the father-in-law.

'Being regularly fed kills it too,' said Andrew. 'That's one more reason why they were as conscious of the seasons as you are.'

'I'm not underfed,' protested the father-in-law. 'Eighteen hundred calories a day. How many calories do you take, Hinley?'

'I don't count them.'

'You're making a mistake.'

I'm making one mistake after the other, Osbert felt like saying. His first mistake had been to look at Linda on his first day at Maidwood, the second to let her warmth invade him. It was useless to count all the others that followed. Here he sat, listening to a lot of nonsense while he was bursting with longing for the cause of his mistakes.

After the father-in-law had departed they went into Andrew's study.

'I was saying to Osbert,' said Patricia, 'he should marry Vivienne. They suit each other in every sense. They've known each other long enough to do nothing impetuous. If you continue as a bachelor some disastrous love at first sight will happen to you.'

'He's old enough to look after himself,' said Andrew who wanted to talk about the Black Death.

What would they say, wondered Osbert, if I told them that I was living in the disastrous depth of love at first sight?

'May I telephone?' he asked.

'It's in the morning room,' said Patricia.

He dialled the flat's number, the telephone bell rang, he let it ring for a few minutes, then disappointed he put down the receiver.

'I'm going to bed if you don't mind,' he said. 'I'd a hectic night.'

'Poor bachelor,' said Patricia.

Hectic night, thought Osbert as he got into bed. It had been the most peaceful night of his life. Tonight wouldn't be. He heard the first cock crowing, and he said to himself the cock had a bad cold. On that he fell asleep, dreaming of Maidwood, the house empty, even the gold stars gone. When he opened his eyes he saw a small creature straight out of a Velasquez painting.

'Good morning, mister,' said the Portuguese maid in a sing song voice. 'Tea morning.' She kept her eyes to the ground.

'Thank you,' he said.

'Zank you,' she said, and ran from the room.

Andrew took him into Tunbridge Wells after breakfast.

'A little pub crawling does no harm,' he said.

However, they didn't pub crawl as they remained in the first pub they entered.

'There's a lot of truth in what Patricia said last night,' said Andrew when they had sat down at a table. Near them sat a young man with his girl, she holding his hand, he reading a magazine. 'You and Vivienne would make a reasonable pair. Ours was a reasonable marriage, and look how well it has worked out.'

'What do you mean by reasonable?' asked Osbert.

'The contrary of unreasonable,' laughed Andrew. 'Vivienne and I could never get on any more because our getting on period is over.'

He thought of the night with Vivienne in Maidwood. Was it that night that he became aware of being in love with Linda? 'Sorry,' he said. 'What were you saying?'

'Simply that you live as you want to and as circumstances compel you. The two are seldom separated. Often we think we want something whereas the circumstances compel us.'

'How true that is. When will your book be ready?'

That gave Andrew his chance, Osbert's also, for while Andrew spoke he could meditate on what he wanted and the circumstances.

'Have you by any chance a cigarette on you, Osbert?' asked Patricia when they returned to the house.

In the afternoon Patricia took him for a long drive. Afterwards some acquaintances came in for drinks, one of them, a stout woman, stayed for dinner, moaning about her daughter who had gone off to Canada with a man she, the mother, abhorred.

'Don't worry, she'll come back,' said Patricia soothingly.

'I don't want her back,' said the woman.

'One of the charms of country life,' said Andrew when she had left, 'is putting up with bores.'

This, said Osbert to himself on his way to bed, is

the end of Saturday, which means tomorrow I'm going back.

At lunch he told them that he would be leaving at three o'clock.

'Can't you stay till tomorrow morning?' asked Patricia.

'Alas, it's impossible,' he said.

Patricia drove him to the station in pelting rain.

'The leaves aren't falling but rotting this year,' she said.

'That's because of the rotten summer we had.'

'It wasn't rotten,' she said. 'Andrew says I shouldn't have mentioned Vivienne. He says it's irrevocably over between you two.'

'Irrevocable is the right word,' he said.

I'm irrevocably in love with Linda, he sighed as he got out of the car, leaving his packet of cigarettes on the seat. Patricia didn't call him back though the packet looked conspicuous on the green leather.

He had a compartment all to himself. Within an hour or so he would see her. He remembered that she wasn't in the flat when he had telephoned on Friday night. As the train approached London he decided to forget that she wasn't married to Mawson. He wasn't compelled to bring up the subject again since all he had said was that he couldn't marry a divorced woman, which by no means meant that he wanted to marry even if the woman wasn't divorced. If he didn't speak about it the subject would cease to exist.

The first thing he did at Charing Cross station was to buy cigarettes. The taxi queue was long and the taxis few. He would walk home with his light suitcase. The rain had ceased, and the east wind was driving the clouds away. The streets were almost deserted, and the smell of hamburgers floated in the air. A real Sunday afternoon, and he hurried to barricade himself in his flat. Perhaps she had come back since with the spare key she could come and go as she wished.

He turned into his street which was empty, not a soul, not a car. He looked up at his windows before inserting the key in the lock: the curtains weren't drawn, but that said nothing as night hadn't fallen yet. He mounted the steps slowly, taking his time. He chose to enter the flat through the kitchen though he didn't know why. Nobody in kitchen or dining room, and the sitting room was empty too. He was angry with himself because of his deep disappointment. In the bedroom he noticed that the bed wasn't made exactly as his charwoman made it, but that hadn't any significance either. He saw that the built in wardrobe's door was ajar, he pulled it open, and there hung a jacket and skirt Linda often wore, a dress beside them. His next move was to go into the bathroom: creams, powder, nail polish and a toothbrush he hadn't seen before were side by side on a shelf. This is too much, he said half aloud in a voice he found unconvincing.

ELEVEN

On Saturday afternoons Mawson pulled on his gumboots, and sunshine, rain or snow he stalked the estate
like a ghost (the farmers said). It was five o'clock on that
Saturday afternoon when Linda heard the front doorbell ring. She got up from her armchair beside the
fireplace, told Nick to stop it, and went to open the door.

'I hope I'm not intruding,' said Tony.

'You look very country like in that corduroy jacket,'
she smiled.

'One must play the part,' said Tony. 'Is Jack around?'

'He's gone for a walk. Come in.'

'What a nice fire,' he said, and plunged forward to kiss
her, for he didn't believe in nonsense. They either re-
sponded or didn't, and Linda would surely respond as
any one could see that not much love was lost between
her and her husband.

'You silly little fool,' she said pushing him away, 'are
you off your head? Stop it, Nick. The house isn't on fire.
Don't try that again, Tony, because I'll get very angry.'

So she didn't respond which he found a pity. 'Forgive
me,' he said. 'It's stronger than I.' He couldn't remember how many times he had said that in his life. 'I
promise I won't try again, a promise that'll cost me a lot
of effort. Don't chase me out of your presence.'

'I don't chase, but don't try again. You couldn't have
chosen a worse time for it.'

'Do you care for someone else?'

'Very much.'

'I'm not one of the lucky ones,' he sighed, and she almost felt sorry for him, so asked him to stay for a drink. 'What do you make of the friend of my youth, Linda?'

'Who's that?'

'Osbert Hinley of Maidwood,' laughed Tony.

Before she could answer Mawson's long shadow came past the window, then the door was pushed open.

'So you've got a guest,' said Mawson. 'Monday morning go to Rock Farm Tony, and tell Yailor that if he lets his cattle stray on the common he'll get into trouble. Don't say it comes from me, say you saw them yourself, and you're warning him in a friendly way before it gets to my ears. I saw a pony in the meadow. He must have bought it for his children, and then he'll come and weep on my shoulder, complaining he's unable to make both ends meet.'

What an intolerant man he is, thought Linda, and in my foolish days I used to think that intolerance was a sign of strength. She looked at him, then at Tony who listened obsequiously, and let out a sigh that neither of them heard.

'Tomorrow I'm going to London,' she said when Tony had left. 'I don't know for how long. If anybody asks say my aunt isn't well, and I'm looking after her.'

'Can't you think up something better?'

'I leave that to you,' she said, and couldn't help laughing.

'Why do you laugh?'

'I remembered you thought up Osbert. Sorry, Jack.'

'There's nothing to be sorry about. Are you taking the dog?'

'Of course.'

'Need the Ford?'

'I won't need it. I think I'll have another drink.'

He took her glass, and half filled it with gin.

'Too much,' she said.

'You can take it.' She laughed again. 'You're in a hilarious mood.'

'I've every reason to be.'

She wondered whether she should tell him that Osbert knew that they weren't married. She decided against because he would soon find out. She beamed at him. 'I'll leave after breakfast.'

'I'm breakfasting with Simpson,' said Mawson.

She packed a large suitcase before she went to bed. 'Nick, it's our last night here,' she said, and Nick wagged his tail.

In the morning she carried the suitcase downstairs, made herself tea, then telephoned to Banbury for a taxi. As it passed the Catholic church she said to herself that soon she and Osbert would be there on all their Sundays which would please Miss Hinley.

A bald headed man talked to her the whole way to London, boasting about his cars, his hunters and his travels. She found it easy not to listen to him. At Paddington she took a taxi to Bloomsbury. Would he be back? The flat looked exactly as she had left it Friday afternoon, the three cigarette stubs she had overlooked were still in the ashtray. She emptied it into the dustbin. She spent half the afternoon admiring the china, saying to herself that the collection should be taken down to Maidwood, for poor Maidwood did need a bit of beauty. At four o'clock she took Nick for a walk, and a man followed her as far as Russell Square.

'Would you like a cup of tea?' he asked.

She gave him a look, and the man fell back. She was sure that Osbert had never accosted a woman in his life. She saw light in the sitting room window, and hurried up the stairs. He was sitting on the sofa they had made love on, an unopened book beside him. He got up slowly as though loth to acknowledge her presence. He would pretend that he hadn't seen her belongings in the wardrobe and in the bathroom.

'What a surprise,' he said. 'I just got back.'

'I took Nick for a walk.'

'When did you arrive?'

'At twelve, my darling,' she said, took off the leash, and threw her arms round him. 'Isn't it wonderful to be together again? You've no idea how I missed you.'

'I missed you too.'

'You won't have to miss me ever again.'

'How sweet of you to say that,' he said, trying to fight against the warmth of her presence, 'but tomorrow will be a very busy day for me. Still, we've the whole night before us.'

She put her bag on Miss While's table before saying, 'What I mean is that we'll never part again.'

'Alas, that's impossible.'

'I'm remaining here,' she said.

'My love, that's impossible.'

'Nothing's impossible for us. I'm here for keeps.'

The awful thing was that he could hardly fight down the joy her words gave him. Yet it was his duty to, otherwise his universe would collapse. 'Understand, Linda, that we can't do it. Everything's against it. Many men live with women, and they're not tarred and feathered for it, but mine's a different case. I love you as I never thought I was capable of loving, but we can't live together because, I repeat, everything's against it.' She was smiling, and the grey eyes shone. Had she gone deaf all of a sudden? 'I'm thirty-eight, and the fact that I never lived with a woman is proof of my not being made for it ... Why are you laughing?'

'Because it's very funny,' she said sitting down on a Queen Anne chair, then kicking off her shoes. 'I don't want to live with you, I want to marry you. You don't know what living with a woman is like, I don't know what being married is like, so we're in the same boat.'

'We're in the same boat in as much as we've no solution.'

'As long as we remain in the same boat,' she laughed. 'I'm going to make tea.'

She put on her shoes, and went to the kitchen followed by Nick. Osbert lit a cigarette, thinking of Patricia whom he almost saw seated in the morning room, chain smoking. He wished he could go on thinking of her undisturbed. However, new thoughts like dark clouds approached, blotting out Patricia and the packet of cigarettes he had left in her car. Suddenly he smiled, and felt almost pleased with himself.

'What did you say to Jack?' he asked when she came back, for it all depended on her answer.

'I told him that I'd be away for some time. He knew what I meant, so he asked no questions. Anyhow, he knows the answers.'

'Is that all you said?'

'There was no need to say more,' she said, pouring out the tea. 'It's lovely being here. I'm not the complaining sort, but it wasn't funny to live with a man with whom you've nothing left in common. It was grim till you came.'

'Still, you were willing to fall in with his plan when the heir appeared.'

'When the heir was going to appear, not after he appeared. I was willing because I owed it to the past, and I'd never do anything to harm him. We harmed each other enough.' She pushed her hair back with both hands. 'Don't think of him, think of me who's yours for good. You haven't kissed me yet.'

My undoing, he said to himself as he kissed her.

'Come to the bedroom,' she said. 'We don't have to do it on the sofa any more.'

They went to the bedroom, and he watched her undressing, so different from the first time, no hurry, no snatched seconds, no fear of time belonging to others. She stepped slowly out of her dress, sat down just as slowly to pull down her tights which she then carried to a chair, took off her bra, put it on the same chair, and lay down on the bed, saying, 'Darling, you haven't undressed yet.'

'I was looking at you.'

When he got on the bed he didn't penetrate her at once, her lack of hurry having communicated itself to him. To expect something without fearing that it wouldn't happen was a new pleasure for him. 'Don't tease me,' she said.

They remained on the bed after they had made love, she stared at the ceiling, he remembering his plan of action. It was she who rose first.

'I brought a leg of lamb,' she said, stretching her arms which made her breasts look almost aggressive. 'That's real life together,' she laughed. 'Making love then roasting a leg of lamb. I'm going to the kitchen, don't move, darling. You stay here, Nick, the kitchen might give you ideas.'

She put on her dress, and went barefooted to the kitchen. Osbert remained on the bed, and found it an effort to light a cigarette. With Vivienne it had always and inevitably been snatched moments. She used to come to the flat about twice a week while Justin was alive. She arrived, had a drink as a preliminary, then he practically jumped on her (that being what she expected from him), and she warned him not to tousle her hair. Generally she came from the hairdresser. Then they came to this same bed, stripped, made love because forgetting to make love would make her visit unnecessary, and immediately she dressed as she wanted to be back when Justin returned from the City. After his death they made love in her flat as if to remind themselves that no Justin was left. There the procedure was slightly different in that they drank and chatted a little longer beforehand, and no reason was left to jump on her. Their love making was an interval between drinks. How different it was with Linda, a revelation in every sense.

The telephone bell rang in the sitting room, and he jumped out of bed afraid that she might answer it.

'Is that you, Fred?' asked a deep voice.

'Whom do you want to speak to?'

'To you, Fred.'

'Sorry, wrong number.'

He saw his reflection in the glass above the fireplace, a ludicrous sight. If one starts jettisoning, he said to the naked man in the glass, one loses everything in the end. He hurried back to the bedroom.

The light touch, he thought while dressing, was the only answer. Evade all important issues, agree with a smile, and let it slowly sink in that her remaining in the flat was impossible for both of them.

She had brought gin and whisky into the sitting room.

'Where's Nick?' she asked.

'Sleeping on the bed.'

'He's more at ease with you than with Jack.'

'Dear dog,' he said with a broad smile.

'Do you know why I didn't object to your going away for the weekend?' she asked.

'Blast,' he said as the telephone rang again.

'Fred,' said the deep voice, 'I don't care for cruel jokes. Why did you say it wasn't you?'

'I repeat there's nobody called Fred here,' said Osbert, putting down the receiver.

'I wanted you to have time to think about us,' said Linda.

'I couldn't get out of the invitation. I told you, I think, that I had put them off too often.' He had every reason to be pleased with his light touch.

'It must have been something of a shock to discover that the woman you love is unmarried and free.'

'Blast,' he exclaimed. 'You answer it, Linda.'

She lifted the receiver.

'Yes,' she smiled. 'Oh, you want to speak to Osbert.

Here he is.' She turned to Osbert. 'It's Mrs Long.'

Oh, my God, he said to himself, the fat's in the fire. 'Hullo.'

'Was that your Linda?' said Vivienne in her best mocking voice. 'Hope I'm not disturbing the idyll.'

'There's nothing to disturb.'

'Can you come to lunch tomorrow? I've got such exciting news for you.'

A real chance, he thought as he said, 'I'd love to. One o'clock.' And for Linda to hear. 'I've a business appointment that'll take up the whole morning. In the afternoon my secretary's coming, it'll be a very heavy day, but I'll be there at one.'

'Very exciting news,' repeated Vivienne.

'So you're lunching with her,' said Linda when he had sat down.

'I couldn't get out of it. She has a guest with whom I've all sorts of dealings. I'm legal adviser to quite a few people.' Very good, he said to himself.

'One day you'll explain to me what you do. All I know is that you're a barrister who doesn't practice at the Bar.'

'But does a lot of other things.'

'If you do the other things as passively as you behave in Maidwood, my darling ... I don't have to finish the sentence.'

'I don't want to think of Maidwood tonight,' he said.

He succeeded in keeping the conversation off Maidwood, Mawson, and the future, which wasn't difficult while she got the meal ready, and afterwards they went straight to bed. 'The pleasantest evening I ever had,' he said.

'There are thousands before us,' she said.

He woke up in the middle of the night as though he had heard somebody calling him. The silence was undisturbed by her quiet breathing. Her arm was flung round his chest, and he was moved by the faith she had in him. Or was it in herself? It had been easy so far because she probably wasn't thinking of the future, the decision to come to him being enough of an effort for the moment. Tomorrow everything would be under control in that his morning and afternoon would, as it were, be free of any discussion. None the less, sooner or later the future would have to be faced. Why not let it ride while he made it obvious to her that neither in London nor at Maidwood they could live together, for wherever they were Mawson and her having lived with him as his wife would remain with them. He touched her cheek, and she woke up.

'Linda,' he said, 'would you care to go with me to Morocco?'

'Morocco?'

'I've been longing to go there for a long time. We could go for a week or so. We both need a respite.'

'I don't,' she said. 'We've got so much to work out here and in Maidwood.'

'Sleep, my darling,' he said, cursing himself.

His next approach was at breakfast.

'What will you do today?' he asked. 'I'll be out the whole morning, then there's the business lunch with Vivienne, and in the afternoon I have my work to do with the secretary.'

'Don't worry on my account. I'll keep myself busy in the morning, and if I'm in the way when your secretary comes I'll go to the dining room while she's here. You must get accustomed, darling, to having me near you.'

Hang the light touch, he should have it out with her right there. He rose from the table, kissed her cheek, and said, 'I'll be back before three.' That, he thought, was surely as husbands spoke when they left for their work.

On the stairs he felt no sense of liberation, in the street he didn't quicken his pace to increase the distance between them, and by the time he arrived at his appointment he admitted that he was missing her. He had an hour to kill beween the appointment and Vivienne. He spent it in a bar he used to frequent before Maidwood and all it brought with it had crashed into his life.

'Haven't seen you a long time, sir,' said the barman. 'Been busy?'

'Very busy.'

The barman smiled because he liked his customers to be busy as that meant coining plenty of money.

Vivienne opened the door with a smile she was certain the Sphynx would envy. Her hair was deep chestnut.

'Do you like leg of lamb?' she asked, leading him into the drawing room.

'Linda brought up a leg of lamb yesterday,' he said. It wasn't a challenge or bravado: he wanted to hear her name.

'She looks after you. I'm glad, my dear, because I won't be able to look after you any longer.'

'I didn't know you ever looked after me.' Would Linda have cold lamb while he ate his hot?

'You're not very grateful,' said Vivienne.

'What's the exciting news?'

'Don't faint, I'm going to marry Simon.'

He should show surprise. 'That's exciting news.'

'He pestered me for a long time, I said no, and now I'll tell you something I find rather weird. The night we spent in your awful house ...'

'The pigsty.'

'Frankly yes. Don't interrupt me. During our little error I realised that I liked Simon. I don't want to hurt your very well developed male vanity but from that night onward I looked at Simon with different eyes.'

'Strangely enough it was during that same night I realised that I was in love with Linda.'

'That's just tit for tat, my vain Osbert.' Let her have that bit of satisfaction, he said to himself. 'Once you look at a man with different eyes your attitude changes towards him. And that's precisely what happened to me.

We ought to lunch. Simon's coming at three, and for some silly reason he's jealous of you.'

He didn't find the lamb as good as the lamb Linda had brought.

'For the time being,' continued Vivienne, 'I won't be able to see much of you, but once we're married I'm sure he'll calm down.'

'Are you giving up your flat?' he asked.

'I have to. Simon's house is far more spacious, and there's no room here for his collection of paintings, one of the best in the country as you know. I'm entering my second marriage with open eyes.' Were they closed, he asked himself, when she married opulent Justin? 'Simon and I have a lot in common which is a great deal. He has immense wealth which is of great help, and I'm not infatuated with him as I used to be with you.' He bowed. 'And that's a great help too. I can start on the level I know I can easily remain on, so there won't be any ups and downs. We'll be able to concentrate on the same things like music, travel and interesting people. I can tell you that he isn't a billy goat as you used to be. That's an advantage too. He won't want to make love to me when I'm dressed for a party like somebody who sits at this table had once tried to.' She laughed reminiscently. 'He wants a soul mate, and I'm a first class soul mate. He needs the perfect hostess, and I'm a perfect hostess in every sense. He loves witty conversation which I can provide, and he's understanding. One of my first conditions was separate bedrooms: he agreed at once. I told him I can't have a husband breathing down my neck: he understood that too. Frankly, I don't see why we shouldn't be the happiest couple in the three kingdoms.'

'I don't see either,' said Osbert. 'This claret is very good.'

'I'm glad. You ought to see his cellar. Once he's got over his jealousy you'll be a regular guest, my dear.'

'Thank you, Vivienne.'

'Admit I've chosen well.'

'Marvellously,' he said, thinking of Linda.

'What was your Linda doing in your flat last night?'

'She came up to spend the night with me.'

'With the husband's blessing?'

'He isn't her husband. They lived together, but that makes no difference in that everybody down there believes they're married.'

'Makes no difference to whom?'

'To all concerned. As I've told you before the situation would be different if he weren't the estate manager.'

'Then you'd live with her openly?'

'I don't know. She isn't the woman who wants separate bedrooms, acting the hostess or specialising in witty conversation.'

'You can be funny at times,' laughed Vivienne. 'One can see at a glance that she's a simple woman. How will you solve it all? You see I'm still interested in the fate of my erstwhile billy goat, or should I say stoat?'

She sat back to let her controlled laughter ripple better.

'I've no idea.'

'Do you enjoy being with her?'

'More than I can tell.'

'Then be with her and don't think of what other people say. Anyway, they won't say it to you. Go on bashing her as long as you pay her husband's salary. Don't wince.'

'He's not her husband.'

'But he remains the estate manager.' Her laughter rippled again. Doesn't she ever get tired of it? he asked himself. 'Your one great fault is that you're a prig, my dear.'

'Don't start about my finicky soul, Vivienne.'

'A prig is a moral snob, a prig is a man who considers himself spotless. Justin was a bit of a prig. If you weren't a prig you'd take it in your stride. You've got a mistress whom you enjoy in bed, the man she lives with is in your pay, there's nothing simpler or easier.'

'That's one way of looking at it.'

'The only way of looking at it. You don't want more than that.'

He wanted to say that what he wanted was always to be with Linda though he knew that was impossible because of his scruples. She would laugh off the scruples as much as his wanting to be always with Linda. 'Perhaps you're right,' he said.

'I know I am. Have some brandy, and then I must chuck you out because of jealous Simon. You ought to be flattered.'

He wished her much happiness as she accompanied him to the door.

'I don't think I've done anything better in my life,' she said.

He didn't take the lift down, preferring the stairs for his thoughts. Vivienne was right when she said he was a prig. Being a prig was like having goitre, no fault of yours despite your having to put up with it. For the prig Vivienne had found the perfect practical solution, and if he were only a prig with nothing else to him he would blindly follow her advice. And why shouldn't he? he asked himself on reaching the front door. The porter touched his cap, and he went out into the mild afternoon. A Constable sky, and remembered that Simon had a Constable which hung next to a Manet, Simon explaining to his visitors that Constable and Turner had a deep influence on the Impressionists. Then Simon took them to his Turner. Vivienne would be happy, but what about him?

Only after he had found a taxi did it occur to him that he was on his way to Linda. She had said she would go to the dining room while Miss While was with him. He ought to point out to her that his bachelor's flat was too small for two. If it weren't it wouldn't be a bachelor's flat. Very profound, he said to himself, slightly despising himself.

Nick received him with loud barks, then jumped up, his eyes full of adoration. 'Dear Nick,' he said, patting him. He looked round the sitting room: Miss While had risen from a chair next to the sofa on which Linda sat who rose too. Never before had he seen Miss While sitting on one of his Adam chairs. It had invariably been the stool in front of the typewriter.

'Enjoyed your lunch?' asked Linda.

'Up to a point,' he said.

'Miss While and I had a very interesting chat,' said Linda. 'Do you want me to retire to the dining room, darling, or can I stay here and read while you work? I'm sure I won't be in the way, isn't that so, Miss While?'

'Not in the way at all,' said Miss While, smiling.

This is too much, said Osbert to himself. What could she have said during their very interesting chat to make Miss While smile? He hadn't imagined that she could smile. 'Let's get down to work.'

Miss While sat down on her stool as pleased as Punch, for her hairy beast had reappeared last night. She didn't dare to ask questions, and not being the talkative sort he didn't speak about his absence. This evening, so he curtly said, he would come to her again. That wasn't all. This terribly nice person, who undoubtedly was her employer's girl friend, had given her the rare chance of speaking about herself.

In the looking glass Osbert could see Linda on the sofa, she seemed engrossed in the book she was reading, now and then patting Nick who lay quietly at her feet.

'This is the American report you are asked to check on,' said Miss While.

'Oh yes,' he said, certain that Linda was listening to every word he uttered. 'I'm going to read it when I'm alone and can concentrate on it.' He hoped that Linda heard the reproach in his voice. She didn't lift her head.

'This letter has arrived today,' said Miss While. 'It's from the solicitors about the death duties.'

'Bone,' he said, looking into the glass from the corner of his eye. 'The list of the houses to sell. What we'll do is to send this list to Mr Mawson, the estate manager.' Linda didn't lift her eyes from the book. 'You send it with the short note I'm going to dictate now. Ready?'

'Yes, Mr Hinley.'

'Dear Jack,' he nearly shouted. 'Here's the list of the houses Bone suggests to sell.' Why did she pretend she didn't hear him? 'Have a look at it, then let Bone know what you think. Yours.'

'Only yours?' asked Miss While.

'Only yours. Now what I want you to do is to make two copies of that report.'

'Before you read it?'

'Before I read it. As it's rather long I leave you to it. Linda, come to the dining room. Miss While can concentrate better if left alone.'

Linda jumped up from the sofa, Nick stretched himself before following her, then the door closed on the three of them. Miss While lit a cigarette.

'I missed you, my love,' said Linda, throwing her arms round him.

'I missed you too,' he said after he had kissed her, only a light kiss so as to keep his distance so to speak. 'Vivienne is getting married to a mutual friend.'

'So she'll be out of the way.'

'She wasn't in the way.'

'What I mean is that everybody's in the way. I want you completely to myself.'

'Sit down, darling,' he said.

'I love standing beside you. Isn't it wonderful that we're the same height? You don't have to look down, and I don't have to look up. You've no idea how happy I am. It was a real treat waiting for you. For four endless years I'd nobody to wait for. Waiting as I waited for you is one of the greatest gifts of God, especially when one knows one isn't waiting in vain.'

He couldn't help thinking of Vivienne's reasons for marrying Simon.

'You're marvellous, my darling,' he said. 'I'm very happy too. My trouble is that I make a mountain out of a mole hill.'

'Am I the mole hill?' The grey eyes filled with mirth.

'I'm thinking about my silly scruples. You and Jack live together as brother and sister, there's nothing between you any more, so we don't hurt him, and I'm sure he doesn't mind you coming up here from time to time. We've no cause whatever to worry as long as we behave reasonably.'

'I've no intention of behaving reasonably,' she said in a quiet voice.

'I forgot to tell Miss While that it's three copies not two,' he said. 'Wait for me.'

Vivienne had advised him to speak to Linda about his Catholic conscience. The result was that Linda told him that she and Mawson weren't married. Today she suggested he should enjoy his affair with Linda without taking it too seriously. That had misfired too. 'You should make three copies,' he said to Miss While, then returned to the dining room.

'We'll go out to dinner tonight,' he said.

'As you like, darling,' she said. 'Miss While told me the story of her life, rather a sad one. She was adopted when she was a baby, her adopted parents died, two years ago she had a baby which got adopted last year. The full circle. I feel very sorry for her. Probably she can't imagine a child living with its own parents.'

'Poor girl,' said Osbert, pleased with the turn the conversation had taken. Miss While the adopted child, was a nice, neutral subject.

'Why did you suggest our going to Morocco?' asked Linda.

'Because I'd like to take you there. You could always invent some likely story for Jack's benefit.'

'Jack doesn't need stories. I'd like to go to Morocco myself, but we haven't time.'

This is a trap, he thought, so he would ignore it. 'You heard me,' he asked, 'dictating a short letter to Jack?'

'I heard you,' she said. 'I repeat we haven't time to go to Morocco. We've got too much to do here.'

'Here? You mean in this flat?'

'Mostly at Maidwood.

'Let's enjoy the flat for the moment,' he smiled. 'Maidwood can wait. I prefer being with you here. More friendly than that huge house.'

'But Maidwood will be our real home.'

'Don't frighten me, my darling,' he laughed. 'I'm going to see how Miss While is getting on.'

'And I'll take Nick for a walk. He's missing the outdoor spaces of Maidwood.'

Miss While banged away on the typewriter, he sat at his table, repeating to himself that Maidwood was their real home according to Linda. What did she mean, that is to say how did she see it? It wasn't difficult to guess. They would go down hand in hand, tell Mawson they intended to get married, perhaps ask for his blessing, assure him that nothing would change in their relationship, then go to the house, informing the Hacketts that from now on Mrs Mawson should be addressed as Mrs Hinley, and Mrs Hackett would smile because she didn't care for Mawson. It wasn't his job to make Mrs Hackett smile. Linda, he admitted, could get away with it; he couldn't. The picture of living down there in Mawson's shadow reminded him of an often recurring dream of his, walking naked in a busy thoroughfare, hoping that nobody notices his nakedness. With Mawson around it would be noticed at once. He looked at his watch: she and Nick were taking their time.

She came back only after Miss While had left.

'What's wrong?' he asked, looking at her serious face.

'Nothing, darling,' she said. 'Aren't I allowed to feel depressed too at times?'

'Why should you be depressed? I never thought that anything could depress you.'

'I'm depressed by your shilly shallying, but don't let's talk of it. So Miss While has left?'

'I don't shilly shally, I know what's good for us.'

'I'm sure you do,' she said in a sweet voice. 'I repeat don't let's talk about it.'

She's becoming reasonable, he said to himself, yet he didn't like her serious mood. 'We're going out,' he said. 'You don't want to be cooped up in the flat.'

'I've just come back,' she said with a sad smile, 'but I'm ready to go out again if you wish.'

'First we'll have drinks in a bar I like very much, then I'll take you to a restaurant where the fish is excellent. Like oysters?'

'I love them. My poor Nick, you'll stay behind.'

She went to change into the dress she had worn at their first meeting.

'When you thought I was married,' she said as they went down the stairs, 'you had an excuse. Now you've none. Don't answer, we don't want to spoil our evening out.'

He was only too willing not to. Nick barked miserably in the flat.

He first took her to the bar he had been to in the morning. Now and then he had been there with Vivienne. Would he find her seated with Simon in the same corner where she used to sit with him? He saw no familiar face. The barman asked whether he was busy, and he assured him that he was. Linda spoke little which he didn't appreciate, and when they went to the restaurant she spoke even less. The sad little smile seemed screwed to her lips.

'Don't you feel well?' he couldn't help asking, immediately regretting it since that might start her off.

'I feel very well, my darling,' she said in a resigned voice.

They took a taxi back to the flat. He grasped her hand which remained limp. Nick received them with loud barks, then raced round the sitting room knocking into chairs. Her face was radiant as she watched him; when Osbert spoke to her it became sad again. It'll be all right once we're in bed, he thought, leading the way to the bedroom.

Love, desire and tenderness too gripped him while she undressed in her slow manner. She went to the bathroom, he waited impatiently, and when she reappeared he said to himself that no woman had a body like hers. Contemplating it was a pleasure in itself. 'My darling,' he said hoarsely.

She lay down, her warmth inundated him, and he put out his hand to touch her. She turned her sad eyes on him, saying, 'Not tonight, it wouldn't mean anything to me, so sorry, my love. Put out the light, please.'

'But, darling,' he moaned.

'I couldn't,' she said in a voice that frightened him.

He switched off the light, and knew that sleep wouldn't come. Was she asleep? He couldn't tell. From the day he met her she had always been happy and gay in his presence, in fact so much so that he couldn't imagine her sad or depressed, yet she was both since she had come back from her walk with Nick. And what did she say on the stairs? He had no excuse left. No excuse for what? To marry her, of course. He closed his eyes and saw old Ramsbottom, standing in his doorway, a ball of cigar ash, calling 'It's cold next door.' He shook himself.

'Linda,' he said, 'are you asleep?' No answer. 'Linda, I want to marry you.'

'Osbert,' she cried, turning to him. 'I didn't think it would be so quick,' she laughed. 'I thought I might have to wait another hour or so.'

'You bitch,' he said with a sigh of relief.

'Take your bitch,' she said, pulling him on her.

He had never thought they could soar as high as that.

'Still want to marry me?' she asked afterwards.

'More than ever. I always complicate things instead of looking for the simplest solution. I'm selling Maidwood.'

'But why?'

'Because that'll be the end of all complications. We'll remain here, no reason left to go down to Maidwood, and once it's sold we can forget it.'

'You can't sell Maidwood.'

'Why can't I ? I don't mind getting less for it as long as I'm rid of it.' If he sold Maidwood Mawson's shadow would disappear. He stretched his legs, then slowly stroked her belly. Everything was beautifully solved.

'You can't sell Maidwood,' she repeated. 'If you sell Maidwood Jack will lose his job. You can't expect the new owner to keep him on. I can't let him lose his job. I took him away from his brother's farm, so I owe it to him to keep him in his job. Besides, I love Maidwood, but now I'm thinking only of Jack.'

The poor balloon has been pricked, he said to himself.

'We have to face the situation,' she went on. 'It looks to you difficult and embarrassing because you're afraid to face it. I'm not afraid. If one loves nothing is difficult and embarrassing. If you want it I'll go to everybody on the estate and tell him that I wasn't married to Jack, but now I'll be married to you.'

Just as I pictured it, he sighed to himself. His hand continued stroking her belly as if it gave him strength.

'Jack's vanity won't suffer,' she continued, 'I mean as

little to him as he means to me. He loves his work and the estate, and being a man lacking completely in sentiments he'll accept the new situation without a murmur.'

'You sound convincing,' he said, wanting her again. 'Give me a little time, a few days, and then with you at my side I'll face the music.'

'There's no music to face,' she said.

The best thing, he thought before falling asleep, would be to send her down alone to see Mawson's reactions. What a prig and coward I am, he added.

They overslept, and were wakened by the noise of the hoover in the sitting room. 'That's the charwoman,' he said superfluously.

'Time she met your future wife,' said Linda.

'This is the lady I'm marrying very shortly,' he said when he and Linda appeared in the sitting room.

'Best of luck,' said the charwoman who was a woman of few words. 'Do you want me to do the bedroom or the dining room first?'

'The bedroom,' said Linda.

While he and Linda sat at breakfast he spoke of Maidwood and Mawson. For a convinced bachelor to leap into marriage was an extraordinary effort in itself. She should, therefore, be satisfied with it for the moment, and not insist on his going down to Maidwood and Mawson before he got his strength back.

'I'll go down in a day or two,' she said, 'to prepare your coming. The doorbell.'

He went to the window, and immediately recognised the Ford. He leaned out a little more: Mawson stood outside the door, wearing a green porkpie hat.

'It's Jack,' he said. 'Oh, my God, what does he want?'

'Jack?' she said, 'I can't believe it. I never told him to come here.'

The bell rang a second time.

'Let's pretend we're not in,' he said. 'If nobody comes he'll go away.'

'I want to know why he's here,' she said.

'I don't want to go down. Linda, I can't.'

She went to the bedroom, and asked the charwoman to go down to open the door. The charwoman's eyes said, can't you do it yourself? None the less, she went.

Osbert lit a cigarette, his hand trembled as he did so, then he sat down in an armchair, listening to the footsteps on the stairs. It was no longer the fear of fear: the great final fear itself was coming into his presence. Mawson should be wearing a black three cornered hat, a black cape, and a grining skull instead of his face.

'Go to the bedroom or the dining room,' he said to Linda.

'He knows I am here.'

The charwoman brought in Mawson through the narrow passage. He wore the tweed jacket he usually wore on the estate, and the stem of his pipe stuck out of his pocket. He put the porkpie hat on Miss While's table. Linda stood with her back to the window, thus he noticed her first. 'Morning, Linda,' he said. He saw Osbert rising from the armchair. 'Hullo, Osbert,' he said. He looked round the room. 'So this is where you live.'

'Why did you come here?' asked Linda.

I ought to leave them to it, said Osbert to himself.

'To see Osbert,' said Mawson.

'You could have phoned before,' said Linda.

How well they get on together, thought Osbert. Frankly, they don't need me.

'It was too early when I left Maidwood,' said Mawson, taking out his pipe. 'There's a lot I've got to tell Osbert. You too, Linda.'

'Sit down,' said Osbert. 'Choose any chair you want, Jack. Would you like a drink?'

'Too early,' said Mawson, remaining standing.

'Do sit down,' said Osbert.

'All right,' said Mawson.

'How's Maidwood?' asked Osbert in a bright voice.

'Bearing up,' said Mawson with a chuckle.

'What brings you here?' asked Linda, approaching him.

'It's a long story,' said Mawson. A pause followed while he lit his pipe. 'You know Linda that we didn't get on any more, I don't know exactly why, but we didn't.'

'You came here to tell me that?' said Linda.

'I've got much more to say. We got accustomed to not getting on any more, didn't we? We could have gone on like that for ages.'

'Luckily Osbert came,' said Linda.

'That's it,' said Mawson. 'Osbert came, and now you're with Osbert.'

'That was to be expected,' said Linda.

'Well, I didn't,' said Mawson. 'I mean not quite like this.'

'I'm sure you'd like a drink,' said Osbert.

'I've got a lot of driving to do,' said Mawson. 'Thanks all the same. When I saw how much you meant to Linda I thought it over. I mean I weighed up the situation and all that.'

'What are you driving at, Jack?' asked Linda.

'Nothing that'll worry you,' said Mawson.

'Give me a cigarette, darling,' said Linda.

Osbert stood up, and went up to her without looking at Mawson.

'Thank you, my love,' said Linda. 'Go on, Jack.'

'Well, I weighed up the situation, and said to myself it wasn't for me any more. It was one thing to live together as we did, but this is quite another. Don't you agree, Osbert?'

'Wholeheartedly,' said Osbert. 'I've said the same all along.'

'Good,' said Mawson. 'Understand that I loved Maidwood, and if the situation wasn't what it is I wouldn't be doing what I'm doing.'

227

'Pray, what are you doing?' said Linda.

'I'm coming to it,' said Mawson. 'This bloody pipe's gone out. I said to myself this wasn't for me. It isn't for you two either, but I'm only thinking of myself. You two can think of yourselves. So I wrote to my brother to say I was ready to eat humble pie and come back. You know my brother, Linda, so you know how he loves people eating humble pie. He wrote to say that he was ready to have me back and give me my share on one condition, and that's taking back Jenny.'

'And you said no,' said Linda.

'I said yes. Don't sneer at me, Linda. She can't give me less than you gave me these last four years or so.'

'I admit that,' said Linda, 'but it does sound very funny to me.'

'It isn't funny,' said Mawson. 'I agreed. I left Maidwood this morning for good. The keys of the cottage are with Tony. When you want to go in take the keys from him. I'll have the furniture removed next week. I'm sure you don't need any of it, Linda.'

'Does it mean you're no longer the estate manager?' said Osbert.

'It does, Osbert. According the law I ought to have given you notice, but in the circumstances I'm sure you'll waive that.'

'Most certainly,' said Osbert.

'You'll miss Maidwood,' said Linda.

'Maybe less than you think,' said Mawson. 'I'd the accountant in, we went through the books together, and everything's okay. Two rents are due at the end of the month, and the matter of Yailor's barn isn't settled yet. My advice is to say no to him.' He took several sheets from his pocket.

'Here are my reasons for it. I wrote this last night.'

He stood up and gave Osbert the sheets.

'You're excellent, Jack,' said Osbert.

'Thanks. Well, I don't think there's much more to be

said,' said Mawson, lifting the porkpie hat from the table, 'but you can see, Linda, that I'm nobody's fool. I will say farewell.'

'Won't you really have a drink?' asked Osbert.

'Haven't the time,' said Mawson. 'Jenny's waiting for me.'

'I'll see you down,' said Osbert.

'Don't bother,' said Mawson. 'I'm sure you and Linda've got a lot to say to each other. Best thing is to advertise for a new estate manager.'

'Thank you, Jack,' said Osbert.

He rose, holding out his hand, but Mawson was on his way to the door which Linda opened for him. She went as far as the landing, and Osbert heard her say, 'Good luck, Jack.' He couldn't hear his answer. Probably there was none.

'Didn't I tell you, my darling, that when one loves one needn't be afraid?' she said, returning to the sitting room.

'Now I can sell Maidwood.'

'We won't sell Maidwood.'

TWELVE

Tony lay in his bed in the inn, thinking of the letter he had received from his French girl in which she said she was tired of his vague attitude and tergiversating, and had decided to put an end to it. The great advantage of being a shit, he smiled, is that people discover sooner or later that you are one. The French girl had discovered it, so he was entitled to forget her. The letter lay on the table beside the fireplace. He would reread it in his time, no hurry since the girl asked him to send the thousand francs he owed her. He would plead exchange regulations as an excuse if and when he answered her letter.

Something stirred beside him. Of course, he had a girl in bed with him, silly to have forgotten her, that too the French girl's fault. He couldn't remember the name of last night's conquest, if conquest were the word for it. He was on his way to Banbury, and she was waiting at a bus stop. He liked the shape of her, and he was at a loose end with nothing in sight.

'Going to Banbury?' he asked, stopping his car.

She said she was, he said, 'Hop in,' and that was how it began. He must get rid of her before they started moving downstairs. Anyhow, it was only six o'clock, he could have another go at her. He touched her ample bosom. 'I'm too tired,' she groand. 'I want to sleep.'

'I must get up in half an hour.'

'Let me sleep till then. I didn't want to come here.'

So he wouldn't have another go at her, no tragedy that.

He found his packet of cigarettes on the bedside table and lit up. The girl groaned again.

There was no getting away from it, he mused, that experience is of no help because the same experience can't repeat itself. When he had arrived in Maidwood he had thought that Linda was an easy catch. He wrinkled his nose remembering the evening he had tried to kiss her, and all the time she was in love with poor old Osbert. Somehow he had never imagined that a woman could fall for Osbert, the self-centred man he was. He couldn't afford to be self-centred any more. What a strange story it was.

It began with Mawson telling him and Rex that he was leaving the estate as he was returning to the farm that he used to share with his brother. 'You've ten more days to go, Rex, so help Tony to get the knack of things.'

'Won't we see Linda again?' asked Rex.

'You'll see her,' said Mawson. 'Now leave me alone as I want to clean my drawers.'

Mawson wasn't the man to have to tell you something twice. They cleared out, and that was the last they saw of him.

Two days later Linda appeared, Osbert only on the following day.

It was impossible not to admire her. Last week she went with him to see one of the tenants in the village, a retired civil servant who suffered from gout. He hadn't paid the rent the last two terms. His wife appeared to stand by her husband in that moment of stress. 'Good morning, Mrs Mawson,' said the wife in an aggressive voice.

'I never was Mrs Mawson,' said Linda, 'but now I'm Mrs Osbert Hinley.'

She said that without raising her voice, so all there was for the wife to do was to throw herself at her mercy, and ask for a little delay.

Linda had suddenly decided to put central heating

into the downstairs rooms. The other day he accompanied the central heating man to the house. Osbert wasn't visible, probably afraid of the estimate. Linda was there, and while she took the central heating man round she beat down the price even before she saw the estimate. 'Do you know why I want central heating downstairs?' she said to Tony after the man left. Tony admitted he didn't know. 'Because I don't want him to be cooped up upstairs as it reminds him too much of his London flat of which I want to get rid. His place is here on the estate, not in London.' She was a remarkable woman, in that she knew where she was going. I wish I knew where I'm going, sighed Tony, stubbing out the cigarette.

'It's cold,' shivered the girl.

'What else do you expect in January?'

'You've no compassion.'

'I've more than is good for me,' he laughed. 'You can sleep another ten minutes.'

Yes, Linda knew where she was going. When Osbert told him and Rex that he would advertise for a new manager, she said, 'There's no need for one. I'll be the new manager. I learnt a lot from Jack.' One ought to have seen Osbert's face. 'But it's an immense responsibility,' he bleated.

'I can cope with it,' she said.

And she did. He found it inconceivable that with him as her only help she managed to do as well as she did. Mrs Durston, who lived in the largest house in the village and had befriended Tony, had said to him a few weeks after Linda and Osbert got married in the Catholic church in Banbury, 'The adventuress has had her way.' Tony laughed, for it wasn't his duty to contradict a woman who was as kind to him as Mrs Durston. The girl groaned, then coughed, not a girl he wished to see again. He ought to switch on the radiator but then she might want to stay longer than she should.

Was Linda an adventuress? And what did adventuress exactly mean? True Osbert was a better catch than Jack which didn't mean, however, that she had been after him because he was a better catch. His own impression was that she loved Osbert. You saw that in her eyes when Osbert came into the office or when he went to dine with them in the house. It couldn't be an act, and she wasn't the acting sort.

'Dearie, we're getting up,' he said, turning to the girl.

'You're a selfish beast,' she grumbled.

'I can't afford to be late at the estate office.'

One morning he had been late, and Linda, who had arrived before him, gave him such a look that he decided like a child that had done something wrong not to do it again.

The girl got out of bed. Her body was pink and white, and she was fatter than he had thought last night. Why had one different eyes in the morning?

'The bathroom's at the end of the corridor,' he said.

'I'll wash when I get home,' she said, beginning to dress.

'I'm going to the bathroom.'

It was nice to be away from her. He thought of Linda again while he shaved. He had dined with them the other night in the study. 'We'll be using the dining room once we've central heating downstairs,' she said.

'It's too big,' said Osbert.

'This house needs being lived in,' she said. 'It hasn't been lived in for a hundred years.'

Then she explained to Tony that it had been the home of lone women for over a hundred years. 'I'm not a lone woman,' she said, taking Osbert's hand. I wish she'd take mine, Tony thought. 'There'll be children too in this house,' she added.

'I don't want children,' said Osbert in a plaintive voice.

'There's only one way of not having them,' she said. 'Now that I'm a Catholic I refuse to take the pill. Understand, my darling?' She looked at Osbert challengingly. I could jump on her, Tony said to himself. Apparently Osbert felt the same because he said in an even more plaintive voice, 'All right, Linda, we'll have children.'

'How many?' she asked, leaning forward, her eyes fixed on Osbert.

'As many as you want,' he said.

She laughed like one, thought Tony, who was having an orgasm, which he couldn't say about the girl who had been reprehensibly placid the whole night.

He finished shaving and got into the bath. Gregson, the innkeeper, and his wife were moving about downstairs.

Linda took everything in her stride, nothing bashful in her make-up as she had shown on umpteen occasions. They couldn't find a file the office needed, so she calmly rang Mawson in Norfolk to ask where the file was. Probably she spoke to Mrs Mawson as Mawson happened to be out. 'This is Mrs Hinley,' she said. 'Ask Jack to ring me in the Maidwood estate office when he gets back. It's about a file I can't find.' Truly enough Mawson telephoned an hour later. 'Is that you, Jack? How are you?' She said that as if she were speaking to a bosom friend. When she had finished with him she turned to Tony, 'It's with the accountant. Go to Banbury and fetch it.'

Tony returned to the bedroom. The girl was dressed, and stood in the bay window. The letter from the French girl wasn't in the same place on the table which meant that she had tried to read it. Luckily it was in French. Why luckily? He didn't care a rap what this girl thought of him.

'I'm waiting,' the girl said, turning back from the window.

'It's no good waiting,' he said, dressing. 'I can't drive you back as I don't want to be late in the office. If you go to the main road you'll see the bus stop. You'll be in Banbury in less than half an hour.'

'You're a mean beast,' she said.

'You're not one of Nature's sweethearts,' he laughed. 'See you to the stairs.'

He went back to finish dressing after he had made sure that she had left the premises. Wasn't Osbert one of Nature's chosen males? He wouldn't mind making Linda a child every night of his life. It might be a case of sheer jealousy (Tony was always in a fair mood in the morning), yet he couldn't help thinking that they were an illmatched couple. All you had to do was to watch them in the ornamental garden which in Linda's words she was bringing back to life, an enthralling picture with Linda using spade and shovel, Hackett standing at a distance, rubbing his back, and Osbert leaning forward, his eyes following every movement his wife made.

'You ought to wear a black jacket and striped trousers with your gumboots,' Tony said.

'How right you are,' laughed Osbert. 'Darling, do you want the rake?'

Tony breakfasted with the Gregsons in the parlour behind the bar.

'I hear,' said Mrs Gregson, giving Tony a worldly smile, 'that Simpson won't renew his lease. Too many expenses, he says.'

'I bet Mrs Hinley will take over the Home Farm when the lease falls in,' said Gregson.

'I wouldn't be surprised,' said Mrs Gregson with an even more worldly smile. 'I've never known a woman more full of beans than she is now. It wasn't like that when we thought she was Mrs Mawson. I often said to my husband, "I've never seen a more bored woman in my life." Nothing seemed to interest her. Now everything does.'

235

'She needed more scope than she'd before,' said Gregson.

'It's love,' said Mrs Gregson, looking at her husband reproachfully.

'My wife's a romantic,' said Gregson.

'I am too,' said Tony. 'Been a romantic all my life.'

He got into his car, drove to the office, and sighed his relief because he arrived before Linda. She came with Nick ten minutes later, her cheeks apple red on account of the cold wind, and the grey eyes sparkled. I bet, said Tony to himself, that they'd been making children the length of the night. Osbert the stallion: she'd turn any one into a stallion.

'I won a great victory,' said Linda, sitting down behind the table that had been Mawson's. 'Hackett is moving his vegetable patch. It was an eyesore don't you agree?'

'The whole garden was.'

'And the house a pigsty,' she laughed. 'I've got some other news too. Osbert has agreed to give up his London flat.'

'I don't believe it. And what about his legal work?'

'I found the solution.' You always do, said Tony to himself. 'Miss While, his secretary, will come down three days a week. I've persuaded her to. I think she likes me. As Osbert hasn't an awful lot of work to do we'll use her a bit here too. That'll save us work, and you, my poor Tony, you type atrociously.'

'I do my best. I saw her in the flat, didn't think much of her.'

'She's a good tempered mouse. Down to work. Simpson won't renew his lease. That was Jack's great hope because he wanted to take over the Home Farm. I've a good mind to take it over myself, an added zest in life.'

'Are you a farmer?'

'I learnt a lot of Jack. Have you checked the builder's bill?'

'Not yet.'

'Get down to it. This afternoon I'm taking it to Banbury.'

Tony sighed because he hated figures and because he preferred talking to her. Now and then he looked up: she was engrossed in a long typewritten sheet, thus all he saw was her thick hair, the puckered forehead and the slightly hunched large shoulders. The telephone rang, she lifted the receiver, and he heard her say, 'He isn't here yet.' Their eyes met. 'Concentrate on your work, Tony.' She does treat me like the family ne'er do well, he thought.

The next time he dared to raise his eyes was when the door opened and Osbert appeared, wearing a tweed jacket, corduroy trousers and gumboots. The wind had played havoc with his hair which he smoothed before kissing Linda on the cheek. Why don't they get down to it? said Tony enviously to himself.

'It's bitterly cold,' said Osbert.

'Why didn't you call me, darling?' said Linda. 'I'd have fetched you in the car. Bone telephoned, he wants you to ring him back.'

Osbert dialled Bone's number.

'Hullo,' said Bone in a jovial voice. 'It might interest you to know that old Ramsbottom died yesterday.'

'Poor old man,' said Osbert.

'Now he knows,' chuckled Bone, 'whether it's cold or not next door.'